I0662846

Introduction

The story's settings for <u>Changing Colors</u> will take the reader back to the early 1800's. The book gives highlights a time period when life was simple yet complex; politically, socially, and economically. As the years progress follow the Chettsburg Family's growth through their careers, struggles and accomplishments.

The stories on the farm are never ending. Every day brings new adventures and events to the family farm. There are oodles of folks, young and old. A place filled with food, fun and flair at times. Let the southern sun guide you to a place of love, romance, diversity and controversies.

As the author, I have used my imagination to produce a variety of characters and settings. Interesting how I see them through my own eyes. Then I wonder how others might interrupt or view the people and places I have created?

This book brings together characters who have a diversity of ethnic backgrounds. While writing this story I tried to stay away from heavy dialoged flavored with foreign accents and southern drawls. The style was to make the reading easy on the reader. A reader should not get tied up in mispronunciations or stumbling on foreign articulations.

As an educator, I have noticed two things at various grade levels. Students at times can stumble and spend too much time trying to pronounce and interact with characters' complicated dialogue. This can lead to losing some of the elements that take away from the actual story. So, I hope the readers can appreciate all the characters as they are detailed and described, along with their simple words.

CONTENTS   PAGE

CHAPTER 1
CHANGING COLORS

This is fall, 1985, and I am seated in my college class, African History. Patiently, I wait for the morning class to end. The day's lecture is very interesting. This professor is one of my favorites, Mr. Seely. He has a tendency to run over on class time. This is mostly due to students having questions and comments about his motivating lectures.

Today's topic seemed to generate some controversies. A handful of the African American students seemed to have the assumption that all the white students had some direct connection in bringing slaves here to this country? Mr. Seely was taken by one student's comments. The outspoken girl's name was Elaine Georgia Walker. Her friends call her Laney. She was a short, sassy, black girl wearing stylish wire-framed glasses. She insisted that all the white folks brought all the black folks here by boat from Africa. Mr. Seely suggested that she do some family history research. Normally he sticks to his class syllabus. Today he announced this subject matter as an extra credit project.

The class was instructed to do the assignment for extra credit. He mainly directed this project to Laney. He suggested that the class trace their family history. Three or four generations of history was challenged to see what the students could come up with. The format was to be in the form of a family tree, an outline, or simply a timeline.

Laney was certain her family came straight from Africa. She did not think she needed to do any family history research project. Explaining to Mr. Seely that her middle name was handed down to her from some great-grandmother? Her middle name was Georgia. Assuming it had ties to the country of Georgia located in Africa? A few students chuckled at her stating that Georgia was also a southern state in the United States. She shot back by telling them that she was certain all her ancestors came straight from Africa.

Meanwhile, Belgium in the early 1820's was intense for agriculture going back to that time. There was the best soil for farming, ample minerals, beautiful forests and mild winters. The coast welcomed the soothing, bordering beaches of the North Sea. The air was fresh and crisp, as if it were spring time nine months out of the year.

Joseph Chettsburg was a handsome stocky gentleman in his early twenties. His thick hair was black like shiny velvet. The face could be that of a Frenchman with dreamy blue eyes and thick, ruby red lips. Joseph was a hardworking man with good ethics and spirituality.

He decided to move north to look for work. He had settled on a job in the coal mining industry. He worked long days at the coal mine, as a laborer. He had experienced several long lonely months of hard work. The days were dark and dreary at times. He dearly missed his family and friends from back home. He yearned for a woman to pamper, feed and care for him.

Outside of work, church seemed to be his only form of socialization. He attended the small local Roman Catholic Church weekly on his own. There he prayed and gave thanks. He was especially thankful for his family although they were far away. He prayed for them and anticipated seeing them soon since they were currently absent from his life.

At church he took notice of a plump, teenaged young woman. The young lady had nice golden blonde hair that dangled all the way down to her waist. Although a little overweight her figure was curvy. She attended church weekly with her family. Every week the family with six children would be there at church along with their parents. The lady's father was a tall, slim man with a very stern look about him. The man never smiled making him almost unapproachable.

Several months later, Joseph approached the somber man. He started the conversation by stating that he admired the man's traditional family. He told him he had noticed that his own family also attended church every Sunday, as he did. So, Joseph introduced himself and asked the man if he could court his oldest daughter? Joseph thought it might be best if he joined the family at church the following Sunday. The father agreed, that would make for a suitable arrangement. The man of few words made no hesitation introducing his oldest daughter to Joseph. Her name was Elizabeth and she was seventeen years old. Elizabeth was a quiet girl as were the rest of the family's children. Joseph had noticed her every Sunday at church. Each week she would wear the same off white muslin dress that she wore the week before. Must be hard to dress eight people, he thought to himself about the large family? Every week Elizabeth would also be seen in that same black hat, just a plain black hat.

The courtship was short for the young couple. The two were married six months later in that little church where they met. Joseph found Elizabeth to be quite the opposite of what he had dreamed his wife to be. She did have some fine personal qualities though. She was a good homemaker and seamstress. She kept a clean house, could cook and on occasion tended to his manly needs.

She appeared so stern, like her father he'd guessed. She was not one for much conversation. Certainly she was opinionated yet gentle. Elizabeth was not very affectionate but was compassionate at times. Many of her sulk qualities were hard for Joseph to get used to. In general, the two were fairly compatible. They both enjoyed her kitchen skills, for instance. They were good companions in many ways. Both were raised that you received an education at school, married, and had children. Neither one really had a clear picture of what marriage really would look like. The couple, now known as Mr. and Mrs. Joseph Chettsburg made a home together in his small log cottage like house. Joseph continued to work as a laborer at the coal mine. A dirty job indeed. Elizabeth took a job at the local textile mill during their newlywed years. She was an extremely good seamstress. Joseph was saving money so that he could purchase a small farm. There the two of them could raise a family. The children could help him on the farm and share chores was his thoughts.

After a few years the industry business in the area began to slow down. Work became scarce in the local area. Joseph and Elizabeth feared losing their jobs. He started considering other options. Joseph did locate a small farm for sale nearby that he was able to purchase. He was pleased with the fertile soil. The farm was equipped with a few out buildings and a small two story house. Money was tight going forward for the two. Both were very frugal and thrifty with money and other resources. The young Chettsburg couple figured they could be self-sufficient living on the farm. They needed to buy some livestock and live off the riches of the land. Joseph intended to grow some produce and staples for their own and the animals' consumption. Any surplus harvest could be sold for extra money, he anticipated.

He knew Belgium provide a long growing season. Hopefully, his crops would get a nine month season. God blessed him with the best soil for farming. He would be able to farm at least nine to eleven months out of the year. The weather was pleasant all year around. The fields were planted and the harvest was anxiously anticipated. The new farmer did not have much money at the time. Thankfully, he was able to purchase a couple of pigs, cows and a few chickens. He already had in his possession two graceful Brabant Belgian horses to help cultivate the fields. The horses were kind and more like pets as he actually named them Buttons and Bows.

While her husband was busy on the small farm, Elizabeth kept active in the house. Thinking to herself, she felt like the luckiest woman in the world. She had a husband who was very kind. Joseph was a far stretch in comparison from what her stern father looked like.

Being late in the morning, Elizabeth wandered out to the barn. In her hand, was a warm cup of coffee for her hard working husband. Assuming he was stacking hay to feed the livestock. She ventured into the barn to greet him. Entering the opened barn door, Joseph was nowhere in sight.   The barn was an area she was not fond of with all the animals and the occasional fresh farm stench that filled the country air. Loudly she called out, "Joseph my love?" No answer was received but only the sound of bales of hay ruffling overhead from the barn's loft. "Joseph?" Again she hollered.

"Up here, my dear." Joseph answered back.

"I brought you a cup of coffee. I will set the cup next to the ladder." She sat the drink down.

"Please Elizabeth, come up here to me." Her husband declared.

"You are silly. You know I am leery of heights!" The wife reminded her husband.

"Take your shoes off and climb up the ladder slowly. Only a short distance?" He assured his wife.

Still hesitant she obeyed her husband's odd request. She climbed the rungs of the ladder grabbing them tightly. Pulling herself up, rung by rung, carefully trying not step on her long length dress. With each step she rested before advancing again. Reaching the top of the ladder she peaked up into the loft a place she never explored before. To her surprise, her husband was sprawled out naked on a worn out tarp. Wadded up underneath his head was an old blanket, a makeshift pillow. Seems the time called for a late morning nap?

A bit startled, Elizabeth blushed staring at her undressed husband. The conservative wife was not as accustomed to her husband baring his all. Let alone out in the barn! Particular she thought? She realized maybe it was a comforting way for him to relax after hours of hard work.

"Please come join me." The husband requested of his bride. Laying there he motioned with his arm for her to come over to him. Elizabeth hoisted herself up onto the loft's wooden landing. She crawled and stood up. Next, she brushed her knees to free them from the little debris. Slowly she wobbled and walked towards her husband. Crunching sounds could be heard from under her feet as she scuffled over the dry straw. Even after years of marriage, the young wife was shy and embarrassed to view her husband's naked body.

"Please, take your clothes off for me, my love." Joseph pleaded.

"Here in the barn?" Elizabeth was puzzled.

"Yes, I am well rested and wish to make love to my wife right now!"

"Can't we go into the house? This seems awkward and uncomfortable." Elizabeth tried convincing him.

"Come on, let your hair down!" He requested of her.

"Seriously, here in the barn where the animals sleep? And it is daytime?" The wife appeared uneasy.

"I am in the mood now. Let's try something different? You may find this to be a comforting experience. Outside in the fresh air. Outside of our confined bedroom walls. I have laid up here in the loft daydreaming of our intimacy. Our lovemaking is so routine, same place, same thing. Come on honey, open up to a new adventure. This is just between the two of us, we are married!" The nervous housewife struggled back to the ladder. She was frustrated in several ways. The trip down the ladder was easier than the struggle up. Joseph just kicked back and giggled. He had appreciation for his wife's prudish and traditional ways. Their lovemaking needed some spicing up were his thoughts. Although he was thankful to have a wife to satisfy him on occasion. Problem was that she was a "woman." The young husband wished she would think more like a man when it came to sex. The crafty man was creative even when there was time for intimacy. A sly smile appeared on his face. He knew over time their intimate relationship would come around. His wife just needed time to develop more self-esteem and confidence in herself, he figured.

Laying on his back he reflected to a time when he was a young teenaged boy. The girls' eyes twinkled when he was around. In time he came to realize his good looks were extraordinary. After all he was a very handsome man. Looks were only skin deep he soon came to understand. He learned fast as a young boy that the pretty girls and cute girls were often snotty. Quite the opposite traits he found in his lovely wife. Yes, she was a polite farm girl on the plain side. Any sane man would appreciate her pleasing qualities; she cooked, cleaned, and at times still a little bashful around her own husband.

Off into a deep sleep the farmer drifted away. A late morning nap came after he manually pleasured himself. An activity he kept to himself up in the loft. There were many other times his wife would not comply with his manly demands. While lying there the cool wind

whizzed across his warm tired body, almost as comforting as his wife's loving arms.

Times were tight and the economy had spiraled downward. The cool winter ahead was not very promising. There was hardly enough food to feed themselves and the farm animals. Meat was a rare item on the dinner plate. The cows were needed to produce milk. The milk was also used to make butter and possibly a little cheese. The hens were needed for their eggs. Elizabeth's body dropped a few pound for lack of sufficient food at times. She prayed to God to never miss a hearty meal again. She wanted to dine and enjoy the taste of foods she savored. Never had she experienced anything like this before! As a child there was always plenty of food for their extra-large family. Living through this time of slight drought and famine she promised herself never go to hungry again. Going forward, she prayed to God that she would never have to eat rabbit again. She just wanted to cook and bake goods that were delightful to her palate and not her husband's hunting leftovers.

The winter brought along time for the two to spend together. The two would sit in front of the warm hearth. There was a pile of poor grade charcoal out back that Joseph had salvaged from work to help heat their home. Joseph would sometimes doze off for a nap in front of the soothing fireplace. Elizabeth would always be seated in the rocking chair. There she would be working on her latest quilt of multiple colors. You could hear them trying to converse in English of what little bit they learned at their jobs. The conversation was good for a laugh or two as they struggled learning the language and trying to understand each other.

Elizabeth reflected on a time when she was not so fortunate. She quietly recalled a time when Joseph had gone hunting and shot a rabbit. Rabbit was not a taste she desired. Again, meat was scarce. She made the meat from the tiny carcass last a few days. As creative as she was, she roasted a rabbit followed by stew and soup all in a week's time.

Joseph kept busy through the winter crafting things out of wood. He was quite the handyman and a gifted carpenter. The farm was loaded with trees. There were plenty of trees and a wide variety of them. He was able to put his skills to use. He enjoyed making furniture out of the oak, birch and pine trees. Once in a while, he would make a special piece for his wife such as a wooden candle holder.

Spring finally arrived along with a plentiful harvest. The fields were loaded with a variety of crops. Day by day the crops continued to color the fields. The fields were sprinkled with sugar beets, flax, hops, potatoes and other assorted vegetables. Later, he would plant some more oats, rye, and barley to keep up with the feeding of the livestock. Along with the harvest came news that Elizabeth was expecting, finally! Joseph had anticipated this moment for years. How wonderful he though, a baby on the way and a bountiful crop on his farm.

The cool winter welcomed the birth of their baby boy. A son named Charles Joseph. Charles was named after Joseph's father. Joseph anticipated that someday his father would meet his newborn grandson.

The season was springtime, in the late 1840's. Joseph had converted the side porch into a tea room. This was where customers could purchase and eat the fresh baked goods that Elizabeth had prepared. In rural areas, a tea room was common to find. Most often they were located within a home. Provided outside of Elizabeth's tea room business were several tables and benches. All made of logs that Joseph had designed and crafted. The outside tables were Elizabeth's solutions to the farmers who patronized her establishment. She did not like the dirty boots trampling across her tea room floor. The beautiful oak floors that Joseph had installed. Yet, she certainly appreciated the farmers' business.

Elizabeth's days began bright and early. First, the coffee pot went on the stove to heat. Next, the tureen was placed back on the stove to simmer. The pot was partially filled with water. Meat, fresh vegetables or leftovers could be added to make a daily soup or stew. Always an extra meal for throughout the day. Then she would start to bake a few signature baked goods. Usually a cake or two, possibly a pie depending on what was in season at the time? The tasty featured items would be served by the slice, throughout the day.

Once the baked goods were in the fire heated oven, she would start breakfast for her husband. By this time, the coffee was ready and the aroma filtered through the house. Then as the day progressed she would make her delightful chocolates. The baker was also a novice chocolatier.

Customers would periodically stop at the tea room throughout the day. Some customers would come for an assortment of chocolates to take home. Other customers would come to savor a piece of chocolate cake with a warm cup of tea.

Then there was a regular customer, Mr. Taras the old farmer down the road. Just like clockwork he would arrive every morning at 8:15. He would be waiting outside for a piece of chocolate cake and a strong cup of coffee. Honestly, his wife never made him breakfast or lunch as a matter of fact. Elizabeth would often make an extra portion of lunch for him knowing his situation at home. He would give her an extra coin or barter with some of his own homegrown produce. At times he would stack wood for her at the rear door. This would help her to keep the stove going. She was concerned for him as he worked long hard days and needed proper feeding. The main reason for the eating area outside was because of him. He was a loyal customer with no manners. His first visits to the tea room were not wonderful experiences. She recalls his first visit.

Mr. Taras stated, "Good morning darling! I hear you are serving up some mighty fine goodies?"

Glad to have a new customer, this gentleman either had to take his dirty, muddy, stinking boots off or wait at the door to be served, she thought.

After hearing her continuous complaints about the old man and his dirty boots, this inspired Joseph to craft the benches for outside the tea room. This idea worked well as long as the weather was favorable.

Maybe that is why his wife did not cook breakfast for him? She probably did not want his dirty work boots in their house either? He seemed not to have a lick of common sense.

Elizabeth loved to keep busy in the kitchen. Otherwise she seemed saddened. She missed her son Charles so badly. She had not seen him in a couple of years. He was their only child, a tall teen with dark, wavy hair. He was extremely smart with a funny sense of humor. That face held the biggest smile ever. His mother loved him and tried her best to spoil the boy. Her life lightened up also since the day when he was born. She treasured him like a special gift.

~Charles Chettsburg, age 16

"Walking down the narrow rural road, my bare feet cringe as they hit the dry, dusty, dirt. The path I have taken so many times. An ever changing trail that always leads the same way. Yet, the scenery somehow changes from time to time; bland fields with a chill in the air, green grass hugging the shoulder of the road on a warmer day, or possibly autumn's leaves scattered amongst the ground accented by the smell of fresh harvested hay.

One day, I will follow my dreams. Unlike the journey I take with my feet. The gift of my imagination creates new ideas in my mind as I travel through life. To move in the right direction, I have to take a look at my mental pictures of how I want to design my own life.

My mind was made up that I needed to reach beyond those farmland walks that seemed to embrace struggles and setbacks. These hurdles will not hold me back. Somewhere, someplace, I will be able to be of service. The directions of my dreams will someday lead me to a colorful life. May God safely guide me and be a witness to my goodness!"

Chapter 2

AWAY FROM HOME

Charles had relocated to the United States to study law in Chicago, Illinois. As a boy he was very brilliant. In school he did very well. Naturally, he had a lot of compassion for people. He was quite the community advocate. He was a problem-solver and very analytical. His mother always knew he would either be an attorney or a priest. At times he was a bit too mischievous to be a Bible thumper?

There in Chicago, he earned a law degree from the School of Lawyers. The big city was not for him though. He was used to the rural areas of farming and warmer weather. Things back home were a bit more laid back then in this big city. He was not sure if he should continue working in Chicago or head back home? He knew there would be greater opportunities in the United States for him.

Charles began to explore his options in the legal field. Maybe he could move somewhere more subtle. Was there a place with climate similar to that back home? The winters in Chicago were brutal. The large plantations in the south that he had heard about sounded more appealing. Maybe this would be an area better suited for him? He grew up on a small farm that he enjoyed as a young boy. Things were different in the states. Politics were not the same. Slavery was still strong in some areas which created tension.

Soon Charles packed up his goods and headed to the southern parts. He did not have an exact destination. He was not really sure where he would eventually settle. He had a vision of a rural area close to a big city.

Charles traveled to the south by stage coach as was spring approached. This was a very long ride for certain. Switching coaches along the way. Sharing the rides with complete strangers. Possibly making a temporary friend or two. The corduroy roads were rough at times recovering from the cold, wet winter. Most of them converted from old Indian trails.

He took in the countryside views along the way. He observed roaming animals such as buffalo and deer. There were ample forests and large farms. Like in Chicago, he was taken by the diverse ethnicities among the people he encountered on the journey. He listened as some could barely speak English. Some not able to speak the language at all.

The further south he traveled the more black folks he noticed. On occasion, he would get a quick glimpse at the black slaves working diligently in the fields. On the outskirts of the fields you could see controlling men managing the laborers.

Charles had two sentimental possessions with him on the trip. The first was a thick warm hand-crafted quilt. The prettiest quilt made from scraps. The covering was thick and comforting. His mother had sewn the quilt for him when he was a young teen. The second possession was an oak trunk his father hand-crafted. The trunk had two metal handles, one on each side for easy toting. Charles had his personal belongings strategically packed in the trunk. In there he stored his clothes, textbooks, Bible and other important papers. The quilt was folded into thirds and then rolled up. He then secured the quilt to the top of the trunk with thick twine to keep it in place.

He did not have a specific destination in mind. He knew he did not want to reside in a big city such as Chicago at the time. Yet, he also knew he could not build a successful law practice living in a rural area with few people. He set out to head south. The south was possibly a good match for him. The area was warmer like back home and housed lot of farm land.

Finally arriving in Atlanta, Georgia, Charles exited the stage coach and grabbed his belongings. The driver of the coach hollered "heading south, all aboard!" Charles walked a ways and checked in at a local hotel. The room was warm, stuffy and small. The room would have to make due for the time. He was mainly anticipating a nice, long, warm bath.

He wanted to mingle with the folks of the city that was new to him. He was interested in learning more about the outskirts of the area. His desires were to settle in a smaller area near this village. He was seeking a town in need of his professional services as a legal consultant.

Throughout his stay he walked and roamed the village streets. Taking interest in the local shops. Once in a while he would eat a hot meal in a diner and visit with the patrons. He also wanted to pursuit and meet with other attorneys in the area. He hoped to make contact with them and associate with them to learn if his services were going to be needed.

After about a two week stay in the village of Atlanta, Charles spent the days ahead traveling to several surrounding areas and small towns. Surprisingly, he took to the town of Atlanta. He would call this place home and establish his profession. He searched the local area for a place to take up room and board. Actually, things worked out better than he expected.

After months of travel, Charles finally started to plant his feet in the village here in Atlanta, Georgia. Things were just as he dreamed. The village was growing and surrounded by rural farm area. Charles was able to purchase a small office building in the sprawling town. The building had enough space to establish his law practice. Upstairs housed a small apartment. The upstairs would be used for room and board tenants for additional revenue while he was getting established. His plans were to temporarily live in his office for a while. Collecting rent seemed like a great enterprise while he was beginning his general law practice. He would have revenue to cover the expenses while he was getting his start. He provided some furnishings for his office. His basic need for the office was a nice cozy bed. His office was equipped with a large oversized wooden desk and a large swivel chair for him to sit in. Two Windsor chairs faced the desk. Book cases outlined the walls. The final touch was a sign that hung out front advertising "General Law Practice

Chapter 3

THE LAW PRACTICE

Charles would sit behind his desk day in and day out. When not occupied with clients dropping in for advice, he would study from his college textbooks. He enjoyed reading and learning. He was always wanting to learn more about the law, as well as, anything of interest for that matter. He had a big collection of books in general, a passion of his.

As weeks passed, he began to enjoy people watching from his big front window. He would sit back in his chair and kick his feet up on the desk. He was fascinated with the local merchants and their daily routines that he took notice of.

One particular person of interest was a beautiful girl from across the street. She worked in the village across from the law office at her father's clock shop. The teenage girl was a bit spoiled and knew how to work the boys. A gentle flirt could result in a trip to The General Merchant Store for some sweets provided by the young gents. Her father was a watchmaker. The unfriendly man named Leon Macher owned The Time Shoppe. He was a fat man with a hard look about him and a bit on the shorter side. The man produced unique pocket watches and clocks. He had special skills in designing the pieces. His watches were timeless pieces of jewelry.

Charles had saved some money to possibly purchase a new pocket watch from the clock shop. This was actually his way of trying to meet the young lady. After months of watching from across the street he was aware of the father's and daughter's routines. She would arrive at the shop promptly at 11:30 a.m. each morning. Roughly around 1 p.m. her father would leave the shop to do banking, run errands, and break for lunch. He would be gone usually for about an hour each day.

Finally one spring day, Charles posted a *"will return soon"* note on his office door. Noticing that the watchmaker had left the shop, Charles bolted across the street to the clock shop. Entering the store Charles was greeted by the young lady.

"Good morning, Sir." The young lady stated in a very friendly voice.

"Please call me Mr. Chettsberg." Charles replied.

"Yes, I know who you are. You are the attorney from across the street. I am Lara." She said in a confident, spoken tone. Quite opposite of her father's raspy voice. So overwhelmed by her beauty, Charles misspoke.

"I am looking for a clock." He stated.

"A clock, Sir?" She replied.

"Well a clock, yes indeed. I need a clock for the office." He chuckled. "I never know what time to close the office."

They both laughed at his comment. Charles was highly interested in pursuing a courtship with the young lady. He just adored her from what little he knew of her. Getting past her cold father is what concerned him.

A few days later around 11 a.m. in the morning, Charles heard someone enter his office. The beautiful young lady from across the street came in. "Good morning Mr. Chet." clutching a small basket with a towel draped over the contents. "My mother has sent me to deliver some muffins to you. Although she does not bake these goods very often, she wanted to share a few with you."

"Oh how nice and thoughtful." He commented. "Please thank your mother for me. Thank you also for dropping them by young lady".

"By the way the name is Chettsburg!" He reminded the outspoken, sometimes sassy girl.

"I know sir. That is not a common name around here. I was just being silly anyways. No disrespect please. You look like you could be named Chet. May I ask what your first name is?" Lara inquired.

"My first name is Charles but I prefer to be called Mr. Chettsburg. I am an attorney of law with a reputation, ma'am." He explained to her, getting a little red in the face.

Lara just giggled and left the muffins behind as she pranced out of the office.

What a wonderful smell he thought to himself? Homemade muffins like his own mother would make? These muffins were unique to him. Some muffins were made with wild blueberries and some had nuts in them. At lunch time he heated some tea to have with a muffin. He tasted the nutty muffin. He was not really sure what was in the muffins? They had a very buttery taste along with the small pieces of crunchy nuts.

He wanted to write his mother and let her know about the muffins with nuts. The muffins with the buttery taste. The problem was he did not know what kind of nuts they were. This was a different taste experience for him. He darted up from his seat and marched across the street and entered the watch shop.

"Ma'am your mother made some very delicious muffins. I am not familiar with the nuts in those muffins?" He questioned Lara.

"Seriously, sir?' she replied. "How can you live in Georgia and not know a pecan when you indulge in one?'

"Ahhhhh pecans!" He exclaimed.

"Yes, fresh Georgia pecans." She implied.

Charles commented "Can't say I've ever tasted a pecan in my life?"

"Lordy, Lordy, are you saying you have never savored a pecan pie either?" she questioned Charles. "Oh yes, pecan pie is quite tasty." Lara commented.

She then continued the conversation. She then invited him to join her on Sunday at the local church's family picnic. Her mother would be baking several pecan pies for the occasion. This would give him the opportunity to try some pie she thought. She let him know that the desserts went quickly though. Hopefully there would be a slice reserved for Charles.

Jokingly, he stated "Maybe I should eat dessert first then? Your parents won't mind me attending the family picnic will they? I have not officially become a member of the Roman Catholic Church yet, being relatively new to town."

She replied "I will ask my parents for permission. I do not see any problem with you attending the church function? For heaven's sake, it is a church, everyone should be welcomed there. Plus, I think it would be a great place for you to meet a lot of the local folks."

Charles returned to his office. He began drafting a note to his mother with his pen and ink. He wanted to tell her about the unique, buttery tasting muffins with nuts. He also jokingly told his s covered his face with his hands. He had a feeling of disbelief.   He told his mother that he met his bride-to-be, a girl named Lara Macher. Everything seemed to be falling into place way beyond his expectations. He kept running the series of events over and over in his head. He thought about his family he had left behind, how fortunate he was to graduate from law school, and finally how he ended up in such a beautiful place in the state of Georgia. His thoughts continued. A young beautiful girl brings him muffins out of the blue. Tasty muffins that he did not even know what was in them. Now she is inviting him to a church function of all places, unbelievable he thought to himself? He continued with the note to his mother whom he dearly missed.

Chapter 4

THE CHURCH PICNIC

Soon the day of the church's family picnic arrived. White clouds filled the light blue sky on the sunny afternoon. Charles got dressed in his fine tailored suit. He dressed in a white linen sack suit. He topped his head with a stylish straw hat. Not wanting to go empty handed to the event, he gathered some assorted flowers from the backyard of his office. He separated them into two bouquets. He attempted to tie the flowers together with some thin twine. One bouquet for Lara, and one for her mother, Mrs. Macher. He remembered the empty basket that Lara had left behind with the muffins. He took the basket and placed the cloth on the inside. Surely he would come across an apple tree or two on the way to fill the basket?

He arrived at the picnic with the flowers and basket of apples. He was greeted by Lara and welcomed by her family, the Machers. Charles presented the two ladies with their bouquets of flowers. Mr. Macher led Charles around the church ground and introduced him to several congregants of the church. First he met the priest, Father Murphy. The priest was hard to understand with his thick Irish accent. There were many others to follow, that he met. Charles then joined the family for lunch. He further got acquainted with the locals.   He met Mrs. Macher, a quiet woman with an Italian accent. She was an attractive thin, well-dressed lady with long brown hair. He then met Lara's siblings. First were her two younger twin sisters, Hannah and Delores who were 15 years old. Finally Charles met her youngest sibling Timm, Timm Macher. He was only 12 years old, the bratty boy was obviously a momma' boys, clutching on to his mother. Timm was a small, petite boy with black hair and long straight bangs. Mr. Macher would tease the boy stating his real name was Time Maker. Mr. Macher wanted his son to also be a watch maker as was his father, back in Germany. Eventually, Charles did finally get a piece of Lara's mother's delicious pecan pie that day at the picnic.

Charles was falling for the young girl named Lara. He appreciated her invitation to the picnic. He like her long, curly blonde hair. She was a perfect Southern girl. Well-articulated, a flair for fashion, yet always kind and thoughtful, were some of the qualities he adored about her. She was also conservative and had a good business sense, a trait she inherited from her father.

One sunny, warm, summer morning, Charles had a plan. He dressed in his cream colored sack suit and put on his brown, low broad brimmed, crowned hat. He went across the street to ask the watchmaker if his daughter could have a few hours off in the afternoon.

"Well, it will have to be around 1 p.m., what's this pertaining too? Oh, I guess it does not matter. A few hours will be just fine" Leon replied to Charles.

Leon thought to himself with a puzzled look on his face. He did like the guy. He knew by the way he was well dressed, he had good character. Besides that, the gentleman was a well-educated attorney. Lara did deserve a little time off from work, if only for a few hours?

Charles then proceeded down the street to the bakery. He wanted to put together a picnic lunch for himself and Lara. He wanted to reciprocate for the invite to the church picnic. In addition, he had a liking for the lady. He purchased some goodies for the two to enjoy. He then proceeded home and grabbed a picnic blanket for the upcoming occasion. Then he proceeded to go out back to get the horse drawn carriage ready. By now the time was only 10 a.m. Charles was a bit nervous, yet anxious. At this time Lara had not even arrived at work yet, nor did she know of the plans the men had set up. Sometime around 1:30 p.m. Charles went across the street to meet with Lara.

"Lara, would you care to join me for lunch?" He asked her as she stood in her floral printed cotton, laced trimmed dress.

She was too timid to ask her dad for time off from work. Besides, she was very hesitant to ask her father to go somewhere with a gentleman!

Charles commented, "It is okay young lady, I already cleared and discussed everything with the boss."

"Father does not mind that I leave the store?" she questioned Charles.

Overhearing their conversation Leon hollered, "Go ahead dear, and whatever it is you two are about to do, enjoy yourselves!" he further shouted "Just keep an eye on the time, dear."

The two thanked the gentleman. Lara placed her wide brimmed decorated straw-hat on her head. The sunhat was decked out with large pink silk flowers on its right side and a wide band of pink ribbon. Her long hair was flouncing from underneath the hat. The two eagerly headed across the street and entered the waiting carriage. Charles politely escorting her into the ride.

The not so shy Lara started the conversation, "Well my father must be registering at 2:50 today?"

"2:50?" Charles noted.

"The truth is that my father, Leon Macher the clock-maker, does not wear a smile often if you have not noticed. This started as a family joke, dad has not figured this out yet. We relate his facial expressions to the face of a clock. For example, a smile would be 2:50. With the hands kinda pointed upwards. Watch out if the time is 7:20, he's sporting a frown. Actually 9:15 is just right for him. I hate to watch when he changes moods so quickly, unpredictable. I am telling you his moods relate to the time on the clock"

"That is silly Lara. Now that you mention this, your father does not crack a smile often. I never really am sure if he is truly that serious or is building up some type of angry." Charles illustrated with a fake grumpy look on his face.

The two new acquaintances laughed as their friendship took off and drew closer. The young pair certainly shared a sense-of-humor. Even when the punch line referred to Leon.

"Where are we going Mr. Chettsburg if you do not mind me asking?" Lara questioned.

"We have reservations at an exquisite, fancy restaurant." He chuckled and laughed.

"Oh really! Well this could be a long ride? Is my father aware of how long my absence is going to be, Sir?" She questioned him again.

"No, just a twenty minute ride is all young lady." He answered.

The carriage ride was quiet. Both of them were feeling shivers of uneasiness. There was a lot of chemistry between them though. Yet, few words were spoken. Suddenly, Charles turned down a small dirt path. The ride was a little rough. The two bounced around and about in the seat of the carriage. Finally they arrived at the location that he had designated as the picnic spot. Charles hopped out of the carriage and tied the horse to the tree. He then escorted Lara out of the carriage lifting her lightweight body into his arms. He twirled her gently and placed her feet on the ground. Then he laid the blanket in his preselected spot near a small pond under a large shaded willow tree.

Charles helped her to be seated on the ground on the blanket. Meanwhile, she tried to tuck her flowing cotton dress underneath her. Both of them were still feeling a bit awkward since they did not really know each other very well. Charles set out to retrieve the goods he had brought for the lunch. He then explained that he wanted to thank Lara for inviting him to the church picnic. He was also thankful for her warm welcome with the muffins her mother had baked. Wondering if she would like what he chose for lunch, he began to place the items on the blanket as he sat near her. He placed the fresh baked bread, strawberry preserves, shiny granny smith apples, and slices of peach cobbler in front of them.

"Hope you do not mind what I selected?" He asked her.

She replied "Everything is just perfect, sir."

The two playmates were ready to feast. The summery scenery was bright and beautiful. The sun over yonder was warm, yet soothing. The fresh air stood still and quiet. A few dancing flies made their rounds overhead invading the picnic, to say the least. Both continued to savor the food and their serine surroundings.

"What a beautiful day Lara? The temperature never really gets this hot in Belgium where I am from. This warmer weather can be a bit uncomfortable, would you agree?" Charles asked.

"No, I am used to this heat. Nothing that a nice shaded tree like this cannot help cool one down. Actually, I enjoy a swim in the water on occasion. I love the water." She commented.

"Belgium has some beautiful beaches." Charles pondered to her.

"Beaches, sir?" she asked with excitement.

"Yes, there are spectacular beaches in Belgium along the North Sea. The weather there is very similar to here but the summers are definitely warmer here in Georgia. My father and I would travel to the sea for a little vacation. There we would do some fishing and get our feet wet. We would have a lot of fun together." Charles shared with her.

Lara had lot of thoughts running through her mind. Since she did not know him very well, she thought it would not be polite to ask questions of him. She wondered why he came to America in the first place. Secondly, he must miss his family back home?

Now she perked up with some enthusiasm. "Can we go put our feet in the pond?" she asked in a childlike manner. Charles did not think she was serious. This seemed completely silly to him. Not to mention it lacked some sense of etiquette. He certainly did not want to do anything foolish nor demeaning, thinking he would have to answer to her father.

"Oooh, you go on ahead and enjoy yourself. I really would not want to get my pants wet. I guess I am not dressed for that." He decided.

"Yes sir, you are right. I too am not dressed appropriately for a dip in the water. Sure sounds like a refreshing idea." Were Lara's thoughts.

They both agreed the water was appealing. She then stretched her legs out on the blanket. Lara then asked him if he minded that she stretch-out on the blanket. He told her to make herself comfortable. Charles was still seated next to her on the blanket. She propped her head up on his leg like a pillow and kicked off her little brown pumps. "Oh, really?" he thought to himself. So tempting he began to stroke her long soft hair, dragging his fingers through the curly mane. He took notice of her stockings and pure white drawers peeking out from under her dress. He moved and leaned a little closer towards Lara's face, in an attempt to remove a fly that had landed on her head. She took this as an invitation. She bounced up and began passionately kissing Charles. He had never embraced in such a kiss before! She continued to kiss his lips and slipped her tongue in his nice warm mouth. They both laid on the blanket and kissed for what seemed like eternity. On occasion, the cool wind would blow through the willow trees releasing them from the warm, blazing, summer sun. Eventually taking them back to reality.

Charles had anticipated giving Lara a gentle kiss on departure. He was startled by this young lady's aggressiveness, one who seemed to be so conservative at times. She fell right into his plan again though. Her kisses grew deeper and deeper. Her hands roamed all over his face and head. Charles was extremely aroused like he had never been before. He wanted to slow down what she had initiated.

"My, is it not time we head back Lara? I do not want to keep your father wondering and waiting?" Charles suggested to her.

"Oh most definitely sir, maybe we ought to go now?" she replied without hesitation.

Quickly, they gathered up their things and loaded the carriage to head back to town. Lara wrapped her arm around his arm most of the way back. Arriving at the store's front, Charles proceeded to drop her off at the watch shop.

"Can we do this again real soon Mr. Chettsburg if you do not mind me asking? Tomorrow?" she asked in a very upbeat manner.

His reply was not to her liking. He reminded her that he had a practice to tend to.

He did not have time to finish his statement. He now had to answer to Mr. Macher. Her father stood in the doorway peering out. He asked Mr. Chettsburg that perhaps he needed a new pocket watch? Mr. Macher reminded the two that they had been gone for over four hours in a loud tone. Charles thought to himself. How am I going to get past this grumpy, pudgy man? Charles just tipped his hat in thanks to Mr. Macher as he escorted Lara to the sidewalk.

"Good day everyone?" Charles cheered as he departed.

Chapter 5

GOOD MORNING SUNSHINE

When Saturday morning arrived, Mr. Chettsburg heard someone knocking on the office door. Figured this must be a client with an urgent matter. He quickly put on some pants and threw on a shirt. There was Lara rapping on the door.

"Do you have time available later on this afternoon for lunch? Father does not need me at the shop today. My mother packed us a lunch but do not let father know about our plans." She said with a grin. "I hope you did not have plans for the day?"

He explained a client was expected early in the afternoon. "I should be done around 2 p.m. Is that too late?"

"Never too late sir!" She exclaimed. "Mr. Chettsburg, it is never too late."

The two watched the clock throughout the morning. The clocks could not move fast enough. The afternoon hours dragged on and on…twelve noon, one, two, three o'clock. Charles was eager to spend some time with his new friend Lara. He changed quickly into something casual and combed his black hair. He darted out the door and scooted across the street to Lara's home located in the rear of the watch shop. Charles told Lara he was ready and hustled back across the street to get the waiting carriage. "I will bring the ride around back, Lara" He called out.

Lara gestured to bring a picnic blanket. She grabbed the basket loaded with food. Again, they loaded into the carriage equipped for another summer picnic. Again, they drove to the country to their private secluded spot near Porter's pond. Neither one knowing what to say to each other. Not much conversation between the two as usual. Both were anticipating the upcoming events of the afternoon trip.

Upon arrival at the secluded location, Charles escorted Lara out of the carriage. Retrieved was the blanket and basket filled with the freshly prepared foods. "That can wait? I mean the lunch, sir." Lara questioned in a soft, lady-like voice. She gazed into his eyes with a very long stare. Charles looked back at her wondering what she was thinking.

Being playful, Lara ran over to the nearest willow tree. There she waited for Charles to spread the blanket on the ground. She was anticipating this get together with Mr. Chettsburg. His sense of humor appealed to her. The European gentleman was handsome in her eyes, along with his dark, black hair. At this time her interests were focused on him focusing in on her. The young lady's mannerism was turning quite promiscuously. This was a man who was attractive and had a prospering profession were her thoughts also. In the meantime, Charles made no hesitation to sprawl the blanket out across the green grass.

Charles was feeling a bit overwhelmed by Lara's aggressive behavior. His mind raced thinking about her. His thoughts were that she must really have feelings for him? He could feel her energy and physical chemistry. The man had to behave like a gentleman in her presence of course. The lady needed to slow down were his concerns. Obviously, she was young and her hormones were obviously sending her lots of mixed signals.

While seated comfortably on the blanket, Charles leaned over and quickly kissed her soft pink lips. After a few seconds Lara initiated a long passionate kiss. She moaned as she intensely kissed the handsome gentleman. The kiss progressed and was longer and deeper. The feeling was sensual for Lara making her feel erotic.

Lara reached for Mr. Chettsburg's hand. Slowing she glided his hand up her dress approaching her breast area. This was a bit awkward for him. Charles was concerned that he needed to act like a gentleman and not be inappropriate with the young lady. He tried pulling away from her but she demanded. "No, no!" He proceeded to take directions from her as he was not experienced with women in that manner. Taking his hand further, she exposed him to her left breast. Peering out of the dress was her dainty, lace, trimmed chemise.

"You are so beautiful!" He exclaimed. A bit nervous as he was not accustomed to engaging with ladies in this way.

She grasped his other hand and placed it directly on her right firm breast. Then she directed his long, masculine fingers to her nipple, offering a touch to him. She begged for him to rub her breasts. Her body began to quiver as he made the suggested motions. Obviously the lady was erotic as her nipples became hard from his gentle touch. Next, she steered his mouth towards her nipple. The invitation was for him to suck and lick with his warm tongue. "Oh Lara, you are truly beautiful. Thank you for sharing your body with me in this way." Charles mumbled.

"Please do not talk now! Just continue pleasuring me like this. I have been waiting for a moment like this with you." She commanded. The top of her dress was lowered over her shoulders. Both breasts, large breasts, were exposed. The passionate kissing continued. She was dreamy yet demanding. Charles was fairly stunned in regards to the woman's intimate behavior. The more intense things became the more excited she became. The lust made her squirm and he felt like a mad man.

At this point, Charles tried thinking to himself. He needed to be more thoughtful of the situation. Slowing things down, he began a conversation with his friend about their courtship. "In God's eyes we cannot continue to carry on and behave like this. I need to make some decisions and plans for us before we take this too far, too soon. You are lovely on the outside, as well as, the inside. My best suggestion for now is to get going and head back to town. Not that I am not enjoying your companionship young lady." Charles lectured with a smirk.

The ruffled blanket was folded and the full picnic basket was retrieved. Off they rode in the carriage for another ride back. Lara announced "I really was not interested in lunch sir. I just wanted an excuse to spend time with you at that nice spot in the country."

"Well I am sure your mother pack a nice basket of food for us?" He questioned his companion.

"Please, take the basket home with you for your lunch or dinner. My mother will wonder why we did not eat. Then she will wonder what we were doing then." She shot back.

During the ride back to town Lara sat close and snug against Mr. Chettsburg. He was still in disbelief about her passionate behavior. He reminded her upon approaching town to keep an appropriate distance between them in the carriage. With her at his side he drove along the bumpy roads approaching town. Finally dismissing her at the backdoor entrance to her home. Proceeding across the street he parked the carriage at the rear of his building. Exiting the carriage, he grabbed the much anticipated basket of food and headed into his office.

He sat at his desk and pondered about the day's events. Thinking back to his own parents' relationship. He recalled never noticing them being passionate. Well, at least not in front of him. His parents were a bit affectionate towards each other, hardly ever passionate. The passion must have been shared discretely? Charles was still puzzled and struck by Lara's act of passion. Continuing to think about all of this, he figured out there must be different definitions of love. Obviously, couples must have other situations as to why they would marry each other?

Chapter 6

A LETTER HOME

As Charles sat in his chair, he figured he would write a letter to his father. He put the packed lunch on his desk. He slowly unwrapped the food Lara had given him. He then grabbed a pen and a fresh bottle of ink and began writing. In between words he would nibble on the freshly baked rye bread, actually a favorite of his. He placed the remainder of the bread on top of his icebox. In the bottom of the food basket he found a beautifully baked pecan pie. After pulling the pie out, he retrieved a fork. Charles inhaled two big bites of the pie straight from the pie plate. The taste was savored as he reminisced about his first piece of pecan pie at the church's family picnic.

Charles continued the letter and told his father about the unique pecan pie. He noted that the pie was so different from any other pie he had tasted before. While writing, he told his father about a beautiful young lady named Lara Macher and that they were courting. His plans were to ask her father, Leon Macher for her hand in marriage. Dwelling on his love for her, he intended and anticipated taking her on as his wife and starting a family. The letter was finished, signed, sealed, and set aside.

After a good night's sleep he was greeted by a beautiful Sunday morning the next day. Hustling for an outfit to wear to church was first on his agenda. He dressed finely in his suit, slicked his hair back, and proceeded out the door to walk to church. As he walked, thoughts of yesterday's events ran thought his mind. He wondered, should he sit with Lara and her family at church? Would that be proper etiquette? Dare he sit next to the girl whose bare breasts were at his lips the day before? Especially in God's house!

As he strolled up the sidewalk to the church Charles heard a voice call out his name. There greeting him was Mr. Macher. Leon actually appeared happy to see him. An invitation was extended for Charles to be seated with his family during mass. Charles gladly agreed. Mr. Macher escorted Charles into a selected pew of his choice. Next, Leon shuffled in his four children with his wife, Fia seated beside him. This was making Charles a bit nervous. Again a plan of his fell into place. Astonished that he was actually seated next to Lara at church!

After service, Mr. Macher invited Charles over to their house for pot roast dinner. "Care to join us for us for dinner this afternoon, Son?"

Charles thought to himself how the situation was getting better. "Son" he recalled? "Certainly, thank you for the hospitality, Sir. What time shall I arrive?"

"What time should we expect our guest?" Leon addressed his meek wife.

"Four o'clock?" She quietly answered her husband. "Lara, please set and extra plate for Mr. Chettsburg this afternoon dear." She added to her daughter.

Everyone offered their temporary good byes. Charles proceed for home. There he heated up some water for a cup of tea. Out of the icebox came the leftover pecan pie to tie him over until he would dine with the Machers.

The Machers' building was similarly arranged liked Charles' office. Half of the first floor made up the store front, The Time Shoppe. The rear of the building made up partly of the family's household including a very small kitchen. The second floor housed the family's bedrooms.

Charles walked down the road to a street vendor selling produce and fresh flowers. This was an unusual sight as most merchants were closed for business on Sundays. He bought two beautiful bouquets of garden flowers. One would be for Mrs. Macher and the other for Lara. He then proceeded around back to the rear of the building where the Machers lived. He knocked softly on the door. Waiting to greet him was Leon. The first bouquet was presented to Mrs. Macher. While blushing, she thanked him accordingly. The second bunch of flowers were handed off to Lara. Speechless, she beamed with delight.

Everyone was seated for dinner precisely at 4 o'clock. Mr. Macher began by reciting a prayer of thanks. The food was placed on the dinner table. Things were a bit peculiar compared to family dinners back home, Charles reflected. Everyone was very quiet. No one was conversing. No words were spoken except maybe when a particular food dish needed to be passed. Charles could not wait for dinner to be over as the seemed to last for eternity. Dinners back home consisted of everyone sharing how their day went or discussing any family concerns. Not at the Machers' household! Seems everyone was a bit intimidated to speak for some reason? Charles also was anxious sitting at the dinner table. His mind wondered. He kept thinking of Lara. Thoughts were geared at placing his frisky hands all over her. Dinner was finally over. The mother and children were expected to clear the table and wash the supper dishes.

Mr. Macher went to sit in his comfortable overstuffed wing chair. Leon grabbed his custom made wooden pipe. "Join me in the sitting area," he requested to Charles. "Business is going well for you, Sir," he complimented the young man. At that point Charles discussed the need for a bride as things were quite busy around his place. Leon knew what he was getting at. So, he questioned Charles about his parent's relationship. What was their marriage like he wondered? Leon reminisced about his own marriage. The marital union was miserable being with that bitch, Fia. Mainly a shy woman, she loved to bicker and argue with her husband. There was not much interest from her to learn the English language making things hard for the two Machers to communicate at times. Seems her way of communicating was to hit and slap her husband up beside his head. Leon became fearful as he recalled how often he stuck back at his wife in front of his children. The kids will probably learn to act that way was his concern now. A talk with his children was in order to discuss their mother's behaviors. Lara would need to be talked to if she was going to become a bride herself he also thought. Leon began to think how embarrassed he would be if one of his children behaved like their mother did at times. He would not want his daughters treating a man the way his wife often would. The often stern man was proud that he took in his wife, fed her, clothed her, and gave her shelter. Thinking about Charles, he assumed the young man must have had a loving kind mother back home considering the way he carried himself.

The two men stood up and shook hands. Leon agreed that Charles could keep his oldest daughter. The man knew Charles would be able to provide well for her. His request was for him to always be kind and affectionate to his bride-to-be. Leon explained that Lara could be challenging at times as he chuckled. The girl was daddy's spoiled, little brat. No more was mentioned about the arrangement the remainder of the evening. The men did not mention a word to the rest of the gathered family, not even Fia. The evening progressed and the gentlemen sat and continued to talk about local topics. The mother and children sat quietly around the dinner table isolating themselves from the men.

Chapter 7

THE CHETTSBURGS' WEDDING

What a beautiful June day in the mid-1840's. God's love must be radiating from the bright summer sun. The sky was blue and full of large fluffy white clouds moving overhead. Today was a very special day indeed. Charles and Lara were to be wed. The groom-to-be was anxious to have a bride to take care of. Both parties were nervous and excited.

The morning started early for the bride-to-be. Her mother and sisters were busy assisting her in every step of the way. First, the mother styled Lara's hair. The long curly hair was combed. The top of her hair was pulled back and fastened with a decorative barrette. Next, the females apply a little amount of cosmetics on her face. Her finger nails were then touched up with a quick manicure.

The most exciting part for them was dressing the bride. Lara put on her white silk stockings, a white chemise, and finally her beautiful wedding gown. The gown was white, embellished with brocade lace appliques. The sleeves were three-quarter length and trimmed in dainty lace. The tight fitting bodice was a perfect fit on the young bride's silhouette. The back of the dress was closed with tiny fabric covered buttons. White boots were placed on her small feet over the silk stockings.

Mr. Macher spared no expense for his daughter's wedding dress. He knew how Lara loved to dress up in pretty stylish clothing. This was a very special occasion for him. The father was proud of his oldest daughter. She was so helpful to him at the watch shop. He often wondered if Lara did not spend so much time there just to be away from her mother. The daughter had grown into a beautiful young lady who was spoiled by her father and Charles. Leon could not have asked for a better husband for her. Charles was the perfect package. He was handsome, educated, professional, and had a good sense of humor were Leon's thoughts.

By now Lara was completely dressed for the special occasion. The others did some finishing touches of their own. The twin sisters, Hanna and Delores were dressed in matching tea rose colored bridesmaid dresses. Mrs. Macher was dressed in her multi-colored plaid dress with a solid jacket. Brother Timm and his father were both suited in black.

The time was now 11 a.m. Mr. Macher loaded his family into their carriage and headed for the church. The family gathered at the rear of the church. The ladies tucked themselves away in a far corner to be concealed. A short white veil was carefully placed on Lara's head. The veil had highlights of small pink and white fresh flowers.

Charles also wore a black suit. His hair was neatly combed under his tall top hat. Somber and saddened though because his parents were not going to be in attendance for this special ceremony. A prayer of thanks was made in silence, thanking God for his wonderful parents and all that they had done for him. The two parents were strong in knowing what was right, respectful, and very religious. Thanks was given to his independence and the ability for him to achieve his education and professional business. At that moment he was most thankful for his bride-to-be Lara that he was about to receive at the altar. He stood proud in the upstairs apartment that would soon be home to his bride also. A big sigh and deep breathe was taken. Later on when he returned home, the gentleman would not be alone. Never again would he be lonely. His new wife would be joining him forever.

Charles slowly came down the staircase and exited the rear door of his home. He took notice of the picture perfect day that God had gifted him. Squinting his eyes at the beaming sun as if he was giving thanks to God. The horses were gathered and he hoisted himself into the carriage. The carriage slowly proceeded to the Roman Catholic Church.

By now, a few guests had arrived for the intimate ceremony. Some arrived by foot, horseback, or maybe even a wagon. Mr. Macher was there to greet and welcome each and every one of them. Entering the church's grounds he saw Charles arriving. Hustling over to him, the two men engaged in a personal conversation. Leon passed on well wishes to his future son-in-law. He assured Charles he made a wise decision marrying his oldest daughter. "The two of you will make a wonderful couple. You both are lucky to have found friendship within each other, as well as, love. May God bless this union and provide me with plenty of grandchildren!"

Leon then escorted Charles to the side entrance of the church. The guests continued to arrive for the occasion all dressed in their Sunday best. Promptly at noon, the pianist began piping out a hymn. The music was a key that mass was about to begin. Father Murphy and the altar boys gathered around the sacred altar. The twins, acting as bridesmaids walk down the aisle first. The bride was then escorted down the church aisle with her father proudly at her side. Her nervous, clammy hands were grasping a bouquet made of fresh cut flowers.

The young bride was greeted at the altar by the priest and Charles. Mr. Macher then stepped aside and sat with the rest of his family. The couple stood facing the priest. Father Murphy began the wedding mass. The marriage ceremony was performed at the tail end of the mass. Again, the music played after the exchange of the sacred vows. "Now I pronounce you man and wife,' the priest uttered in his thick Irish accent. "May I introduce everyone to the newly married Mr. and Mrs. Charles Chettsburg," he added with his expressionless face. Lara shed a few tears. Her new husband whisked the tears away from her face with his white linen handkerchief. Then he hugged and embraced his bride. The two stood nervously together in the church. Charles took a deep breath as he was now legally married in God's eyes. With the music as a backdrop, the bride and groom were first to exit the church. The rest of the worshipers followed behind.

The celebration extended into a casual reception for the now married couple. An afternoon social was hosted outdoors on the church grounds for the family and guests. The bride and groom stood solemn and mute near the church's entrance. A common activity was to extend best wishes to the newly married pair. Guests gradually made their way to greet them. Seems people were more interested in roaming the grounds picking up on the latest news and gossip. Quietly, soft music filtered in the background. A trio of men played their string instruments, singing a song or two.

Leon stood proud next to his wife. His face sported a permanent smile. A sight rarely seen by anyone. Mrs. Macher was not as happy though. She feared her daughter moving out of their home. Things would not be the same there without her. She hoped for her daughter to have a happy marriage if that was at all possible? Reflecting back on the hard times and struggles she encountered with her own husband.

Mr. Macher then announced to the small crowd, "It is now time to wish good fortune to the newly married couple and our guests. At this time we will BREAK THE CAKE. I do not want my beautiful daughter Lara to be humiliated," he chuckled. "So, may I request Mr. and Mrs. Charles Chettsburg to cut their wedding cake?" Charles stepped aside as Lara cut into the flat single layered white cake. The dessert was frosted with dense butter cream frosting. The sides of the cake were coated with freshly chopped pecans. Lara removed a piece of the cake and placed the portion on a plate. The bride took the first bite savoring every sweet morsel. Then the groom dove a fork right into the rich frosting. Both of their faces lit up with delight. Both enjoyed their special cake along with a cold cup of apple cider.

The couple moved aside of the church. Charles quietly spoke and promised his bride something. He explained that one day she would meet his mother and be able to taste one her freshly made desserts. Preferably something chocolate!

The wedding cake was not the only cake at the social. There were many others. Charles wanted an assortment of cakes for his wedding. He requested cakes like his mother would have prepared. There were several more cakes for everyone to enjoy. Chocolate cakes similar to the ones his mother baked were on his menu. His mother would frequently bake single layer chocolate cakes. When cooled she would take a long bread knife and slice it evenly into two layers. In between the chocolate layers she would spread homemade raspberry jam. Creamy frosting topped the cake. His mother would then place a few fresh raspberries on top of the cake. The berries would be a hint of what was waiting inside. The other cakes resembled the unique types his mother also made.

After several hours the wedding celebration came to an end. The Macher family, along with the bride and groom left the church. They headed to the Machers' home for a wedding dinner. The family was joined only by a few other people. One guest was the priest of course. He would be over to give the wedding couple a special blessing.

Mrs. Macher had beef pot roast simmering all day. Along with the meat she roasted white potatoes, carrots, and onions. Topped them off with a few spices including salt and ground pepper. The day before was spent baking fresh bread and muffins. Charles noticed the pecan muffins on the table. He thought about the day Lara delivered muffins to his office. He inhaled the aroma of the beef pot roast. He chuckled to himself wondering if this is what married life would smell like?

The guests were all seated along with the immediate family at the dinner table. Father Murphy who was seated at the head of the table stood for grace. A prayer and a blessing were not only recited for the food but for the newlywed couple, Mr. and Mrs. Chettsburg. Leon began the dinner by serving a big crock of beef noodle soup. The bread and muffins were also passed around to everyone at this time.

Everyone ate and conversed at the crowded dinner table. The behavior was unusual for the Machers as supper time was always quiet. This was a good time for everyone to get acquainted. Every person shared their hopes and expectations for the new couple. Father Murphy lectured the two on the importance of keeping up with the Roman Catholic Church's practices within their marriage. Leon talked and expressed his thanks for having his family extended. He was so very grateful, yet relieved to have such a well-rounded husband for his daughter. His wife, Fia did not have much to say. She kept busy serving food and clearing plates and platters from the table. As dinner ended the children helped their mother clean off the table. They also helped wash dishes which was a production.

Charles thanked his new mother-in-law for the delicious dinner that followed his wedding. He explained he enjoyed her tasty dish of beef pot roast. Not sure of Mrs. Macher's sense of humor, Charles had an additional comment, "Well, Mrs. Macher, I have had a very similar dish in the North. Except they call it Yankee Pot Roast!" Mrs. Macher blushed of course but Leon and Father Murphy broke out into a huge roar of laughter. Lara and her siblings just glared at each other not really getting the joke.

Leon commented trying to keep a straight face, "That is one thing I enjoy about my new son-in-law, he has a good sense of humor."

The gentlemen joined Leon in the sitting area. The bride was also invited. Fia continued to serve tea to the dinner guests. As the table was cleared, leftover cake from the afternoon celebration was put out for a second round of desserts. Leon commented to Charles that he really enjoyed the chocolate cake that he had suggested. "Charles, I like the fact that you have a unique flair for things. I have never had such an interesting cake?"

Charles explained, "These chocolaty cakes are similar to the recipe of my own mother's. She is very good in the kitchen I might add. Maybe someday you will have the opportunity to taste her goods. At this point I would like to give a word of thanks to my parents who are not with us today. Because of them, I have progressed this far in life. They encouraged my educational pursuits. Secondly, I thank God for blessing me with wonderful parents, my new family of in-laws and a journey that has led me to this beautiful bride that is seated next to me."

Father Murphy intervened as Charles finished. The priest broke into a quick prayer directed at the groom. He detected a sense of emptiness about Charles knowing how he must have missed some very important people on this special day.

Leon addressed Charles as he was curious about his folks back home. "Hopefully your parents can come to America for a visit sometime soon? We would like to meet them my son."

"Actually, I would foresee them joining me here permanently. I have already requested this of them. I know my mother would love it here with me." Charles added.

As the evening turned into night the few guest began to depart. Charles expressed his gratitude to the Macher family for all their hospitality and welcoming him into their family. He reached for his top hat and headed home across the street.

The custom was for the father to deliver the bride to the groom. Leon instructed Lara to gather her things. She placed a few personal belongings in a cloth muslin bag. She packed her hair comb, a few items of clothing, and her sentimental locket that she almost always wore around her neck. The father and daughter walked together across the street to meet the groom. Lara was still dressed in her wedding attire. Leon was not sure what to say to his daughter. The two were greeted at the door by Charles. Mr. Macher wished the newlyweds a good night as they proceeded into their home.

As Leon started to walk home he pondered and questioned himself. Should he have had a talk with Lara as she was just a teenager? Did she know what to expect on her wedding might? Hopefully she would be a tentative wife he hoped. Possibly his wife Fia had a discussion with their daughter. Unfortunately he thought, his wife did not know how to obey and tend to her own husband's needs. So how could his wife advise Lara on marital expectation? These thoughts of his wife only put him in a bad mood. Actually this was making him angry. How did he end up with a wife who was so cold and bitter most of the time? After three months of marriage he wanted to return her to her father. Fia's father advised him that legally she was his.

At this point Leon did not want to go straight home. A brisk walk might be nice he thought. The warm evening air was cooling down a little bit. Along the way, he shuffled his tired feet. With his hands in his pants pockets he strolled back towards the church. Once he reached the church he was seated on the front brick steps feeling lonely. As time passed, a couple walked by with a dog. Moments later an older gentleman paced by. The man's name was Lester, a village vagrant. The fella had no real known family, no place to call home, and smelled of booze. Sympathetically, Mr. Macher knew Lester's story.

Lester lost his wife during childbirth. The baby was born healthy and Lester was left alone to raise his son. The boy named Franklin was the world to his father. His son made the stars shine at night in his eyes. Lester previously work as a clerk in the village. His mother-in-law at the time helped care for the child until her death. Franklin grew up and married a very nice lady named Charlotte. After a few years of marriage, Franklin enlisted in the military to assist in the war. Off the young man went and never returned. No one ever heard from him again since his departure. This drove Lester to drink heavily and he was unable to keep his job as a village clerk. Fortunately his daughter-in-law Charlotte owned a hothouse at the west end of the village. Lester was able to do odd jobs for her to make a little bit of money. Most nights he slept out in her toolshed. The other nights he probably was not able to find his way there after nights of drunkenness.

Charlotte herself was confused. She did know how to categorize her situation. Was she abandoned or a widow? Did Franklin get injured or could he have possibly found someone else? For certain, he would not have intentionally left his father? Years had passed since he left for the battling war.

Knowing Lester was headed west of town, Mr. Macher headed towards Charlotte's home. The two knew each other since they both were local merchants. Matter of fact, they knew each other very well in some ways. Leon stepped up the steeped stairs leading to her place. He knocked on her front door that displayed a sign stating *"CLOSED"*. Peering through the lace curtains Charlotte's face lit up delight. Her lover had finally came to take her again. In the background soft music could be heard. Leon took Charlotte by the hand and started to dance with her. Dancing and prancing from room to room they went. The two lovers enjoyed every second of their companionship together.

They had started the discreet affair years ago. Leon had not been intimate with his wife since the conception of their son Timm, he calculated. Charlotte was a lonely war bride. During the day she enjoyed tending to her flowers and wares. The nights had become lonely and she was needy. The lady missed the intimacy of a man. The two seemed to fill a void in each other's lives.

Still dancing playfully around the house Leon chuckled and addressed Charlotte, "Will you marry me? Be my wife!"

"Let me ask my husband first you silly man." She teased back. "Please spend the night with me Leon? I promise in the morning I will make you a stack of pancakes a foot high, along with a pound of crispy bacon."

"Charlotte I just hope God forgives me for my infidelity. Joy is in the Bible and celebrated during Advent. I myself, celebrate joy all year long with you my love, Charlotte." He expressed.

Charles and Lara were not the only ones celebrating that night. On the other side of town were another pair of lovers. The father of the bride made love to his mistress as he expressed joy and love on his own daughter's wedding night.

Chapter 8
THE CHRISTENING DRESS

The autumn fields were picked and the holiday season became a busy time for the local merchants. Mr. Macher needed more of his daughter's valuable time working at The Time Shoppe. As always, she agreed to help out her father of course.

The long days were tiring for the retail duo. Although this was a temporary arrangement. Lara wanted to spend more quality time with her husband. By saving time, the newlyweds would have dinner at the Machers' on most work nights. Certainly the two were not imposing on her mother who stayed home all day. Two more mouths at the dinner table was not an inconvenience. In fact, Leon teased his son-in-law Charles for joining them so often for supper.

"Basically, my wife Fia is a terrible cook. I sneak down to the diner for lunch as often as I can. At least I know I will be getting a tasty meal." Leon laughed. "I know my daughter does not cook much but she knows how to spend money I must warn. That is why she is better off in the store earning money than being a disaster in the kitchen."

Poor Fia spent the afternoon preparing and roasting a few ducks. The twin girls helped set the table precisely placing the linen napkins. Warm apple cider was served with a splash of cinnamon added to the drinks.

Dinner was promptly served when the head of the household was seated. Crackling logs provided a background noise for the very quiet family meal. Spontaneously, Lara stood up. She made her announcement not as planned. "Everyone I want you to know, I am pregnant." Lara abruptly blurted out. Charles wiped his face with a napkin. Standing up he turned and kissed his wife. Leon darted over and hugged his daughter. The three other children were lifeless as they really did not seem to know how to react.

The often timid one quietly asked her daughter, "When will be expect the new arrival Lara?"

"Sometime in late spring I am guessing, Mother," was the excited young lady's calculation.

Charles politely excused himself from the table and rushed home. He returned within minutes. In his hand was a bottle of corked wine. "Time to celebrate Leon, where are the glasses? Can't say I ever tasted the crap before."

Leon was just as quick to celebrate the new news, "This shall be a special occasion, and one of many." The soon grandfather-to-be proudly pronounced with a glassed raised in his hand.

Lara was excited about being pregnant. A designated area would be set aside for the expected little one in the upstairs apartment. The small space would eventually stage a bassinette and eventually a crib. A baby doesn't need much room does it? After all, her parents raised four children in their household and managed well.

Lara was especially interested in planning for the baby's christening. She looked forward to the event that would be a huge occasion. The spoiled mother-to-be would only want the best for her newborn. Along with her husband, she needed to discuss who the God parents were going to be.

The local merchants were scouted to purchase fabric and materials for the baby's christening gown. The Roman Catholic Church required babies to be christened in a white garment. The color white was a symbol of purity and innocence. Lara purchased a couple of yards of white glossy satin. Along with that, were assorted white lace trims, ribbons, and other needed notions for the outfit.

Next, the pregnant mother needed to find a local seamstress to assemble the christening garment. Not having access to a sewing machine the project would be too time consuming for her. In addition, Lara was too spoiled to take on such a big job that would have to be hand-stitched. She did not want to bother her mother with such a large endeavor. Thinking ahead Lara wanted the garment to be worn by the next baby and then the next baby after that. The gown would have to be perfect of course. The garment would be a precious piece that would be passed on from generation to generation. Across the street she went to pay a visit to the town tailor, Mr. Perkins. He would be the one to take on the special sewing project known for his detailed skills.

Lara stood clutching her purchases and took in a deep thought. She wondered what her own christening dress looked like. She did not even dare ask her mother about this. Her mother was not the sentimental type. *"Why my mother would have had us children christened in a white silk pillow case if she could have. Maybe she did?"* Laughing to herself she as amused with her own sense of humor.

Along with the late spring harvest a beautiful baby girl was born. A daughter was welcomed into the arms of Charles and Lara. The family named her Melissa after Charles' paternal grandmother. Several years after her birth she somehow inquired the nickname Missy. Her grandfather Leon did not take a liking to the pet name. One way or another he justified this as an abbreviated version of Miss Melissa.

Chapter 9

LEON'S FAMILY SECRET REVEALED

How could the news of a family member be so troubling for
Leon Macher? The birth of his beautiful granddaughter Melissa was a
blessing for all. Somehow the baby's delivery brought back some mixed
emotions for the man with a hard personality.

There was a disturbing history behind the strong, stern man. For
years he tried to bury parts of his earlier life deep inside his mind to
shield the hurtful memories. On the other hand, the birth of his first
grandchild gave him greater appreciation for his immediate family, as
well as, his extended family that now included Charles Chettsburg.

For days Leon held back the tears that only he felt. Reminiscing
and reflecting only made his feelings worse. The sadness on his face
was something only he knew about. His hurtful heart apparently had not
healed over the years.

The skilled craftsman could not concentrate on his family business it seemed that day. His mind wandered and kept him off track at The Time Shoppe. The morning sun was rising as he peered out his store's window with a somber look at a road that seemed to lead nowhere? He dwelled back in time when a young man named Charles opened a law practice directly across the street. This man would forever change Leon's life as he became his proud son-in-law.

The previous mishap in Leon's life was long gone. Private prayers were constantly said as he tried to get past this phase of deep depression. Now was the time for him to rekindle his feelings and give thanks for what he had now. Of course, the praying continued. At times he was jealous of his own son-in-law's upbeat, free spiritedness. *"Come on, how lucky can I be for my dear Lara to marry such a well put together gentleman?"* He prided.

Leon quickly exited his store front. He dashed across the street to pay a visit to Charles at his office. The confused man confronted his son-in-law upon entering the building. "Charles, you have shared so many interesting memories and stories with me. I'll bet you miss those times spent with your father whom you have not seen in years?"

"Why certainly, sir?" Charles replied with a puzzled look.

"I recall your stories of your father, you as a young boy, going fishing together. Maybe the two of us could spend some time doing just that! I have to admit, I've never fished a day in my life. Maybe my son Timm would enjoy an activity like that?" Leon continued.

"Yes sir! I personally would relish that. A little relaxing time away from the office would also be appreciated. Let me check my schedule for the week." Charles noted with a pen in his hand.

"This week!" Leon yipped. "I was thinking about right now, well today?"

"Now?" Chuckled Charles. "Give me a few minutes as I need to get ready? Why, we will need poles and some bait. I can put off what I am doing now until later today I guess."

"Oh, I hate to be so spontaneous and abrupt, Charles. Certainly I did not mean to impose on your work. I myself was working hard early this morning. I thought it would be kind of nice to spend some time together, you know just us men?' Leon nervously added.

"No problem sir, not a problem at all for my magnificent father-in-law. I'll change my clothes as you should too. Then I'll gather some fishing gear. Can you ask your wife to pack some food for us hungry men? As you know the kitchen is not always Lara's specialty. Leon do you mind displaying the *"closed for business"* sign on your way out? Meet me around back in about 20 minutes and I will be ready, buddy!" Charles put his hand to his forehead and thought to himself, *"Buddy?"* Leon was usually a far cry from being a "buddy." The thought of going fishing with his father-in-law actually got him enthused.

The time was essentially about an hour later when Leon appeared at Charles' office rear door. Standing there was a mustached man in a dingy white undershirt, plaid brown linen trousers, and boots that were high to his knees. The pathetic outfit was accented with a casual tan hat. In hand, was a wicker basket containing something tasty for later.

"Leon, you could not have picked a more beautiful, sunny, day to go fishing. Just enough clouds for a little shade. The wagon is packed. Let's hope the fish are biting this time of day?" Charles snickered.

The two men hoisted themselves into the wagon. Charles suggested "Maybe we should have brought the little guy?"

"Little guy?" Questioning with a raised eyebrow.

"The little guy, meaning your son, Timm. Does that name ring a bell, Sir?" Charles kidded as always.

"Never been fishing, nor has he. I'm German, I eat real meat." The two men laughed at the silly comment.

"Fishing is for the men. Gets us away from the women. Not that I do love your daughter, sir. A man needs his own time. Away from women and work."

Leon had his own thoughts about his *"own time."* His precious time alone was certainly not spent on fishing. His private getaways were spent with his dear lady, Miss Charlotte.

"Where is your boy?" Charles inquired.

"Manning the store."

"On his own?" Charles asked in disbelief.

"Yes, he'll likely mess something up." Leon commented shaking his head.

"Now why would you say that about your son?"

"Probably the same reason I did not bring him fishing. The boy is clumsy. I am always fixing his mistakes and you know how I hate rework Charles? Timm will never be an expert like my father and I have been, designing precious clocks and such. Charles like I have stated before, the boy takes after his mother, not his father. Maybe someday you will have my grandson who will follow in your professional footsteps or maybe mine? Timm is not going to be a likely candidate from what I can tell!" Muffled Leon about his only son. "Lara has not been working at the store with having the baby and all. I have been trying to mentor Timm more and more. God bless him, maybe the skilled craft is something he will grow into? Enough, Charles, enough! Let's enjoy this sunny day!"

The traveling horse drawn wagon proceeded and turned down a very narrow path. Leon was not exactly sure where they were headed. "Headed to Porter's Pond are we?"

"You must know the area well?" Charles grinned.

"Been out here a few times for a social gathering or two. The secluded area is actually quite peaceful at times." Leon explained and Charles agreed. "Obviously you have found your way out here before and done a little fishing? You may have fished but did you catch anything?"

"Yep, caught a few little ones. You know there was a time when I had to fend for my own supper?" Charles reminded his father-in-law.

"I admire your sense of humor, always being funny. You rarely complain, that's a strong trait in a man, Charles. Not to sound mushy but at times I feel grateful. I am fortunate my daughter has found a loving husband and I have a son-in-law that I can't register any complaints about."

"Leon, it has a lot to do with personality and upbringing. My parents are kind hearted and my father is so easy going. My mother's parents were stern folks. She was so blessed to have met and married my father. There were too many demands and expectations of her at home on her family's farm. My father opened up a whole new life for her from what I am told. Since I was an only child, our family was less complicated compared to the large family she came from. Father wished for more children. Like my mother always said *'it was better to have one golden egg than a bunch of rotten ones'* was her pride and joke."

Both men laughed hysterically about the comment. Leon laughed so hard, tears streamed down his chubby cheeks. "You, a golden egg?"

Arriving at the pond, Charles stood up in the wagon and pronounced, "Oh yes, all these willow trees. Something odd about them."

"Odd?" as Leon was not so quick to agree.

"They just look weird and creepy. The tree limbs are long and dangling. Not so pretty like a blooming apple tree I suppose," was Charles' opinion.

Leon shrugged his shoulders as if the trees characteristics did not matter to him. All he knew was that the willow trees were plentiful with strong branches offering a bit of shade. "Willow trees around here always survive the storms. The limbs bend but don't break. Once the thunder and lightning pass the trees simply bounce back into shape. Kinda like myself I guess?"

"Come on, let's catch some fish, Macher!" Charles unloaded the wagon as Leon stood nearby waiting for instructions. The poles were ready with line and baited as Charles gave Leon ongoing directions. The two proceeded to the pond's edge with the poles in hand.

"This is just nice to be away. Honesty, I have a lot on my mind, Charles."

"Anything you care to share to relieve that load?" Was Charles compassionate request.

"Matter of fact there is. First, you are part of my family being my son-in-law. Secondly, you are an attorney. I know I can consult and confide in you like a priest, meaning this is very personal Charles. I must share this troubling story with you if you do not mind?"

"What better place and time, certainly in confidence." Leon was assured by Charles.

"Well, I know you have vaguely asked me how it is that I ended up here, here in Georgia."

"Yes, I have been so curious? It is awkward, you do not speak much of your family back home in Germany."

"I need to tell you this story as there may be a time you need to share this with my daughter. At this time I only want you to know this troubling piece of my past."

Charles was quick to comment, "Are you sure a priest is not needed?"

"No, no, I did not do anything wrong. Just want to disclose a special time in my life that I have kept a secret from my family."

"War or prison?" Charles began to guess.

"No, this is not a guessing game. I am going to reveal this only to you, Charles. Back home in Germany I was fortunate to attend school. But attendance was not regular. The family's farm always needed tending to. My father also insisted I work with him in the shop learning the skills he had acquired, making and repairing clocks. Guess I turned out to be quite the craftsman. I have taken the skills and tools I learned from him and ventured into other areas. How proud I am of the unique jewelry pieces I have designed over the years. They are truly priceless creations."

"I believe this is the first time you have spoken of your family, Leon?"

"Yes, Charles that is true. I rarely talk about my family back home."

"Please, share some more about them with me!" As Charles was in suspense.

"Of course. One thing about the two of us, we have completely different backgrounds. Yet, we get along so well. I know it is not an easy task getting along with me." Leon acknowledged. "Why we seem to understand each other well considering our language and culture diversities. I'm a skilled craftsman with a grammar school education. You are a highly educated attorney.

The story I need to share with you is about my own family and not an easy one to tell. When I was a teenager, oh about 15 years old, I met and fell in love with a neighbor girl named Olivia. Her father was the local blacksmith and her mother tended to their four children. Olivia wore the most beautiful smile that accented her big, bold, blue eyes. Her personality sparkled with friendliness. Just the site of her made me feel chilly inside and out, all the time, every time! At 15, I felt like a grown man. My father had given me the tools to support myself. I had approached my father for advice and blessings. He approved of me courting Olivia. We both headed to her family's farm to speak with her father about this. With her father's approval, I immediately starting getting better acquainted with her. A few years later her father granted me permission to marry his daughter. Of course she had no say in the matter but clearly we shared love for one another. After we were married, my father and I built a small one room cabin about a half mile away from my family's farm. The home was placed on a few acres my father owned."

Charles interrupted, "Oh Leon, I did know you were previously married back home?"

"There is more to the story, Charles. About a year later, my young bride gave birth to our infant son, Leon Timothy Macher Jr. The baby was our pride and joy. Olivia was a wonderful wife and caring mother. She tended lovingly to the baby and me. Not really sure how she put up with me though?" Leon's smile grew. "She called the baby '*Little Leon*'. That little baby actually made me a bit nervous as he was so small and precious. My wife and infant son made me proud to be a man.

The following winter, my wife became ill. Days later her petite body weakened. The doctor was called upon. Apparently she contacted a serious disease or plague. The doctor told me to keep her warm and confined to the home. Her sick condition worsened quickly. Then the baby cried for days and quit nursing, although I think it was his mother who gave up? The pain was unbearable to see my young vibrant bride bedridden, along with a now sick, starving son. The brutal, winter weather hindered me from venturing to my folks' house that particular day. Nor did I dare want to possibly infect them if my family's illness was contagious. Only a few more dreary days went by and they both perished." Leon's eyes were loaded with tears. "Excuse me, for this is hard for a man to express."

"No apologies needed." Charles patted Leon on the back to console him. "This is an isolated case. Understandably, any human would show some sort of remorse?"

As Leon sobbed he continued with his story. "I eventually went to my father's farm and scouted around for a shovel. At his farm I dug a grave for my wife in the hard, cold dirt. Then I proceeded to dig a smaller one for the baby. I was so angry at God for taking them both from me and at the same time. I tossed the shovel aside. My thought was to bury them together in one grave and not side by side. I believed Olivia would have liked that better anyways. Her son forever cradled on top of her, the pairs' eternal home. After their burial, I just could not go back home to that empty cabin. I moved back in with my parents. Charles, I was extremely miserable. Losing my wife was devastating, losing my baby son was heartbreaking. From there, I felt like I was living in a dark hole where the sunshine would never reach.

Months later, my cousin had plans to move here to America. He was interested in the ongoing wars. He invited me to join him on his journeys. All I wanted to do was escape my past heartbreaks and somehow move on. Our travels lead us to the northern states. I did not care for the colder climates. Local folks told me to keep going south and I'd surely find warmer temperatures. So, I took off leaving my cousin behind to do what he set out to do. Traveling for weeks I ended up here. At the time, not really knowing where *"here"* was? Something felt peaceful. The area had a few established merchants among the rural farms. Most importantly there were no known clock makers in the area.

From ther,e I set up shop in an old abandoned barn where I actually lived for a long time. Eventually I saved enough money and set up business in a small space in the village."

"Wow Leon, I did not know you were carrying these troubling circumstances around with you? Certainly sheds some light on things. Now I know why Timm is not named after you, a son had previously been named in your honor?"

Leon continued, "I miss that family dearly. Things were perfect then. My wife Olivia was adorable. The baby was cute and cuddly. The loss was unbearable and overwhelming. My first wife, Olivia and I had a tight bond. Oh how I long for her and my son, a son I never will get to know. I was so young and proud of him. A son named after me. Charles you are the only one besides the folks back home that are aware of these circumstances. My current wife Fia would not understand if I even tried explaining this to her. This is something Lara needs not to be bothered with either, I guess?"

"No, no, she does not need to know. This would be upsetting. No need to add the pain to her life. The untold story is just that, untold. There is no reason to tell her from what I understand." Charles complied.

"Now I hope you also understand why my marriage to Fia is so troubled. Not that it is completely her fault. Just seems I can't get back what I once had. Do not take me wrong, I am thankful for my new family. Maybe God has blessed me twice? Charles I feel that you and

Lara have a marriage something like I once had with Olivia. I am happy for the two of you. I hope you never have to experience what my troubled past has produced for me. Poor Fia, she could never compare to Miss Charlotte either. Fia is not at fault. I blame her father who was giving away his daughters like leftover puppies."

"Leon what did you mean to compare your wife to Miss Charlotte?" Charles was a bit muddled by the comment.

"Miss Charlotte?" Answered a surprised and confused Leon.

"Yessss, you mentioned her also! Come on!" Charles smirked, "Is there something else to tell or clarify?"

"No!" Was Leon's feisty reply.

"Maybe another secret story to share?" Grinning from ear to ear with annoyance.

"Using your attorney skills on me are you?" Leon shot back.

"Leon you spilled the beans. Is there a little something you have to share about the flower lady? This has to be a better story, meaning pleasant? Come on, Miss Charlotte is always so delightful and I am sure you would agree?"

"Charles, you will never be the man I am. I am now confessing my sins to you. Maybe I do need a priest now? My life was so empty. Any man would appreciate my life, I am a businessman with a pretty wife. There are four well behaved children along with my grand-baby Missy. Miss Charlotte came into my life and filled a major void. Her upbeat personality drew me to her. The lady is just plain fun!" Leon explained briefly.

"I will agree with you, she is very pleasant and quite pretty also."

"She was alone and I was lonely. We just fell into each other arms spontaneously one rainy afternoon. I was down at her hothouse and it was drizzling rain outside. Apparently she was scared of thunderstorms which drove us inside. We stepped into her house. With the first boom and crackle of the storm, she was in my arms seeking comfort like a toddler." Leon joked. "She has been there ever since, Charles. Gee, may be about five years or so by now? My friend, my lover, forever. The women in my life have come in a strange sequence. Charles, at times I have had a hard time understanding and appreciating God's love and gifts for me?"

"Things have been complicated for you I will agree. What are your intentions with Miss Charlotte?" Charles further interrogated his father-in-law.

"Just to keep things going as they are and quietly." Leon sadly admitted.

"Are you not afraid that you have broken one of God's Ten Commandments?"

"No damn it! God put her in my arms to comfort us both." Leon demanded.

"You are a strong souled man sir!"

"I can't be afraid nor fear God. I have too much responsibility for my family, business, and friends. Those things keep me going. God is understanding, I know it says that somewhere in the big thick book?" Leon referring to the Holy Bible.

Charles replied playfully, "I promise you I will never stray from my wife. 'Cause I would not want to have to answer to you, oh no Sir!"

"Funny, Charles!" Leon acting irritated.

"I am being serious, I truly love my Lara!" Charles exclaimed. "Well Leon, guess the fish are not biting today. Maybe we scared them away with all the mushy women talk and all. Let's call it a day. Maybe next time? We will need to go fishing more often."

"Seriously, you want to fish with me again?" The look on Leon's face was puzzling.

"Certainly, we learned a lot today. I hope Lara was not planning on fresh fish for dinner this evening."

"You know that daughter of mine would not touch a dead fish let alone eat one!" Both men again laughed.

"Leon I am thankful for one thing. Your troubled past has lead a path to me. I have been blessed with the best wife ever. To prove this, I would never want to trouble her with the story of your loss of Little Leon, and the baby's mother. Why bring sorrow into her life when it is unnecessary. That is your story and shared only to me and the two of us will keep it that way."

The two men gathered the fishing gear and loaded their things back into the wagon. Back to town they headed nibbling on the baked goods from the wicker basket. The conversation was strictly business, no sentimental stories or confessions. Leon's spirit was lifted with the time he spent with his son-in-law. His only concerns were that he shared too much about Miss Charlotte. Charles could be a trusted individual Leon presumed. After all, his well-liked son-in-law was an attorney! Leon's final comments consisted of a thought of comparison. "Charles, seems your life is like the blossoming apple tree. Mine has been more like the willow tree."

Chapter 10

THE ADVOCATE VISITS A TROPICAL ISLAND

Several year later in the late 1850's, Charles was offered a short-term position by the American government. The mission was for him to visit a specific tropical island. Mainly, he was going to meet with a government official and discuss immigration laws, if there were any there? The journey would be a rough one but a challenge for the attorney was always acceptable.

Once the small ship arrived at the tropical island, Charles was taken by its beauty. The sky was a medium shade of blue he had never seen before. The big, pure, white puffy clouds acted like a coated ceiling to the heavens. Feeling the hot, the steamy air was a bit discomforting. The sun was blazing and beating down hard on the sandy earth.

There was no time for recreation. Charles was here strictly on government business. He took notice of the active slavery in the area. Personally he did not like it nor did he understand the oppression. His job was to compare these slaves' conditions to what was gradually diminishing in the southern states.

By chance were these slaves ever going to see freedom? Charles recalled the rural area in which he was raised as a child. There were no colored folks around. One thing his mother taught him was to love every man equally. As a young boy he did not even know men of color existed. His mother's spiritual expressions made no exception for anyone.

Moving to America he faced new ideas and concepts. Quickly he learned to be a stronger advocate for what was right and slavery was wrong in his opinion. For a while he kept these views to himself. He was not hesitate to help out when needed though. Abruptly, he learned again that man was being categorized by specific stereotypes that solely included the color of their skin.

Charles wondered about a misunderstanding. "Why did God create such a diversity among mankind?" Some people seemed to gain and benefit from the mixture. Then again others suffered based merely on their skin color and culture.

The next few days were filled with meet ups. Charles was getting overwhelmed. The trip involved a lot of work involving legal issues. Also, he was not accustomed to the culture on the small island. All the black people were servants of some sort. The food selection was definitely different.

Upon his arrival Charles was assigned to a local man that acted as a guide and chaperone. The dark-skinned man spoke very little English but knew his way around the village and some. The local folks called the man "Doc." He was known for his healing skills. The story was told that he once set a dog's broken leg with sticks and twine. Doc had an ailment for every illness. The local folks knew he was not an official doctor or anything close to being one. In his early years he wanted to be a caretaker for animals. He had a liking for nature and animals and always observing his surroundings. For a man with no formal education he certainly was knowledgeable and loaded with common sense.

The last night of Charles' stay on the island, Doc escorted him to the beach. By dusk the tropic temperature had cooled down by only a few degrees. On the sandy beach were a group of black mean gathered around a small fire. "Eat." Spoke an elderly man motioning the act. The blazing fire was cooking some type of charred meat.

"You eat Sir?" Doc requested of Charles. But Charles was reluctant. The food smelled good but he was unsure what was actually cooking. Charles was more interested in prying into Doc's past. He began by asking if the man had a wife or family. "Yes, I do." Was Doc's reply.

"A wife and children?" Charles inquired.

"If you must know, I have two motherless children."

"And…?" Charles was interrupted before he could continue.

"I feel pain in my heart." Doc held his hand over his chest.

Charles compassionately placed his hand on Doc's shoulder for comfort.

"My wife, stolen from me, to become another man's servant. My wife is gone forever with two of my own to raise alone."

"How old are the children Doc?" Charles eagerly asked.

"Boy 12, girl 10. I fear for them. I fear they one day will be captured or sold as slaves. They are too young. I try to keep them in my sight all times and isolate them from the community. They are a target for the greedy man. I want the family together." Doc explained to the curious white man. "I know you have a good life. Things are bountiful in America and more politically structured. You are fortunate, white man."

Charles tried to explain his life was not always so perfect. "I had a long journey to get to America. I once lived in Europe and moved to get an education. My goal was to always help people. Doc, would you like to come to America with me, move there?"

"Impossible, I have no money." Shaking his head.

"I will arrange for you and the children to return with me tomorrow. My family is in the process of purchasing a large farm. The work is never done on a farm. Live as a family, finding shelter will not be a problem as I knew just about everyone. You would be helpful with the farm animals." Charles knew Doc could be handy in other ways also around the farm. "Come Doc, you will never have this opportunity again in your lifetime."

"I will go if what you are telling me is true. I do not believe you are a white man trying to trick me. Your eyes are sincere, aren't they?"

"Doc, I am an attorney. I represent the laws of the land there. Your children can live with less fear, get educated and learn skills.

Seems your children have suffered enough with the loss of their mother. My family will welcome you. I have a wonderful wife and one very special daughter. My parents are arriving soon to live on the farm also. I have not seen them in a long time. The farm was actually purchased for them. My father is a hard worker. He loves animals also." Charles lengthy invitation was convincing.

"I will go, Sir."

"Pack as very few things as possible. Everything your family needs will be provided. We are adding three extra passengers on the return so there will not be much room for personal belongings. No word to anyone. No one!" Charles demanded.

Charles knew he was doing the right thing by relocating Doc and his children. The man had qualities that Charles could appreciate. The farm could always use an extra set of hands and eyes.

Chapter 11
CHETTSBURG'S FAMILY FARM

The ambitious attorney was anxious to have his folks move to America. The area was searched for a small farm for Joseph and Elizabeth. Charles hoped to find suitable soil to grow crops like those grown back in Belgium. The land would also be used to cultivate nut producing trees. Just a few trees would do as Charles was fascinated with the local pecans. The nuts that were first introduced to him years ago. Pecans baked in the inviting muffins by his now mother-in-law, Fia.

The farm needed to be located near a town or city. The idea was for Elizabeth to establish another chocolate shop and tea room. Thinking ahead, Charles needed to calculate how many acres were needed to harvest peanuts and sugar cane, as well. If the crops were plentiful the extra crops could be sold to local residents or merchants was Charles' thinking. He was always thinking of ways to make more money. The soil was rich in the area. Charles was interested in a garden of his own to help feed his family.

The idea of moving was beginning to be an overwhelming task for his father, Joseph. The farm in Belgium would have to be sold. All their personal belongings would need to be sorted through. There would be decisions on what to keep and what to pack. Everything possibly could not go with them, just a few tools, clothing, furniture, and of course Elizabeth's baking and candy making supplies.

Surprisingly the perfect farm to be purchased was stumbled upon. Charles approached the owner of the slightly run down homestead, meaning no one had taken up a vacancy there in a while?

The young man offered the farmer a small sum of money for the farm. The older gent accepted the offer as he was ready to move out of state and head north. Word was the farmer was a mean and cruel Master named Thad Davis. Mr. Davis feared retaliation from the slaves he previously owned and mistreated. Ironic thing was most of his freed slaves had already headed North. "I heard from my former colleagues that a system is in place for some former slaves? A discrete plan is to help them move through the states moving towards the state of Michigan. Many of them are crossing over to Canada."

As usual, Charles thought to himself in a comical tone. *"I'll laugh if the old man Davis moves north and runs into his some of his former slaves. He's funny, he'll never make it as a Yankee. His deep southern drawl will be the first thing to give him away."*

Charles had few concerns about the man. He put the fear in Mr. Davis so that he would leave town quickly. The older farmer was eager to start packing up his household. The attorney offered his legal advice and assured Mr. Davis, "I do not think you will get a very fair price for your farm since the place has a lot of stigma attached to it. First thing I'd do is tear down those old shanties outback. That is a dead giveaway the place housed slaves. A prospective buyer would be turned off knowing colored slaves lived and worked here. That's like damaged soil." The old man nodded in agreement with the bluffing Charles as he tried not to laugh aloud. "Well maybe I can come up with some cash and buy the farm from you? Might not be much. At least you could move on. Not sure if this would be much of an investment on my part. Being a local I might be able to find someone who might take an interested in the run down place. Please let me go back to my office and balance my record keeping books."

"Oh, I will take whatever you have to offer Mr. Chettsburg. My wagons are packed. I really need to get out of town." Commented the concerned and frightened man.

"Stop by in the morning. I'll have some paperwork drawn up on the property. You can sign the deed over to me and officiate the purchase," stated a confident Charles.

"Thanks sir, you have saved my soul," the farmer replied.

Charles thought to himself about how the man was about to hand over a great opportunity, knowing his parents were in the process of moving to the states. In the back of his mind, he hoped they started all the necessary preparations to come America.

The large farm appealed to Charles. The house was real nice when things were kept up a few years ago. Beautiful trees landscaped the yard and the soil was rich and fertile. The farmer had a very plentiful corn crop at the time. Probably the only thing that kept him going? Charles had plans for that place! The farm was going to open new doors for his family. The day would come soon when he could get his parents' feet planted on that soil. The thought of his father loving to farm thrilled him even more. Possibly fulfilling his mother's wish of opening another tea room and chocolate shop was a thought dear to him. The biggest sentiment was for his parents to meet his beautiful wife Lara and his adorable daughter Missy. What a feeling of completion that would be.

Morning could not arrive fast enough for the attorney. *"Maybe I will have to sleep with a pen in my hand?"* he snickered to himself. Soon enough the farm was sold dirt cheap to Charles. The old brutal man stated he was headed to California. He was not going north as they catered to the freed slaves there. Charles being good natured prayed for the guy. The spiritual man understood the comment he once heard and took to heart, *"The events of our past guide our future."* Not

even Charles could save the old farmer's soul with prayer.

Chapter 12

REUNITING WITH THEIR SON

Joseph shared a vision of farming in America like his only son, Charles. Quite possibly he could grow produce to be used in his wife's tea room or chocolate shop. He knew the weather was warmer in the south. Could he convince his wife to change her venue? He sat back and smoked out of his packed pipe. Dreaming about farming in America was on his mind. There would be acres and acres of peanuts and sugar cane. His yard would have walnut trees taking up space and shading the yard. Daily he would pick fresh nuts and deliver them to his wife were his exact thoughts. He was not too sure about those peanuts and sugar cane. *"Produce is produce."* He proclaimed to himself. After all farming was what he knew. His pipe went out and he headed back to work.

There were years of saving and scraping. Joseph and Elizabeth felt they had enough money to make their big move. The decision was to sell their home and farm to a sibling of Elizabeth's. Anticipating this would give them ample financing to make the major move to be with their son. Joseph dreaded leaving behind his family and friends knowing he would miss them dearly as he already did. Rarely did he get to see his immediate family anyways as the travel was a long one. Elizabeth was going to miss her own parents and siblings but a wife must stick with her husband's decisions. This is what makes a man, he thought. At least he knew meeting up with their only son was going to be beneficial to his wife who yearned for him.

Elizabeth was well beyond her time as an entrepreneur, especially for a woman. She dreamed of moving to America to be with her only son, of course. There she would have access to better varieties of ingredients for her chocolates. There would be fresh nuts and sugar cane.

Joseph farmed and saved to get money to move to America. The best produce and crops would be sold. The couple would eat the farmer's seconds while they scraped and saved. Joseph cared for his wife dearly. A woman who at times was hard to get along with. When she did have something to say, at times the conversation was as if she was yelling. By now, Joseph was very use to her demeanor. He did not take these actions too personally. He figured this was a bad habit she had inquired from being brought up in such a large family. The husband looked at the brighter things. Elizabeth seemed to tend to everything including meals on his table, a well-kept house, and a yard full of beautiful flowers and bushes. She was a God fearing soul, living as if the Devil sat on her shoulder watching every move she made. Next to her wooden recipe box, one could find a tattered Bible. Matter of fact, the book was located near her at most times.

Months later, Charles' parents Joseph and Elizabeth finally arrived to America. The journey continued towards their new home in the state of Georgia. A very large farm with lots and lots of acreage. Ahead, a home sat waiting that would be very big in Elizabeth's eyes. The house had five bedrooms and something very unusual to Mrs. Chettsburg. Confused, she did not understand why there was a kitchen detached from the house? Charles had some clearing up to do. He explained to his mother that most of the larger homes built a separate cooking quarters, apart from the main house. The reason for this was, in case of a fire the flames could be detained in the isolated area and hopefully not damage the house. This was a clever safety precaution when it came to cooking and living in rural areas.

Outback was a huge barn possibly for animals and equipment. Attached to the building was a dwelling that Charles referred to as the "*backhouse*." To the far rear of the farm were several little tattered shanties that once housed slaves.

"Lordy Charles, what is this all about? This farm is huge, is this affordable?" Joseph question his son.

"Father, I got the best deal on this here farm. The previous owner wanted to head north. He said things are far more settle there. He can go there and stay there as far as I am concerned. The weather is much too chilly there for me," joking as usual.

Charles further explained the farm had been somewhat idle for the past few years. The acreage needed some tending to such as the over grown weeds. The house was basically in excellent condition. A woman's touch was needed; a few curtains, more furniture, and some laughter to make the place feel like home.

"Father, I have hired a handyman for the farm. He and his two teenaged children," Charles explained.

"Who is this gentleman?" Questioned Joseph.

"A man with knowledge of care for animals and who seems to be able to treat them well. I met him while I was on business in the tropical islands, he is called Doc. Hopefully you received my letter detailing my extended government assignment there a while back. I knew you would need some extra help once we got things up and running here on the farm."

"A man of medicine, a doctor?" Puzzled Joseph. "What does that mean, is he a doctor?"

"The man is remarkable, he can set a broken arm or leg with sticks and twine. He is kind and compassionate when this one comes to animals. There is a fruit called a banana. Doc has used the outer peelings as remedies for infections and rashes. A very well rounded man indeed. His children are beautiful, loving beings. I have offered him a place to stay in the backhouse in addition to a small wage. Heads up Father, he is a very dark skinned man. I know you and mother have not been acquainted with these types of folks as of yet."

Joseph nodded in agreement, "Interesting, I have a man of color with two children who are going to reside in something called a backhouse. The gentleman is a man of medical knowledge as you state, and a handyman? As always Charles you make things interesting and complicated. Now son, please tell me what are we gonna do with those shanties way out back?"

"My thoughts are once we get the farm up and running smoothly we will definitely need additional labor for the fields. The laborers can be housed in them. The shanties could use a little maintenance though?"

His father was obviously still confused, "Where are you gonna get all this help?"

"I know a plantation owner south of here who has some displaced freed slaves."

Joseph was quick to respond, "I am no slave owner!"

"No Father, they are freed. He claims they are good workers in need of work and housing. They are currently living in poor housing conditions with lack of food and other daily necessities. I figured we can put them to work, house them, and pay them a little money or barter for food."

"Make sure they get paid a fair wage, Son. I know what the situation is like to work a hard labor job. I worked long hours before you were born. I do not want to insult these folks," Joseph continued.

"Father I have things all work out as usual. Housing will be provided along with some pay. The wages will allow them to eat. The farm will be plentiful when the setting comes to crops I imagine. Terrible how they are living in rash conditions now."

"Son, we moved here to farm a small farm and to eventually establish a small chocolate business for your mother. She is fascinated with the crops grown here. Looks like you've created a major enterprise here in this town? At my age I am looking to slow down Son, not take on such a big undertaking," the father confided kiddingly.

"Father this is an opportunity! I am here to help. There will be hired help. I now have a partner in my law practice where I act as the senior attorney. Lara takes good care of our child and home. The farm land is going to harvest lots of peanuts is my plan. Behind your house I plan on planting more and more pecan trees."

"Son, your mother can only use so many nuts in her baked goods?"

"Father are you not getting the big, overall picture? We are going to mass produce peanuts and maybe pecans? The abundant crops will be sold. Peanuts are in high demand. We can sell the surplus. The sales and profits will also help run the farm, the farm is a business. Do you get it now?" Charles was enthused about the proposal with his father.

"Since when has my very successful, well-educated son become a farmer? I thought that was why you left Belgium for

America to seek your dreams as an attorney?" The father drilled his son.

"This is becoming my dream. I have my whole family with me now, a law practice, a part-time position as a professor at the university, and now a huge farm." Charles grinned. "Where will I find all the time, Father?"

Chapter 13

PLANTING THE SEEDS

~Welcome to Chettsburgs' Farm~

~Where Pecans Are Plentiful~

A new wooden sign, crafted by Joseph was hung at the farm's driveway's entrance. A symbol that shared Charles' vision and passion, acres and acres of bountiful pecan trees.

First thing on Charles agenda was to hire some farm help. There were several freed slaved housed in an old barn down the road. Charles and his father set out to gather some workers for hire. Joseph again assured his son that he was not a slave owner but an employer, Charles was certainly in agreement with him. Next, a small orchard of pecan trees were planted in a vacant yard next to the house. The first crop of peanuts were sowed and harvested, a far better harvest than expected. The new laborers highly appreciated their new lifestyle arrangements. A somewhat safe place to live and call home. To think they were actually getting paid to work even though the amount was very little. Actually they did not need much money. Most of their food was produced on the farm which seemed self-sufficient. The group was eventually given a designated area near the shanties to cultivate a large garden for themselves. Money did not mean much to them anyways. Not like they had anywhere to spend their wages?

Elizabeth had an opinion as usual, "Not nice to treat folks differently based on skin color or looks alone! On this farm, the policy will always be that everyone works for a fair wage and gets the same opportunities. There will be an elimination of segregation on this farm, darn it!" A surprisingly stern statement.

The freed colored slaves would appreciate the self-contained safe haven and security of living on the Chettsburgs' farm. Everything they needed was provided. No other daily necessities were required except for a lot of prayers.

The men of color were able to enjoy an evening of fishing there on the farm. Out yonder behind the corn fields were small running streams. The back woods delivered wildlife for trapping small animals. Beyond the farm's borders some cruel people still existed. These were people who distributed labels to people based on their skin tones and centered on their trying pasts.

The closer these folks were to the Chettsburg house, the safer they felt, even though they were still on their farmland. The group of laborers were highly religious. A fortunate feeling was among them as they knew they were a select few. Their prayers gave constant thanks to God for the new found freedom.

All the prayers in the world could not give enough gratitude for the way of life the Chettsburgs were providing.

The biggest benefit was that some of the colored folks' children were able to attend Missy's makeshift school. Seems Missy turned her playhouse into a "*playschool*." The young girl who was about twelve years old, dreamed of being a school teacher. She was bright like her father, Charles. On the farm, she played and pretended to conduct school. In an essence, she was teaching the colored children. The opportunities were rare for children of color to attend a real school to learn how to read and write. Word of the playschool actually made some of the local town folks mad. Charles was an advocate for everyone. He allowed his only child to continue with her childhood school-like play. His thoughts were these town folks were just jealous. Maybe someday these colored children might be smarter than them, one day. With Missy as their mentor they probably would be, Charles chuckled with pride. The parents of these children loved Missy for her free spirit and compassion for everyone.

Missy would conduct her school sessions daily. Not having many playmates, her small group of students usually consisted of the offspring of the farm's workers. This was a unique opportunity for these beginning black children. The young teacher taught the alphabet. There were sounds, sight recognition, and writing of the alphabet's letters. A few letters were put together to be read as words.

When the weather was extremely hot outside the group could be seen sitting in the shaded areas near the schoolhouse. The activities consisted of songs, games, and Missy reading aloud. The school only had one book, the Bible. Seemed to be the only book that was necessary for her? Missy loved to read from the big book. Although the Bible became part of her daily curriculum this helped her learn new words also. She liked to flip through the thick book finding passages suited for the other children. Her main purpose with the Bible was to apply the verses to real life experiences.

Also in attendance at the school were the new arrivals on the farm. The family from the Islands that had moved into the backhouse. The three of them shared the household quarters on the farm. The father was only known as "Doc." A nickname Charles brewed up since he had a hard time pronouncing the man's real name, whatever that was? The son was called Peiter, pronounced pay-tare. A well-built boy with tight, curly, black hair. Finally, there was Kemica, a dark, brown skinned girl with beautiful, long wavy hair. A unique name pronounced kem-eek-a.

Planted Seeds in My Garden*

The time is now to plant the seeds.
But first I must cultivate with my hands and knees.
Place the seeds in the dug holes.
I help the tomatoes stand with poles.

Days pass by and I see them sprout.

They appear so green and healthy, also very stout.

Weeks pass by and the food begins to bare.

I must fertilize my plants so they will have extra care.

Months have gone bye, now the seeds have ripened well.

It is time to pick them? Or should I let them swell!

The time is now, I pick them to eat

Fresh garden vegetables are better than any candy treat.

I wash them carefully and put them on the stove to simmer.

That great garden has helped make a wonderful dinner.

The growing season is over, I'll can these leftover few.

So, throughout the year I can have vegetables as tasty as new!

* *This poem was written by the author as a teen at age thirteen.*

She was inspired based on a local newspaper contest.

The prize she was awarded allowed her spend several days on campus at Michigan State University and attend summer classes that were in progress.

Her mother held on to that poem and framed the gift for a recent birthday.

Years later, the poem seemed suited for this chapter.

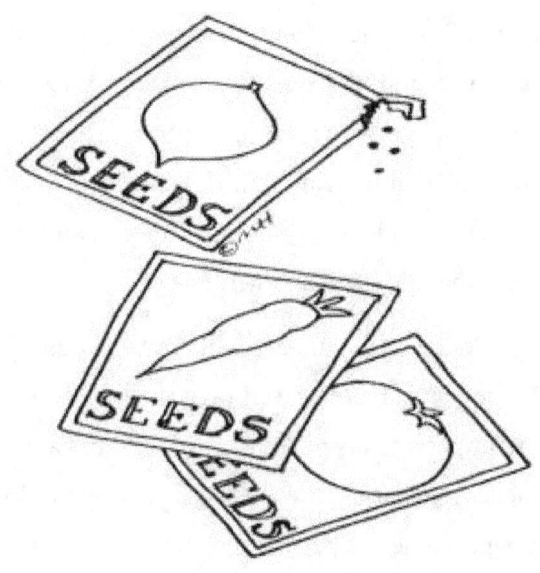

Chapter 14

CHANGES AT THE FARM

A few years later, Charles' father Joseph needed to slow down as he seemed to tire easily. The farm was too much for him to manhandle even with his son's help managing. In the meantime, the old law office had outgrown the small space. The building was about to make a big transformation into his mother's new shop.

Charles was excited about his move to a newer and bigger business location down the street. His law practice did not seem to occupy enough of his time though. There was plenty of time for him on the farm that was acquired for his family. Soon after, the large house and the farm became too much for his father, Joseph. That was fine with Charles. The challenging man knew how to delegate and get things done. The thought of his family living with his parents on the farm was delightful. But that idea was short-lived.

Charles' parents eventually took up housing in the old office's upstairs. The newlywed's old dwelling was now home to Joseph and Elizabeth. Even though his parents moved a short ways into the village, they were closer to Charles' law business. The main floor of the old office building became the perfect set-up for his mother's inspirations of baking goods and making chocolates. The new store front was quite upscale compared to her tea room back home. Like the old place, the location was welcoming and homey.

The signage on the store front had to be updated. Another cheerful chore for crafty Joseph. The new store's insignia was proudly displayed, "Chettsburgs' Farm's Chocolate Shop & Tea Room." The subheading read like the one at the farm itself, "Where Pecans Are Plentiful." The pecans were just another signature feature of Elizabeth's, along with the chocolate delights and baked-goods. The modest owner mainly referred to the store as the "tea room." She did not care for the term "customers". The openhearted host preferred to call her patrons "*guests*," well most of them?

Elizabeth's store had a counter to display a few baked good for the early arriving guests. This same counter divided the dining area and kitchen. Yet, the kitchen was pretty much visible to the customers. This allowed for Elizabeth to keep an eye on incoming patrons. She tended to those seating in her receiving area enjoying her goods. In between time, the host kept an eye on anything baking or brewing her special kitchen.

The receiving area was a cross between a living room and a dining room. Against the west wall was a flaming hearth to keep the front of the store warm on cooler days or into the brisk nights. A large, oval, handmade, braided rug filled the center of the rustic wooden floor. The rug was accented with two small round tables surrounded by wooden Winsor chairs. Neatly placed was a lumpy couch. Two wingback chairs were tucked away in the corner with a dainty end table placed between them.

"How much business would there be for this type of store here in town?" Back in the kitchen Elizabeth was busy baking and wondering. She anticipated being much busier than back home on the rural farm's tea room in Belgium. At least the store's set up was comforting with home only a few steps away.

The fresh bread could be smelled by late morning. The baker was busy with a few new ideas for her store. With lunch time approaching the menu needed something extra in addition to her special sweet treats. First, a batter of shortbread was whisked together; butter, sugar, and sifted flour. The final touch was a cup of chopped, roasted pecans. When baked, she had a tasty, buttery, cookie type dessert. The newest lunchtime item was Elizabeth's flip bread. Again, no eggs needed for this appetizing feature. Basically just starting with flour, water shortening, salt, and a pinch each of baking powder and baking soda. The fresh grilled bread was usually served smothered with creamy butter and homemade jams. Made for a great side with a bowl of steamy soup. The scrumptious, seared bread was delicious on its own if customers were real hungry and in a hurry. New to Elizabeth was the idea of warm flip bread coated with creamy, melted, butter and topped with a blend of sugar and cinnamon. Gee, could she possible add crushed pecans to the mixture? This is the place where the buttery pecan nuts were plentiful!

Her husband Joseph still helped managed the farm on his own time. He would make time to help out his wife at the tea room, if needed. Stacking wood at the back door. Organizing supplies in the kitchen. Joseph was enjoying the flexibility between the venues of the tea room and the farm.

Charles enjoyed spending time at his new home on the farm with his wife and daughter. There were many activities for him to love and the surroundings were beautiful. The farm was somewhat like a mini village with all the people living there along with the animals, shanties, barns, buildings and an abundance of ever rolling land. With his father at his side, he continued to fish on occasion outback in the running stream. His most valuable treasure on the farm were those pecan trees he planted near the rear of the house. For many reasons the young man prized his crops.

Charles was living a big dream indeed. He now owned an oversized, expanded farm. Nothing compared to the small one he enjoyed as a kid. By now he had achieved a lot of other goals. First, he arrived in America to attend law school, had a growing law practice, and a beautiful wife and daughter. Sitting back in his favorite chair he crossed his arms. The smile on his face expressed that life was good, very good for the young attorney!

Chapter 15
MISSY PLAYS SCHOOL

What is school really like? Missy continued to play the game of make-believe school. Or was there real life lessons going on in the playhouse? All the neighboring children living on the Chettsburgs' farm were invited to play along. The student count could be six or a dozen or so on a given day? The summer afternoons tended to get very warm in the south. When the playhouse warmed up inside, Missy would take her students outside. There they would sit under a shaded tree for a story to be told. Their creative teacher Missy, was good at making up stories. Most of her stories had an underlying lesson, actually like a fable.

There was a broad range of subjects to be taught. Math included counting with counters of small stones or dried beans. Letters of the alphabet were taught and recognized as symbols and sounds. Her long tales of other places could easily be a lesson in Geography.

Missy did not have many friends of her own. Most girls her age were going to boarding schools. Although her parents and grandparents could easily afford to send her, they chose to have her schooled locally. The young teen also studied a lot independently. Coming from a diverse background, she learned a lot from her family and their adult friends. Considering, her father was a well-educated attorney who also taught sometimes out of state at a university. Grandmother Chettsburg was a creative cook and baker who enjoyed sewing also. Her Grandfather Macher was a wise businessman and a skilled watchmaker. On hand was Grandfather Chettsburg, a man who farmed and crafted items out of wood. A wide variety of talents and role models surrounded the only child.

By age sixteen, Missy stood about 5'3 and was a petite young girl. The sun would reflect red highlights flowing through her brown hair. Her overall appearance was that of a youthful woman. Yet, she possessed a childlike charm. Most folks still address her as "Missy." She did not like being addressed as Miss Chettsburg. "Missy" suited her just fine, a bit less informal.

Missy continued to be the playful type. At times she was like a tomboy. Constantly dressing up or down. She dressed very sophisticated when the occasion was appropriate, bows and frilly lace. A skill for sewing in time was acquired as she took an interest in making those fancy dresses.

The young girl's main passion continued to be education. By now she had completed grammar school. Her parents allowed her take some time off from her studies, a year or so. Then, she was expected to further her school work to be a teacher. Her heart lead her to this discussion. There were children who needed and wanted to learn and that was her passion.

Fortunately, her family was wealthy enough that college was an option for her. Not too many woman had the opportunity to further their educations. The funding was just not available for most local folks.

Missy loved her father and wanted to follow his footstep in some ways. The attorney who was also a university professor. Actually, his first and foremost passion was managing the family farm. The man was known for harvesting pecans and planting peanuts.

Then there were her grandparents, the Chettsburgs who migrated from Belgium. Deep inside of the grandmother was a hardness about her. The overweight woman was avid about her chocolate specialties. Guess that is what made her a successful business woman. Joseph was mainly a farmer. Crafting wood was his relaxing hobby. His goal was to produce and grow quality crops suited for his wife's shop.

There was depth to Missy's daily school schedule playing out in the yard. The sessions began outside if the weather was fair enough. All players would gather and stand in a circle and hold hands. Yes, everyone held hands no matter the color of their skin. Missy began with a prayer of thanks. "God, thank you for all your gifts and blessings that you have showered us with." Other children would join in and recite the passage as they learned and memorized the prayers.

Then an additional request would be made. "Lord hear our special individual prayers." A moment of silence was given so everyone could peacefully pray to themselves. Missy knew each person had their own ideas on how they wanted their life blessed. Reaching those goals sometimes seemed impossible to many. The young woman inspired the children to pray and ask for special gifts from God.

After the prayers everyone would be seated in a circle on the ground. Often Missy would read aloud from the Bible.

Sharing the words, she tried to give more depth and interpretation to the book's phrases.

Chapter 16

A TRUE CARPENTER

Why was Joseph spending so much time in the back barn lately, Charles wondered? Charles had to investigate and see what his father was up to now. Maybe his father needed help with whatever was occupying his time all of a sudden. What was he doing?

Charles ventured out back to drop in on his father. Along with Joseph, there stood four of the farm laborers. As Charles looked around in amazement, something appeared to be mass produced? He took off his hat and scratched his head as something very interesting was going on in the barn.

"May I ask what is going on here, Father?" Charles was curious about his inquiry.

His father began to explain he had an ongoing project with the men. Most of these laborers were older. "We are assembling coffins." Joseph spoke up with pride.

"Coffins!" Charles yelped.

Yes, Joseph had begun assembling coffins in the cooler months to keep himself occupied. His new found hobby began when a poor family could not afford a coffin for their ill son. The five year old boy named Jessy knew he was sick from disease and was going to die soon. The optimistic child knew a little bit about death. The fact was dead people were laid to rest in coffins. The boy told his parents he wanted a special little "*dead bed*" that would be drawn by a big, white horse and wagon. A white horse, like an angel that would take him to see God in Heaven. All the coffins Jessy had seen were way too big for his little fail body. The parents obviously could not afford one for their dying son, let alone a customized child-sized one.

When Joseph heard about the situation he quickly assembled one out of some scrap wood. He was not alone on the project. As ill as Jessy was, Joseph invited the little guy to the farm. The two gathered odds and ends of pieces of wood. They put together and built a tiny coffin that fit the boy to his likings. The boy was puzzled about a few things as he laid in his customized coffin. "Mister, why are there crooked pieces of wood in the corners, there is not much room for my head or a pillow? How can I sleep forever without a pillow or blanket?"

"The corners are tapered and slanted, Jessy. This helps the body stay in place. You will rarely find a coffin in the south designed like this. I have made a lot of things out of wood. At times I fascinate myself as to what a good carpenter I am. When you reach Heaven, God will give you a special pillow and blanket made out fluffy clouds." Shaking his head with a smile.

Charles was so proud of his modest father. This was the first he had heard anything about this situation. Joseph further explained that locally inexpensive coffins were not available for poor folks. He felt some of the dead were not being properly buried nor respected.

Scrap wood, or good, salvageable, old boards were being used to assemble wooden coffins. The few pieces of needed hardware were purchased at The General Merchant Store. There was not much cost in making the coffins and the labor was cheap. The sale of the goods would be very profitable. The uniquely, crafted, wooden boxes were sold for a minimal price compared to other business manufactures. As Joseph started his new little enterprise, he found there was a greater need for the coffins than he anticipated.

The wood-working training began for the new enterprise. A few older laborers were selected to help build the coffins. Joseph was pleased to prepare the men with a special skill in crafting wood. These were men that were getting to old to work the fields, he thought. The only things needed were a few handsaws, lots of nails, wooden boards, and a little guidance were Joseph's thoughts.

His newfound project gave him an appreciation for all the great natural resources provided to him in America. The thick forests reminded him of his home in Belgium. Joseph explained to the workers that for every tree he ever cut down, he planted three more. "The forest of today need to be the forests of tomorrow. Trees are just like the crops on the farm, they need to be planted, grown, and harvested."

The workers were taught a lot about carpentry from their mentor. Joseph expressed that being a carpenter made him happy. Further explaining he told them to try and have a good mental attitude. A good attitude produced good quality work was his philosophy. Mainly, he enjoyed his craft and it took his mind off of the troubling things life had to offer at times. He addressed the men "Always be alert and awake when working with wood. Practice safety, make sure your shirts are always tucked in. Enjoy!" were the instructions. Easily said for the white man. The colored folks appreciated Joseph's enthusiasm and were praying to share in on his positive teachings.

All the coffins produced were constructed step-by-step. Some had flat crosses attached to the top for those who believed in God and Jesus. Some were actually designed quite beautifully from the way Joseph arranged the varieties of wood.

Charles was taken by his father's warm heart. Not totally surprised though. His talented father was sharing his skills by teaching others. A skill the men would possess forever. What a diverse crossover for his father, from farmer to craftsman. Charles was mostly proud for his father who had not placed any negative judgment on these men. A trait he found in all his family, a true lack of prejudice.

The son was quick to congratulate his father on his accomplishments, including making the coffins. He was thanked for sharing his skills with the other men. Charles knew this was a great opportunity for the somewhat suppressed workers. He was so surprised and taken by the coffin business that his father was establishing. The training was an unselfish gesture, Charles thought. He wanted to make sure to take the situation a step further. Going forward, there would be additional small groups of laborers trained in this unique skill also.

Although a brilliant man, Charles stood clueless. Never had it occurred to him that there was a need for coffins. Especially for the poor folks. As a businessman and attorney, Charles himself was always looking for opportunities. Seems his father was one step ahead of him this time.

Charles placed his hat back on his head. Exiting the barn, he crossed the dirt path that lead to the house. His thoughts were about what an amazing father he had. Now he knew what was going on in the barn!

The newly skilled carpenters were very grateful to Joseph. The men were proud and thankful that he taught them how to use tools they never had their hands on before. Along with the skills came a little bit of money also. Mostly appreciated was that they were attending the new church formed on the farm. A lesson they learned at a church service was to tithe money to the church and God. Meaning, a donation or small portion of their earnings should be given to the church. If they had no money one could give of their time and talents to their religion.

Chapter 17

DOC'S SON PEITER

Why would a son want to change his given birth name? Doc sat outside the barn on the ground, pondering in the blazing summer's heat. The usually strong natured man was deep in thought about his two children. The biggest concern was his son's enormous interest in a new found religion. Seems Peiter was interested in sharing what he had learned from other people. The father did not share his son's enthusiasm. Doc had grown up to believe differently. Ancient ancestors had rituals and beliefs. Some he followed, others he deviated away from.

Back home as a younger teen, Peiter was curious to listen to the foreign missionaries whenever they arrived on the island. A few locals would gather on the sandy ocean's shore to learn about people called Christians.

Doc closed his eyes to replay his son's requests. "Father if I could, can I change my name?" Asked his son. Doc recalled being irritated and upset by the suggestion.

"Why would anyone want to change their name, Son?" Replied a hurtful father. "You do not like the one your mother and I gave you?" His children had never seen their father so upset and mad. "What is this? Just tell me! I do not believe someone would want to be called outside of his own given name. You are being strange son, very strange."

"Father, you do not know my feeling." Peiter tried to explain.

"A name gives you feeling now?" Doc was confused. "Must be bad. Real bad. This is making you unpleasant towards me son."

The two children chuckled at their annoyed father. "You have misunderstood me, this is all wrong." Laughed Peiter. "I would like to take on a Christian name. My name Kelvin makes me feel attached to my culture and its ways. I want to be separated from those customs. I want to be like the men the missionaries described in the book called the Bible. They call themselves 'priests and ministers'. I would like to be like them, telling the stories from their big book. I listen and listen so I can retell the tales. They are like legends. I want to be like the man named St. Peter. Peter was a fisherman asked by the special man Jesus to join him in his ministry. I like to catch fish too."

Peiter asked his father to go for a walk without his sister Kemica. The boy wanted to share a few things and confess them privately with his father. "The religious men have taught me new ways about the girls. You know how the girls like to play at night on the beach? They are just being promiscuous with their bodies and being overtly intimate. They are trying to make babies to get husbands using their bodies as playgrounds. I thought that having sex is what boys do with girls for physical comfort. The feeling is like no other sensation. The warmth of a woman sends bumps up and down my skin.

These men have taught me a new way. The book has given me a second chance to find a wife. I have learned that a man should take on virgin for a wife, an untouched female. Now I can put my past behind me and start over and be forgiven, Father. I will know when God sends me a wife by the special sparkle in her eyes for me."

"Please Kelvin, tell me your sister is not involved in these games you have been describing at the beach? I am sure she has not, as I rarely let her out of my sight." The concerned and demanding father interrogated.

"No, my sister is too shy." Giggled the boy once named Kelvin.

After reminiscing, Doc opened his eyes to be greeted by bright, sun light. He recalled a son mature enough to rename himself '*Peiter*' for lack of not knowing how to properly spell, '*Peter*'. A boy who wanted to be a minister, something he had never heard about before. Doc was amazed at the things his own son was teaching him. There was no more time to reflect as there were plenty of chores to be done around the farm.

Along the way, Peiter would find his new name to not be so welcoming. Seems there were a few colored laborers on the farm who teased the boy. "Funny name for a colored boy, "pay-tare", as Peiter's name was slowly pronounced and mocked by one of the older gentleman. "You are different anyways, Island Boy." The chuckling continued from several male farm laborers.

Peiter knew to stick up for himself. "Most people from my island and the Caribbean have African ancestors. Do you men know what you are talking about most of the time?" Sputtered the young boy. "You need to spend more time learning about Jesus and quit picking on me. Every one of you on this farm is lucky to be here. Mr. Chettsburg is a lot like Jesus." Peiter just went quickly on his way ignoring the small group. He set out to find Charles as there was something on his mind.

Peiter surmised that most of the former slaves had knowledge about the Bible and prayed together. One thing he observed they had no church building to attend. Nothing available like Charles and his family had at St. Michael's Roman Catholic Church. The laborers would gather around behind their shanties. The group could be heard singing, clapping, and tossing their hands up in the air. This was a way of expressing thanks for their freedom and faith.

In the past, these same people had invisible churches. The slaves were encouraged by their slaveholders to attend these gatherings. The main message then was to '*Obey your Master and be good to him.*' This practice assured the slaveholders that their slaves were getting the correct message about them being obedient to their owners.

With Peiter being relatively new to the country, he did not truly understand a few things. There were a few cultural hurdles he was learning about. "Who really is a Master?" He continued to look for Charles to find some answers to his concerns.

The young boy still held on to hopes of becoming a minister. What better person to console in? Mr. Chettsburg! Charles continued to have a compassionate personality and was approachable by all, Peiter surmised. He knew Charles was the "go to" person to help get his start. Charles was always inspiring to people and gave them hope.

Peiter sat near Charles' house under a shaded tree waiting for his presence. Sitting there, he pondered about his ideas for a church and wanted to share them with Charles. Along come Mr. Chettsburg, a short time later.

"Sir, can I talk to you about something?" Peiter quickly approached the always busy Charles who abruptly stopped to listen.

"Certainly, what might that something be?"

The boy began explaining how he wanted to be a minister. He wanted advice on how to buy a small plot of land to build a church building on. Possibly an acre or two. The structure in his mind would be small, probably have a dirt floor like most of the shanties outback. The church could be constructed out of old barn boards, scrap wood or cheap milled plank. Pretty big was thinking for a poor colored boy. Charles seen some depth in the boy's ideas as he continued to listen.

"The church building doesn't need to be much. I want a church for everyone, colored, and white folks. Anyone who needs religion, even those drunk ones. There are people around here who are needing the Bible. I want to tell the stories to individuals who can't read either. I want to be inspiring like you!"

"Well, thank you for the compliment but those are some pretty big ideas you have?" Charles was not really sure what direction to take the conversation. He wanted to encourage the boy yet did not want to disappoint him either. There was no way a colored, teenaged boy was going to buy land and construct a building.

"Come for a walk with me Peiter. I have a few things to tend to in the barn. You can help me out. As we walk, we can discuss your ideas and concerns." Charles assured the ambitious youngster. As the two entered the barn, Charles found two empty metal buckets and turned them upside down for them to sit on. Charles began to explain, "Church is not for everyone. I have even seen a few torched around here. It would be a shame to spend money to buy the land and build a church for the hoodlums to destroy. No sense putting all that time and effort into something that is not going to be secure? These same mischievous people could surely benefit from what you are trying to promote. You are still young and have not seen all the wicked ways of man. I know there is a solution to your goodness, Peiter." The two sat as Charles continued to listen to the boy's admirations.

"Come take a walk with me." Charles again instructed Peiter. The two were headed towards Missy's playhouse. Being a problem-solver, Charles was going to resolve the boy's request. They entered the well-constructed, over-sized playhouse. "Do you know what this is?" Asking and inquiring.

Peiter nodded and answered, "Yes, it is now a schoolhouse."

Charles began to explain to Peiter how the big playhouse was built for his beautiful daughter. Missy did not ask for much but when she did, her father made certain he spoiled her just as he did his wife. With some help from his father-in-law Leon, the two men built and erected a playhouse twice as big as most of the shanties outback. Eventually, Missy outgrew the playhouse that grew into a makeshift one room schoolhouse. The teenaged girl had ideas of her own, similar to Peiter. Although playful, Missy wanted to reach out and be a teacher to the children she played with.

"Take a good look around this room Peiter and notice what you see. Benches, tables, coat hooks, shelves, may not be much but it truly is a school in Missy's eyes. All the resources she needs are right here. Do you know what the biggest possession this schoolhouse contains?" Charles franticly drilled Peiter who had an empty look on his confused face as his eyes roamed around the place. "No, you are not going to see it! The largest, most prized element to this school is my special daughter's loving heart. There is no reason why you could not have church services here also. Missy does not have school on Sundays. No one would dare step foot near the place in acts of retaliation. As you are aware this farm is secured with armed men. Always two armed overseers stationed on the farm. Usually the stocky Buck Edwards manages the property well as he knows every nook and cranny around here. His partner Whitey has his 44 long packed at his side along with eleven rounds loaded into a 4470, along with extra bullets for the rifle in his leather sack. More apt to find Whitey dangling a pole in the stream at times, he loves to fish. I personally would feel better with your church services held here. This building may be small but the school has provided humungous opportunities for Missy's students. Maybe the same thing can happen for you, Peiter?"

For the boy who started the conversation, there was no chance for him to intervene. As always, Charles had the situation resolved. By now Peiter's head was spinning as he was a bit overwhelmed with the information that was shared by Mr. Chettsburg. The creation of a new church was somehow transforming in a very unusually way for the eager teen.

Chapter 18

THE MINISTER'S NEW SUIT

"What should a minister look like?" Charles asked himself after the conversion with Peiter. He knew they usually do not dress like the Catholic priests. Recalling he knew some ministers dressed in black clergy type outfits with white collars similar to the priests'.

Thinking ahead he knew Peiter should not minister in the apparel that he often dressed in, shorts, T-shirts, and leather sandals. "Where do you get minister's clothes made?" was another question he thought about. "Does a teen boy really need a special outfit to preach? Of course he does!" Was Charles' answer. The clothing did not have to be special or uniform with any other church's requirements.

Now Charles was looking for Peiter near the backhouse. He knew the boy was so sincere and dedicated to starting a ministry and a church of his own. A new tailored suit would be in order for the boy's new career giving him a professional look. Something Charles knew about being an attorney. Charles assured himself the teen never had worn a buttoned-shirt, let alone a suit coat or jacket?

After retrieving the boy, Charles asked. "Boy, you have time to head into town with me?"

"Town, Sir? I never go into the village," Peiter answered with fearfulness. "Do you need help with something?"

"Nah, just come along. Let your father know that you will be with me for a few hours." Charles got a wagon with horses ready, then the two guys headed to town together. Upon arrival, the wagon was parked. The farm cart was tied securely to a wooden post right in front of a store named Perkin's Tailoring. Peiter was not sure why he was to be included in this trip to town.

"Why did you want me to come along with you here Sir, may I ask?" Peiter lingering far behind Charles. He had never been inside a tailoring shop before.

"Looking to purchase some new clothing today, Mr. Chettsburg?" Mr. Perkins inquired to the customer.

'Yes, I believe so," he promptly replied.

Entering the store, Peiter felt out of place as he sensed the owner's cold stare. "Good afternoon, Mr. Chettsburg. What can I do for you today?" Mr. Perkins asked in a snooty demeanor.

"I'd like you to measure up the boy and design a custom suit for him. Black or a nice, dark gray one," requested a confident Charles.

"I respect you but I cannot service this colored young man in my proprietorship," demanded the owner.

"Why?"

"I do not service coloreds here in my establishment! Not good for business." Mumbled the condescending elderly man.

"A person's skin does not color their heart or soul, Sir."

"I refuse to go along with this ploy of yours. Bad for business. He is colored, not a customer, probably just a measly farm-hand? I am a well-respected tailor and will only service customers of my own liking," ranted the gentleman. "Good day, Sir!"

"Come on boy," Charles requested as the two men exited the tailor's shop. He shook his head trying not to laugh at how he upset Mr. Perkins. Peiter was not so cheerful about the situation.

"Hope you were not too embarrassed or uncomfortable. That was really awkward I must admit. I have patronized Mr. Perkins' business for many years. Time for a new tailor. My intentions were good. I only wanted to surprise you with a new suit."

"But why would you have a suit made for me?" There was a puzzled look on the boy's face.

"A minister should be a role model for his congregants. A suit and tie will make you feel good and look good. A professional like myself," stated the proud man.

"Now what, Sir?" As Peiter was feeling distraught.

"Wait in the wagon, I will keep an eye on you."

Peiter hustled into the wagon as requested. Charles dashed back into the tailor's shop. "How much fabric would be needed to make a suit for a man of my size, Sir?"

"Oh, about five and a half yards. Are you now thinking of a new suit for yourself Mr. Chettsburg?" Mr. Perkins calculated.

"Not exactly but thank you for your time, Sir."

Charles headed down the street a bit walking to his mother's tea room and store. Entering the store he kissed his mother on the cheek. Usually he greeted her with a hug but this time a hug would not be sufficient. "Mother do you have a few minutes for your handsome son? We have some shopping to do."

"Why yes, please go out back and call for your father. He can watch the store while I step out with you." Elizabeth grabbed her coin purse and proceeded out the door with her son. Together they walked to The General Merchandise Store. As they walked he began explaining to his mother that he wanted a suit coat and trousers made for Peiter. He did not want to trouble his mother with such a lengthy task as she did not have a sewing machine nor the time. The thrifty lady did make one suggestion. She wondered if her son had an old suit that would properly fit the boy. Charles was open to that good idea. Peiter was not yet as tall as Charles and was much more slimly built. An old suit would need a lot of alterations to fit the boy properly.

Charles needed his mother's assistance. He wanted to purchases everything that would be needed to make a suit for Peiter. His mother was a seamstress and could certainly help pick out the needed materials.

The duo entered the store that had the aroma of cinnamon and other spices. Several colorful bolts of fabric were displayed along a back wall. A bolt of gray wool would be their selection for lack of any other appropriate choices. Elizabeth scoured the store for other needed accessories and notions. In the hand-basket she placed some buttons, thread, and a metal zipper.

While walking through the general store, Charles began explaining his intentions of having a suit custom made for Peiter. The conversation continued as he explained Mr. Perkins' refusal to service the colored, teen boy. Charles really wanted his mother to sew the clothing but he knew time was a factor also. She was busy enough running her own business.

The items to be purchased were taken out of the basket and placed on the counter. Adding to the order were a pile of assorted hard candies, a treat for the ride home. The fabrics were wrapped in paper, secured and tied with string. All the other things were gathered and paid for. Charles hugged his mother good bye as they exited the store. The two would venture their own separate ways. Elizabeth was on her way back to her tea room. Her son, continuing to help out someone as if he had all the time in the world, to solve one problem at a time.

Charles hoisted himself back into the waiting wagon. The look on Peiter's face revealed that he was relieved Charles was back so quickly. The two headed out passing the west end of town. Kind of weird were the thoughts of the few local town folks. Mr. Chettsburg tooling around in the wagon with a colored boy? Nothing too surprising came from Charles' actions.

Peiter was uncertain where the two were going now. Too humble to ask. He sat back and enjoyed the scenery of the short journey as they passed by St. Michael's Roman Catholic Church. The boy knew this place to be Mr. Chettsburg's church. Sure enough the wagon passed the church and continued down the winding dirt road. Peiter had never been down this particular road. Where were they off too?

About a mile and a half down the road the two arrived at a small farmhouse. This was the home of Mildred Miller. She was a fairly poor woman that Charles knew from church and around town. He knew she would be able to sew a man's tailored suit. The busy mother was also a seamstress. With six children, a large garden, and some livestock, this lady was too short on time to hold a job or profession.

Her husband was gone more often than he was home. Mildred claims he is in the military. Rumor has it that he tends to his other woman on the east side of the state.

Charles hollered from the wagon as the six Miller children gathered around to gawk at the unexpected guests. One to be exact, a colored boy they had never seen before. Who was this teen boy with the local attorney, the family wondered?

"Good day, Miss Mildred. I have a small request for you. I have little job that will pay a fair wage," requested the friendly man.

"Doing what, Sir?" Mildred was puzzled of course not knowing any details yet.

"This young man needs a tailored suit. I know you are a fine seamstress." Charles gave her a compliment.

"Thank you Lord! I could always use a little work to earn some food or money, Sir. Things are always tight around here. Always needing something. Shoes, hairbrushes, lamp oil, and tired of making soap," the tired lady responded.

All six children had gathered even closer to the wagon. Every eye on the colored boy observing him carefully. They never had a colored person at their farm before. Seen a few pass through. Who was this darker, skinned, teenaged boy and what made him so special to be riding around with Mr. Chettsburg? Everyone was curious, though not too concerned. Charles was just as interested about something also. With all six kids lined up, he noticed a pattern. A tall, thin, brown haired girl named Natasha, with two teenaged brothers, Mark and Mike. To the right, were three younger girls with blonde hair and rounder faces, Allie, Piper, and Alyssa. Natasha welcomed the little sisters as she once was outnumbered by the two older boys. Charles smirked to himself as he had another mystery figured out. "Looks like the children of two different fathers?" He was getting to see a bigger picture of what was really going on at Mrs. Miller's house.

"Yes, I'll gladly sew the suit for you, Mr. Chettsburg," Mrs. Miller spoke up.

"Boys, get the fabric and materials out of the wagon for your mother." Charles happily demanded. "Am I rushing you, is two weeks enough time to make a suit?"

"Maybe the top coat alone, Sir. Less than a month I suppose for a man's suit? Do you not see I have six children?" A little smile crept came upon Mildred's bashful face. "Let me get some twine and get a measurement on the boy now. You know you will need to stop by every now and then to try it on? In case I need to make some adjustments or alterations." She continued to measure Peiter with pieces of twine making knots to mark off her calculations. Charles handed Mildred a few coins. As generous as he always was, Charles wanted to leave the mother some money in case she needed anything extra for the sewing project.

"Let's make out a schedule now. You know I am a busy man." Charles commanded with his eyes still on the children. He addressed them all, "Feel free to come over anytime during the week. You know Missy would love for you to join her any day for school. Get all loaded up in the wagon and head over to the farm, maybe even play? Usually my housemaid, Hattie Mae will make lunch. There will be enough for everyone to enjoy." Wasn't much response from the fairly, quiet, half-dozen, bunch of Millers.

Back to the farm the wagon went. A nice, dry, sunny day with a few bugs to smack along the ride. Charles was delighted that Mrs. Miller took on the project of making the boy's suit with no unknown prejudices. Secondly, she sure could stand to earn some extra money. Charles could not image a woman raising all those children alone, or was she? He surely had this figured out, there was more to that story at her farm.

The wagon took them along the gaping dirt roads. Again approaching the church of St. Michael's. The boyishness came out in Peiter. He began to plea with Charles. "Is the church open now?"

"Peiter, this is a church for heaven's sake. A church is always open. What if someone needed to pray or take shelter?" Charles tried frantically explaining. "Why?"

"I had never seen a church until my family came here with you, Sir. I wonder what the church looks like on the inside. I only have a picture in my mind. I've seen white people dressed up nicely and go in there. The ladies all wearing hats. Can a colored boy take a look inside or will the Devil or a Master get mad?" Peiter's tone was convincing to Charles.

Charles pulled the wagon around to the rear of the church building. Up the steps was a single wooden door with a glass pane. The two headed up the narrow steps together. Charles offered a peak to the curious teen. The sun's summer rays gave gentle lighting to the dimly lit room. Peiter's eyes observing every square foot within sight. Rows and rows of wooden pews faced a platform altar. An upright piano took up space in the far right corner. Books and ceiling beams seemed to finish off Peiter's visual tour.

"The place is dark and gloomy, Sir?"

"What were you expecting a frilly ladies' powder room?" Charles snapped.

"How do I know? Jesus always talked about a beautiful place called Heaven. The church is not bright and sunny, like I thought. You were right, this reminds me of a big school like Missy's, nothing too fancy."

The two hustled back to the wagon and headed again towards the farm. Peiter was excited to share more about his own vision of a church. Charles suggested to the boy that a church does not have to be a fancy building. He assured the boy that St. Michael's church was a very nice church for the area. "You know it is not what the church looks like on the inside or outside. What is most important is to be a Christian and that comes deep in your heart boy. You are truly a Christian. You have not ever attended church service in a building structure. Yet your heart proclaims your love for God and Jesus everywhere you go. Do you understand a church is a place to gather, pray, and hear the words? Anyplace in the world, one can pray and God is listening."

"I see Father Murphy has his own house on the church grounds. I am almost eighteen Sir. Will I be able to ever have my own home, my own space? Hard for a minister to live with his father and sister." Peiter was hinting.

"You having trouble sleeping out there? Or your father snores too loudly?" Charles tried to resolve the issue.

"No, I really want my own room. Can I someday buy a shanty?" The teen pleaded.

"Could you settle for the schoolhouse for now if it is that urgent? No one uses the building at night. A new outhouse is going to be built nearby. Why, everything you need is practically in place there. Just make sure the schoolhouse is kept clean and you are awake and properly dressed before Missy arrives for school. All you need is a mattress or a pile of blankets to sleep on. All your things can be stored in the loft."

Peiter just sat back in the wagon and went over what Charles had expressed to him. He sometimes compared Charles to Jesus as he was always kind-hearted, shared words of wisdom, and common sense. Peiter knew the man was a blessing to his family and was fortunate to have crossed paths with Charles. The boy was growing up fast and learning a lot of life's lessons from another mentor, Charles, in addition to his own father.

Charles also had something on his mind. He was still thinking about the Miller children. There was something odd but who was he to judge. As always Charles had the puzzling thoughts figured out. Six children that seemed to be made up of two sets of three was his math? Quite possibly two fathers? Nah, that was not nice thinking. Putting his thoughts together he realized the oldest three teens were probably Mr. Miller's. The military man had not been around much over the past eight years or so, if at all. There must be more to Mildred's story? She was obviously a poor farm woman but was not doing too badly on her own with six kids. Charles did not want to make any false allegations but he figured there had to another man involved. For his own sake he was curious about his accusations. Would not be Christian-like if he were wrong?

Back to the Chettsburgs' farm the two companions traveled. Both having their own stories playing in their heads. A boy who wants to minister and help mankind through the words of the Bible. Then an adult who helps out those in need of legal assistance, in a land filled with structure and the words of the laws to keep peace for mankind.

The next few weeks were followed by numerous trips to the Millers' farm. Each time Charles and Peiter approached Mildred for a fitting of the suit. Step-by-step the tailored suit was pieced and sewn with progress.

Peiter started to enjoy the trips to the quiet farm. The secluded place was peaceful despite the children and free-roaming livestock. The Millers' actually started looking forward to the occasional visitors. Not many folks came around to the very rural home. Seems like the younger children were actually trying to make a new playmate with the much older, Peiter. Although he was older like the eldest Miller children, the younger kids were naïve and curious about the somewhat friendly, dark-skinned teen.

There was one trip to the Miller's farm in particular that caught Charles by surprise. As the wagon come up to the home, he noticed an adult male beside the chicken-coop. To his astonishment the man was Lester. The man who was always caught stumbling around town, apparently drunk.

Mrs. Miller was quick to justify Lester's appearance on the farm. "You know the man comes out here to give me a helping hand on occasion. Considering the circumstances with my husband who is gone all the time. Nice having him around for company and to help tend to the children. The chores get over bearing at times for me and the youngsters."

"Yes!" Charles thought to himself. "The children! God will punish me for just thinking so. Lester and the children. This explains my theory about the children. Yes indeed. Those three little children had to be products of Lester's offspring. He had been coming around for more than chores! Poor Mrs. Miller wasn't so lonely after all. There was a male companion keeping her company. But Lester of all men? Guess I do not know him very well?" Charles just shook the thoughts right out his head and shouted out a greeting to the busy man. After all this was none of his business unless they cared to make him aware of what was actually going on?

After weeks and weeks of laboring on the suit the final fitting approached. Charles had brought along a white cotton shirt and a black silk tie. These were clothes he no longer wore and was passing them on to Peiter. Mrs. Miller gathered the finished suit coat and pants. Charles and Peiter toted the rest of the accessories and followed her to the barn. A trail of six children also joined the procession. There in the barn, Peiter put his new clothes on. The boy looked handsome and stunning in his new custom-made suit as he exited the barn to a final showing of the outfit. Sounds of tiny hands clapped as they seen the finished project their mother had been so busy working on. The youngest one jumped up and down with pride because of her mother's creation. "Looking good black boy!" shouted one of the younger children. Mrs. Miller was embarrassed and quick to silence her youngest named Allison, often refer to as Allie. Charles assured the blushing Mrs. Miller and Peiter the youngster's comments was truly a compliment.

Peiter approached Charles privately as he wanted to confront Lester. He wanted to share a few words with Lester in an appropriate manner. The boy wanted to invite Lester to his new church. Charles did not see any harm in the boy asking although he was not certain how the older man would react.

The young inspiring boy explained to Lester that he was trying to build a ministry. He described how a church service was going to take place in Missy's schoolhouse on Sundays. "You know she is teaching me to read the Bible, Sir? I want a church that brings unity and love to all people, peacefully. I have seen you around on Sunday mornings. Does this mean you do not go to a church like Mr. Chettsburg?" Peiter inquired.

"Boy, I have not been inside a church in years. Doesn't mean I don't believe. When I lost my son, I lost my faith." Lester grumbled.

"Please then, find your way to the new church. Bring a friend or some of those children with you. From what Mr. Chettsburg said, Mrs. Miller doesn't always attend St. Michael's church every week. Too much work getting ready and heading to town with so many children?" Peiter looked down at the dirt path with his head hanging for fear of rejection from the older drunken gentleman.

Lester had nothing else to say to the handsome boy standing there in the new suit and just walk away. Peiter felt like a salesman who just lost his biggest sale. Slowly he walked back to the wagon and climbed in. He was not even certain if he was supposed to personally thank Mrs. Miller for sewing the suit. After all, Charles was the one who made arrangements for the suit to be tailor-made and was paying her for the services.

Charles was also impressed with the farm woman's skills of designing the clothes. The suit was well made and of good quality. Not quite as detailed as the suits Mr. Perkins tailor-made. The price was far less expensive though. Charles felt especially proud to have given the woman a chance to earn a little extra money and show off her seamstress talents.

The process of getting Peiter's suit sewn turned into a series of learning events in many ways for Charles. A tailor who was more concerned with a customer's skin color than making some money. A bunch of isolated children who welcomed the thought of a new companion on the small rural farm no matter his color. Finally, a struggling mother with little means but a whole lot of admiration for a variety of circumstances.

Chapter 19

BUILDING A MINISTRY

What would a church building be without a sign? How would the local folks know that the schoolhouse was going to conduct services on Sundays? The go-to person according to Peiter would be Joseph. This is the man who was always making something out of wood.

Together the two crafted a wooden plaque. Joseph spoke in great lengths in order to assure Peiter had a great understanding of what the sign stood for. Indeed he did! According to the young want-to-be minister the sign was to read "Christ is Here, Colossians 3:11". From what Peiter learned the statement meant that his church would welcome people of all races, social status, slaves, and freed slaves.

Joseph was quite impressed with Peiter's familiarity with the Bible. To be certain, Joseph called upon Father Murphy to make sure what Peiter understood was totally correct. The priest was somewhat fascinated with what Joseph was explaining to him. "Where did the boy gain such knowledge?"

Joseph explained only what he knew, "The boy lacks in reading skills. He loves when my granddaughter Melissa reads the Bible to him. His interest began back at the island where he came from when the missionaries came to preach. Peiter has a good memory I might add. The message in Colossians 3:11 seems to be his signature statement, Father. He has had an interest in religion the whole short time I've known him. By the way, I must add this young boy actually renamed himself because of the Bible stories."

"Meaning he changed his name?" Father Murphy asked with a puzzling look.

"Yes, the story is interesting I may add. He learned to like the stories of Saint Peter. With his father's permission he changed his name to P-E-I-T-E-R for lack of knowing how to properly spell Peter. The pronunciation is off a little bit along with his accent, '*pay-tar*.' Quite interesting if I may add? The boy is very smart considering his background or lack of it. He and my granddaughter make a great pair. She is the inspiring teacher and he is the inspirational minister. Both are advocates in their own little worlds to make big changes." Joseph chuckled. "My how the Bible's words really work. Did Jesus ever dream of a playhouse that would be a school to mostly black children? Then on Sundays, there will be real church services conducted there by a young colored minister? To be honest, I am in total misbelief. This could be a serious crime in some counties around here." Again, the two men broke out in heaping laughter.

"God bless me, I need to watch out, the boy may be after my position here at the church!" smirked the priest. Father Murphy ended the conversation with a short prayer to shed light and good will blessings on the teen boy's new ventures. Both men agreed they had learned something enlightening from the talk. "I am here with an open heart and arms should I be of service again, Joseph." He concluded with a firm handshake.

Joseph's next stop was to see his son at the law office. There seemed to be a few things he needed to discuss in regards to the "new church." First, he wanted to share his discussion that took place with Father Murphy. Next, he wanted to be reassured that the playhouse was actually approved for Peiter's plans of conducting church services. Joseph grew a little leery. The circumstances of Peiter hosting church on the farm seemed confrontational? The man just shook his head knowing Charles always had everything thoroughly figured out.

As Joseph entered the law office, Charles sprung up with delight to see his father unexpectedly. "Must be lunchtime?" Charles insisted.

"I guess? I am ready for something to eat." Joseph agreed.

"Come on, let's go visit Mother and see what is on the menu today," Charles insisted.

"Well Son, I came to discuss a few things actually," Joseph appeared a bit distraught.

"Shall we talk first or eat first? Or can we do both?" Charles grabbed his hat. "Let's walk and talk, come on Father!"

The two men headed towards Elizabeth's tea room. Joseph briefly began explaining about making the sign for Peiter's church. Then he consulted in his son about having met with Father Murphy.

"Father Murphy?" Questioned Charles, "Why on earth did you meet with him?"

Joseph continued to explain he wanted to be certain that Peiter was on the right path with his ministerial interests. The two guys had the biggest laugh yet. Who was going to attend these services? As always, Charles had his analytical skills at work.

"Father, do you really think folks are going to travel out to the farm to hear a colored teenaged boy talk about the Bible? I think the only people in attendance will be a few bored colored kids that live on the farm? Peiter actually did invite Lester and the Miller children to come. Highly unlikely I think. The boy has a good head on his shoulders. He expressed the church was open to everyone regardless of color, education, or religious background. So far he is reaching out to alcoholics, illiterates, and those that are isolated. The odd balls I guess? He is very inspired to give hope to these people. I know one thing for sure, his church service is going to have to take place sometime after our morning church mass and before Sunday supper!" Ending his opinion with a sense of humor as Charles usually did. "You know Missy will be right there at his side with the Bible wide open. She will not miss attending her own Catholic services nor our Sunday family feasts!"

Finally, the two come upon the tea room and entered the store. Behind the counter stood Elizabeth beaming with a bright smile as she wiped her hands on her floral, calico apron. "Two of my favorite customers here at the same time? What is the special occasion? Or is there one?"

"Every time is a special occasion when you are cooking, Mother." Charles assured his now blushing mother.

"Seems we have started a new community committee and Father and I are the only two team active members." Charles jokingly stated. He further explained his father stopped by to discuss Peiter's ministry plans. Elizabeth was quick to intervene with her opinion. She did not think it was right to mess around with religious matters. For her there was only one religion and that was the Roman Catholic Church's! Her compassionate son gave insight to the fact that the colored folks really did not have many options for religion in the area. The three were aware the colored residents on the farm practiced their faith freely there though. Elizabeth was still a bit fearful of God's understanding of Peiter's mission.

"Come on Mother, he is just a kid. How could God possibly punish him for trying to share hope to those who lack it?" Her son expressed seriously. Joseph spoke up as if to agree with their son since he knew his wife could get a little feisty at times.

"Well what are the town folks going to think of you Charles, hosting a non-traditional church on our family farm?" Muttered Elizabeth.

"Do you think I really care? The judging is in God's hands not ours mind you Mother."

"I trust you as always my son. I just want you to be aware of the doors you might be opening. Everyone is not as open-minded as you are, and smart I may add. You are always the expert. Son, I am so proud of you for being a unique individual."

"Oh Mother, if I did not have such encouraging parents I wouldn't be the wonderful person I am today." Charles stood proudly knowing and believing his own words.

"Enough, let's get my men something to eat! How about a nice warm bowl of chicken noodle soup and freshly baked soda biscuits? Or, can I start you out with a piece of my signature chocolate pecan pie?" Elizabeth offered.

In unison the men chatted "Both please." Like two little children.

Chapter 20

ANOTHER SUMMER BEGINS

The leaves on the pecan trees showed signs of a new summer approaching. Soon the nuts would be showcased from the branches. Charles' little orchard behind the farm house had begun to flourish as expected over the years. As the time passed, many other things started to grow also.

The two older teens continued with their goals of school and church. Peiter scouted around for people to be part of his newly found congregation. The young school teacher was hard at work educating the laborers' offspring. Closely they worked together like best buddies despite their diversities.

Their relationship was certainly unusual for lack of having many other friends. Together they grew up on the Chettsburgs' farm almost like siblings in a way. With Missy being the only child, she had no sisters or brothers to play with. Peiter and his sister Kemica were to some degree shunned from the other colored children and their parents. This was a matter of reverse discrimination. Although their father Doc was well respected by the farm's community, his children were treated as foreigners. The two kids from the tropical island were not seen as "one of their own" when viewed by the colored folks. In several ways, they were right. Doc's family had special privileges on the farm. Their physical appearances were also somewhat different compared to the other dark-skinned residents on the farm.

Quite possibly these differences were what bonded the two grownup teens. Side by side they played as children and invested in each other's dreams and goals. At times maybe they dreamed a little too much together. Interesting how a child's playhouse had turned into a school and church building that they unselfishly would share.

In the pint-sized one-room building the two friends were always working on something. Together they organized and rearranged the furniture most of which were log benches crafted by Grandfather Chettsburg. Once a week, the housemaid Hattie Mae would come out and sweep and dust as instructed by Charles. In the cooler months, the farm laborers made sure there was plenty of wood stacked for the school's stove.

As time went on, Peiter's liking for Missy grew deeper. Basically, she was his only true friend. He did not fit in with the other colored children that roamed around the farm. His sister Kemica was the other child companion of the boy. Certainly he did not blend in with the few colored children on the farm that came and went.

Peiter admitted to Missy shamefully, "My wise father once stated when I was younger, I would have a difficult time making friends here in America. I am like the interracial child, a man of two lands."

His friendly feelings were turning into romantic interests towards his best friend, Missy. Deep in his heart he had fallen in love with his dear companion.

"What are you doing?" shouted Missy as she was really stunned.

At some point, Peiter had grabbed her by the hand. Quickly she pulled away.

"You touched me?" Missy scolded in anger.

"I love you, Missy. I think I have loved you for a long time? I want to be closer to you. I just wanted to feel your white, pale skin." A somewhat strange acknowledgment came from Peiter.

Missy assured him that they were friends, very good friends to be exact.

"But I am attracted to you not only physically but spiritually. Tell me your feelings are the same!" The teen boy's requested.

"Honestly Peiter, I can't say I have had any thoughts like that. You are my very close friend is how I would label this relationship. We could *never* court if that is what you are implying?"

"Why are you talking to me like this Missy? Do you not sense that God has united us?"

"You know and understand exactly what I mean. You are of color. Family and folks around here would never accept that. Nor would anyone respect God's wishes if he did want us united." Missy tried to disagree acknowledging the truth.

"The color of our souls is what matters the most. Please, I am a man of the Holy Book, I am a Christian. My life changed when I was younger and was introduced to Christianity. I have been blessed with so many wonderful things. Your father gave me a whole new life to live by bringing my family here to the farm. The most magnificent thing is that my life includes you, Missy. You have grown-up to be a special lady so pure and innocent. I want to take you as a virgin, a gift from God. Marry me! You will be my wife." Peiter demanded with confidence.

"You are scaring me with this unexpected request. Yet, I am a little flattered hearing all of this for the first time. We have been acquainted for a long time like siblings and playmates. Maybe I never considered you as a husband. I am really scared about how you feel. There are many judgmental folks. What would our families think?" Missy was not convinced.

"What matters is how God views our relationship. Not people, nor the government. Our hearts and souls can still be joined and melded together. Please! Please meet me tonight out back in the flower garden. I need to have some time alone with you to feel the comfort of your warm hand. Standing before you I am a man of God with needs and goals. God had guided me to you and I believe in his guidance. Promise me, tonight?"

Missy agreed nervously to meet later on that night. Her body trembled almost as if she had been violated into agreeing. As the day went on she did not feel well. The teen was overwhelmed with uncertainty. She could not let her friend down. Nonetheless, she had an uneasy feeling as she did not know what to expect later in the garden with her friend Peiter.

The love struck boy hastily exited the building. His trail took him to his living quarters attached to the barn. The home was not big enough to house his raging feelings. Off again, he dashed to over the flower garden. There he sat on a decorative wrought iron bench. Surreal, secluded, and surrounded by a beautiful array of blossoming vegetation.

His face was aimed at the bright beaming sunlight as if he was seeking answers to his thoughts. Pondering, he reflected on his friend Missy. The female companion was always so kind and nice to him. The teen boy felt embarrassed. He thought the two teen friends had been sharing the same romantic feelings for each other all along.

Peiter may have misjudged Missy's feelings. By nature, she was kind and compassionate to everyone, he noted in his thoughts. This in itself made his heart grow fonder of her. Disappointment and frustration came over him as he thought for sure the attraction was mutual between the two of them. Then he started to sort out his feelings. Was he mistaking this state of mind as a sexual interest? Of course not, he convinced himself. He was in love and she also had to be, he persuaded himself.

Continuing to think, he knew there were answers. Maybe Missy had not grown into the role up till now that was destined for them? Definitely present was something special going on between them. Was there enough extraordinary feelings to consummate a marriage for the pair?

With the sun still beaming in his eyes he continued to visually reproduce images. The two had continued to build a congregation for the ministry. Both worked hard at the school and church to educate and teach and to help others grow. Why wouldn't the two be suitable for each other in marriage? The fall and darkness of the night could not come fast enough for Peiter who had so many unanswered questions.

Meanwhile, Missy headed back to the house taking big steps. In through the house's side door she scuffled and headed upstairs yelling, "I'll be in my bedroom for while Hattie. Can you please bring me a cold drink and something to eat?" Missy hustled up the steep back staircase and darted to her room closing the door behind. The small black buttoned shoes were taken off her dainty feet. Up on the bed she jumped and laid down.

Laying facing the foot of her bed she held her head up with her hands against her cheeks. The two long, ponytail like braids dangled on each side of her flustered face. Staring at the floral designed wallpaper, she reminisced.

Seems the sixteen year old girl had many conversations with her father. Usually talks that a child would have with her mother. Her father Charles could converse with a horse, if need be. Then the memories focused on her wishes to become a schoolteacher. Her father was the one she mainly shared her ambitions with.

Her compassionate father was always supportive of his daughter's childlike goals. The playhouse conversion was the beginning of her teaching career. The only child was highly accommodated in regards to achieving her objectives by everyone. One thing for certain, Missy was provided well for but not in a spoiled way like her mother, Lara.

A few years earlier, her father gave her detailed expectations of what being an employed teacher really meant. Teachers were held to high moral standards and were expected to remain single and never marry. Her choice would mean no husband nor children. If indeed she decided to marry she would have to give up her teaching position. The rules came with some contradiction. Why would a teacher not be able to marry and have children if her passion was a love for children in the classroom? Quite puzzling for the rural farm girl. As long as she was a teacher she had to remain single and have good moral character, which she always did of course.

The conversation continued that day with her father. She recalled him telling her teachers could start working at age sixteen, an age she was at now. She had all the needed credentials; good penmanship, read very well, knew arithmetic, and studied the Bible.

There were other teacher responsibilities the father explained to his daughter. Fresh water would be needed daily for the drinking bucket. The lamps would need to be filled with oil.

Coal and wood was to be hauled for the cooler days when the stove needed to be fired up. Sweeping and cleaning was mandatory for the building. All these rules were understood by the young teacher. As usual, things on the farm ran a little differently. Most of these responsibilities would mainly be passed onto the laborers. The Chettsburgs were fortunate to have so many handy and helpful residents with their unique family farm situation.

Five dollars a month would be Missy's starting salary according to her father. He would be the one paying the wages. When she turned eighteen he promised her an increase of fifteen dollars per month. There were more schoolhouse rules according to the experienced attorney. Playing school as a younger teen was full of fun with good intentions. A paid teacher had to apply higher expectations and standards according to her father. The students would need to be disciplined, taught proper manners, and language. Missy would have to learn to be firm at times with her students going forward. This was not typical of her but something she knew would have to learned and incorporated with her teaching skills.

On the other hand, her father explained with the usual smirk on his face. The farm's school is unique and did not have to run like the other local ones. This was a private school that could have some rules of its own. There was no headmaster or government official to oversee the daily operations. Missy was in charge with her father and family backing her choices and decisions.

Together they agreed the school would teach a variety of subjects. Penmanship, the alphabet, reading, geography, and arithmetic were to be included. Recess would be filled with songs, games, and Bible readings. The promise of a new outhouse was already in the works. Obviously, something closer was needed for the students. There was an inconvenience of the children running back to the shanty area when nature made its call. The new addition was to save classroom time being located nearby.

Finally, Charles had one last comment for his dear daughter. He explained how he and her mother dreamed of sharing grandchildren someday. Should she ever want to leave this career path and marry, they would be supportive. "Maybe one day a special man will enter into your loving world, Missy? You may choose to move on, marry, and have children of your own? My parents were blessed with one child, just like we are. I feel like I am having a talk with you that a mother should share with her daughter, not a father. You know how much I love and adore you. I was fortunate enough to have found love not once but twice. First I met your mother, a true gift from God. Then I was given a second loving treasure. That was you, Missy! Over the years your mother and I have prayed for another blessing to come along. At any time I would take another blessing from

God. I have a hard time understandings God's distribution of them. Look at Mrs. Miller with all those kids. Sometimes at night I worry about that family way out there alone on their farm." Charles confided. "Don't worry love will find you Missy. I firmly believe that. You know your Grandfather Macher hardly knew your grandmother a day before he planned on marrying her. An odd arrangement at the time. Marriage relationships can develop in many different ways. Guess your Grandfather Chettsburg and I were one of the truly lucky ones, dear."

"Father, can we get back to the schoolhouse?" Missy interrupted.

"Oh yes as usual, I am off track. I will make one promise to you. In addition to the pay raise at age eighteen, I along with your Grandfather Chettsburg have agreed to construct a bigger school building. In a few years, there will be more children to educate here on the farm. Your grandfather has designated a plot on the east side of the pecan orchard for the new school one day soon. I know Peiter is not going anywhere either. He and his family will forever live and work here with us. The schoolhouse as it stands will then be his to conduct his ministry from, given he has a congregation?" Chuckling as usual.

Missy shook her finger at her father playfully scolding him for the negative comment about her friend.

A knock on the bedroom door disconnected the dreamy girl from her reflective thinking. Hattie Mae appeared at the door with the requested refreshments. "Come in Hattie, you can set the tray on the trunk at the foot of my bed." Missy ordered the house maid. "May I ask you something, Ma'am?"

"I guess? I hope I have the right answer for you little one. You are the smart one around here" The bubbly colored woman stood with her hand on her hip.

"Well, can we talk? This is personal I guess. Have you ever been in love or been courted by a man?" Missy bashfully asked. She knew this was somewhat inappropriate.

"Where am I supposed to meet a man, little one? You know I do not go nowhere. Gee, at times I think you and Mr. John are my only people. Folks outback think I am too good for them 'cause I live here at the big house. Golly, I live like a princess compared to them. I have the best living quarter's ever, little one. The day I found out Mr. Chettsburg, your grandfather was building me my own room on the porch, I cried myself silly. I was accustomed to sleeping in shanties with dirt floors. No colored folks lived in white peoples' houses. I have a dang palace my dear and all to myself. Top things off, I work in this beautiful big house. Lots of jealousy."

"I mean, even before you came here? Was there any special man for you?"

"Nah, nah, nah! We are not having these words. You talk to your Mamma or Granny. We probably should not be talking like this." The worried woman cautioned.

"Hattie seriously, would you like to be married and have children of your own?" Probed Missy.

Hattie Mae's eyes watered up, "Honey, things have not been so easy for me. There was a time when life was very hard for me. I am down on my knees at night thanking the Lord that your father found me down the road with the other freed slaves. I had been abused by men, both colored and white." Tears rolled down her rounded cheeks. Reaching for her pure white apron she dried her face, feeling embarrassed. "Child, there are things you will never understand or know. Trust me that is a good thing. Your father hired me to plant seedlings for those pecan trees that he is so very proud of. He seen what a hard worker I was. Being a bit overweight, I had trouble bending over and shoveling. He did not dare put me in the fields to work!" Hattie laughed. "Plenty of work up at the house for me. Never did figure out why I was the special one?"

"Oh Hattie Mae, I am sorry to have made you sad."

"Actually, I am crying because I am happy." Confessing Hattie as she sat on the bed next to Missy. "Please do not tell anyone. I would not want to be fired for being disrespectful to your family. Men have treated me so badly that have I hated all men. I mean all of them! Then I met your father. I was shocked that a white man could be so nice. The man did not have a mean thought in his soul. Why, I have known him for a long time now. Then he brought Doc and his children to the farm. Doc and I were in the same situation. He did not fit in with the laborers either for other reasons. Folks on the farm did not like him. His background was different and they were not very welcoming. Shame on them! They know what it is like to be discriminated. Doc and I stood out like sore thumbs around here. Because of our jobs we became close, do you know what I mean?" Asked the sobbing woman. "Not sure if it's called love but we got something 'special' going on. Doc started sneaking over to the back porch late at night. My body would tingle with delight having him touch and hold me the way he did. Kissing me with passion. However, I feared God would punish me for a good thing. Was not like I was a virgin anyways. Some boy robbed me of that years ago when we were young teens. Doc and I have been going at it ever since." Finally a smile came on her face.

"Going at it?" Missy questioned.

Hattie leaned in and quietly spoke, "You know what the married folks do?"

"But you do not have any children?" Missy again questioned Hattie.

"You can do that and not get pregnant if you are very careful. Something Doc taught me actually. He is the man with a spiritual and medical mind. He knows a lot about stuff, you know?"

Missy was surprised about the conversation with Hattie and grew more confused. She was not aware that Hattie Mae and Doc were discretely intimate partners. How could they not have children? After all, having marital relations is how babies were created. Even more puzzling, Hattie seemed to imply that being intimate made you feel really good?

"Tell me how you never had a baby doing that?" The curious naïve teen asked.

"Little one, you really should be talking to your mamma about this. Not my place, no, no, no way!" Hattie sprung up off the bed. What Hattie did not want to share was Doc had a method figured somewhat out. He knew there was a safe period of time according to a woman's monthly cycle. That was when he and Hattie would be intimate. At the time when he was married the husband had this all figured out. If he only had cherished relations with his wife up to five days after her monthly period, she would not get pregnant. He stopped there! Knowing what he knew and only that was what he knew. So, he stuck with that schedule. They already had two little children and that was enough for the family's poverty ridden conditions. What he knew worked and he was sticking with that method, "the five day rule." Doc told Hattie that was why men had two hands with five fingers. After the fifth day of counting fingers, the relations were over for the month and time to use the other hand! Hattie smiled to herself as she recalled how her lover made her laugh about his counting method. Next, she knew what that really meant about using his other hand. "Don't think Doc ain't up in here trying to sneak a big kiss at times either. He may act like he's after some vittles or something at the house's out-kitchen. Nothing finer than a pair of lips on lips, mmmm" The house-maid sighed then burst into laughter.

Hattie Mae proceeded to leave the bedroom giggling loud. Missy was more confused and frustrated after reflecting on her father's own conversation about marriage. "Hattie Mae, get back here! Why ain't you and Doc married then?" Missy questioned the house servant. "Don't you want to have children of your own someday?"

Hattie Mae sat back down on the bed. "I have dreamt of having my own children. Maybe six of them? Have fun singing to them." Hattie Mae chuckled loudly. "I am getting old for that maybe being twenty-eight years old already? All the good young men are married by now."

"Doc doesn't have a wife? Maybe one day you will become his wife?" Missy suggested.

"He already has a family," Hattie Mae disagreed.

"A family includes a wife, two parents, and maybe more babies? Certainly Doc's children would welcome you into their family. Maybe some younger sisters or brothers for Peiter and Kemica?"

"You are a smart girl, maybe too silly at times. Is that at all practical? That's for the men to figure out how his family is gonna look?" Grinning with a big smile Hattie Mae hustled out of the room for fear of being caught and goofing off. "I have to get downstairs, little one."

Now Missy was baffled by the information Hattie Mae shared. "Should she meet Peiter in the garden tonight?" Trying to convince herself one way or the other.

In the meantime, Peiter sat tucked away at home. His sister Kemica knew something was concerning her older brother. He had a secret to disclose to his only sibling who he truly trusted. "I want to marry Missy!"

"You are a crazy boy," She shot back loudly.

"Shhhhh, Kemica! My feelings for her have intensified. I want to do right by God," Peiter spoke quietly and softly.

Kemica started to pace back and forth in the small living area. "Hadn't I told you before that girl is going to make you unhappy? The two of you are like two buds on a rose bush I tell you. The beauty and pretty smell of the flower is attractive but the surrounding thorns on the stems are going to hurt you." The sister cautioned her brother.

"You are the crazy one, what are you talking about?" Peiter insisted.

"Missy is nice but get some sense. A colored boy can't be with a white girl? I like her and I am jealous of her. She is the Plantation Princess. That is what all the folks outback call her. Everything about her is perfect, her hair, clothes, even her family. You will be hurt and others would never accept the two of you getting married. You are stirring up trouble for even thinking about her like that." Pacing up and down the floor. "She'll want some nice white gentleman, get married, have babies, live in a big house, and wear her pretty fancy dresses. You can't do that for her. A white man will want her for a wife. She'll stay home, nurse those babies, while the maids clean, cook, and sew. Now you are making me afraid Peiter, do not do or say anything stupid. I know how trusting you can be."

Peiter was angry about the information that his sister shared. He sat on the floor with his hands covering his face, almost in tears. What his sister told him was not of his liking. He was looking for support from her, not ridicule.

He left the house and ran back to the flower garden. Again, he sat on the bench looking to God for guidance and answers. His thoughts were overwhelmed. The two closest friends of his were both females. Who could he talk to about this situation besides God? He needed some real advice and soon.

Suddenly he jumped up and headed towards the big house. Arriving at the backdoor of the home he called out. "Hattie, Hattie!"

Moments later the housemaid peered out the door. "What you need boy? Don't you know this is suppertime around here?"

"Please give Missy a message. Tell her I will see her in the morning as usual." Peiter quietly relayed.

"Well if you are going to see her in the morning as usual don't you think she would know that boy?" The housemaid inquired with a raised eyebrow.

"Just tell her that for me when you see her!" Peiter demanded and darted across the green lawn looking back. "You better tell her, Hattie!"

Chapter 21

LET THE CHURCH SAY "AMEN"

The smell of freshly cooked bacon scented the early Sunday's summer morning air. The aroma trickled from the big house as Peiter crossed the lawn as he headed to church. Proudly, the teen boy walked in his newly tailored suit sporting a Bible in his hand.

Arriving early, he placed the book on the front table. Next, he opened the Bible, a book he could hardly read. Yes, there were a few words he could recognize and sound out. Maybe a passage or two he had memorized. But word for word he was unable to actually read the book from beginning to end. In time, he planned to continue to learn how to read. With his teacher Missy always at his side for instructions he certainly could reach that goal someday.

Alone in the church he felt isolated and nervous. Today would be his first actual day of ministering. How many people would be in attendance he thought? Who was going to come? Would anyone show up? Certainly Missy and Kemica would be there to support him. Missy for sure! Who else was going to do the readings from the Bible?

He scoured around for a blanket or towel. An old coat hung from a nail near the side door. The coat was usually worn by whomever retrieved more wood for the stove on chillier days. That was not the case on this early Sunday morning.

Peiter placed the worn coat on the floor in front of the table that was holding the Bible. He knelt on the jacket to avoid the knees of his new suit pants touching the wooden floor. Next, he folded his hands together and prayed in silence.

Hours passed as he now sat alone in the quiet building. Outside the echoes of the chirping birds filled his ears with song. An occasion sound of a cow mooing in the distance offered a disruptive enlightenment that he was not alone. Peeking out the window in hopes of spotting a potential congregation member.

With time to spare he thought maybe he should stand outside the church? He grabbed his Bible as if to use it as a prop. Outside he stood proud next to the nicely crafted sign that read "Colossians 3:11" with the words inscribe underneath "God is Here."

First, he spotted a few colored children playing under a large willow tree nearby. Peiter called out to them, "God's children please ask your parents to attend church right here. Service will be an hour after noon time, one o'clock. You come, everyone is welcome here." The kids seemed to avoid the minister's request as they continued to play. He hollered over to the tall, black man sometimes referred to as *"Big Don."* "Donnell, let me remind you I am conducting church service this afternoon. Right here!" Donnell seemed to ignore Peiter's invitation and went about his work of delivering the freshly gathered eggs.

"No time for church now, son! Got a job to do. Said my prayers early this morning." Muttered the old man.

Peiter continued to stand proud in front of the building not knowing exactly what the time really was. "Really wish I had money to buy a time piece from Mr. Macher in town. How am I gonna know when it is one o'clock? That is the service's starting time. Certainly Missy will be here anytime soon! A minister really should have a time piece." Peiter grew nervous about the time. He was ready to deliver his first sermon with or without Missy.

Frantically, Peiter ran back to his home quarters in search of his sister Kemica. "Hurry, you need to follow me to the church. I know I can depend on you to be there for my first service?"

"Yes Peiter, I have plans of meeting you over there shortly. Anyone show up yet?" Kemica was uncertain about the whole new church thing but was going to support her brother and Missy's efforts.

"Father has been busy all morning trying to deliver a new calf out back. Doubt he'll make it, plus he's skeptical about new religions? Please hurry! I am nervous and no one has shown up yet?" The teen hurried back to the church that was just yards away.

Minutes later his sister arrived for the initial service. In her hand were two long, slender, candles made from bee's wax. "What's the candles for?" Peiter inquired with a he seen old man Donnell carting eggs to the out-kitchen. Peiter confused look.

"Candles are usually lit in a church. I know there is some explanation but I really do not know." As she handed them to her brother as if he knew what do with them? "Maybe they should be placed on this front table? One on each side. Either way, they will look nice?" She retrieved the candles, set them up and then they were lit. "Where is Missy?"

"Guess she is not back from church yet?" Peiter spoke nervously.

"This is church!" Kemica joked.

"Please Sister do not kid around. We are in the home of the Lord at this time. We have to pay respects and mind our best manners." Peiter was harsh to discipline his sibling.

"Hard to take you so seriously, Brother. Do you get a special name?" The sister inquired.

"I do have a special name, it is Peiter."

"What I meant was like the priest at the Catholic church. You know Father Murphy?" Kemica tried to clarify. "You need a minister name, like Minister Peiter, Brother Pieter. What are you going to call yourself? You have to have a fancy title to go with that fancy new suit, Brother! What exactly are you?"

"Yes, you are right Sister." Peiter started to pace back and forth. "You have good ideas and are creative sometime. What do you think?"

"Well first of all, are you like an official church minister? How did Father Murphy get to be a priest?" Questioned the teen girl.

"Must be official? Yes, it has to be! Otherwise why would Mr. Chettsburg offer the building to me to conduct church service from? He is the lawyer." Peiter grew more nervous as the goose bumps on his arms were shielded from his clothing. His new venture had big responsibilities as he continued to think about this. His efforts were being supported by a very important man. "Do you think Minister Peiter sounds appropriate Kemica?"

"Father Murphy uses his last name, shouldn't you?" As if his sister did not agree at first. "Yes Minister Peiter! Everyone knows you as Peiter, so why not?"

Suddenly there was a knock at the side door. Kemica peered out the door to find Louise, hand in hand, with her two young daughters. The farm worker wanted to know if she could drop the two girls off for Sunday church service like she did for school "You do not care to stay ma'am?"

"No, I figured the girls would not mind taking in an extra Bible lesson. They enjoy coming to school here all week long with Missy. Figured this was for the children?" Louise explained.

Peiter politely intervened. "No Ma'am, this church is open to everyone! You are welcome to stay."

Feeling a bit awkward the mother entered the building with roaming eyes. "Never seen the insides here. The girls talk about school and Missy all the time. Blessed to have this place for us folks."

Peiter directed her to have a seat next to the girls. Seems they already had assigned seating from attending school during the week. The mother sat on the wooden bench beside her daughters feeling a bit uneasy for lack of knowing what to expect.

The new minister started to feel more at ease. He thought there were sounds of the Chettsburgs' carriage coming up the driveway's path. This was an indication that Missy would soon arriving for service. Things were starting to look up at this point for Peiter. Surprisingly, Peiter was wrong.

Standing at the front door was Lester. Behind him was two of the youngest Miller children. "Went to pick Mrs. Miller up from Mass this morning. Mr. Chettsburg reminded me of your church service. Figured I'd grab a few kids and head over and get them introduced. Maybe they might like the new church? Good way for them to see the schoolhouse as well." Stomping to clean off his dirty boots. Lester then took off his dirty, grubby hat and hung the floppy thing from one of the hooks made of nails.

Kemica welcomed the new trio to sit on a bench. Seems she had taken on the position of being usher or host to the newcomers. Quite an accomplishment for the somewhat isolated girl. The teen rarely had the opportunity to interact with people outside of Missy's school.

One more person flocked in. This time the new guest was Hattie Mae looking nice and refreshed. "Mr. Chettsburg sent me over here ya'll. He figured I'm always over here sweeping the place. Might as well come and enjoy some prayer and company. Can't get enough prayer?" The woman announced loudly.

Peiter quietly approached Hattie to ask if she had seen Missy. He was quite antsy by now waiting for his counterpart.

Hattie assured Peiter she would be on her way shortly. "Just added a few hair ribbons to those braided tails of her. She'll be over shortly I assume."

The room was quiet as a church should be. Maybe a tad too calm. Peiter became uncomfortable for lack of knowing what to do. The few guests were like strangers to each other. This made the minister feel awkward. He did not want to keep them waiting any longer. Nor was he certain anyone else would be attending. He began the service with hopes of Missy coming to his rescue soon.

The young preacher now known as Minister Peiter approached the front of the makeshift church's room. The Bible was placed again on the table mainly for security. He feared the fact, knowing he could not read the book very well. The small crowd was greeted and thanked for joining the minister for his very first service.

"Christ is here!" Peiter proclaimed and by the sounds of the side door, so was Missy. A relief and prayers were answered for the new minister. Missy slowly took a seat near Kemica. The young preacher began with his first sermon he had practiced all week long. For one who had never attended church himself, he was not sure how the orientation would be perceived.

"Coping with life! You cannot look for happiness. First you have to be happy. You can be the person you want to be but you must first have to act like that person. Everyone is not perfect. God knows and understands this. What he also knows is that you are capable of making changes.

Want to be more beautiful? Then be beautiful! Fix your hair, make a new dress, borrow a dress, buy one if you have money for that?

Want to feel powerful? Feel confident and strong about yourself then! You have a strong government, feel the strengths God has given you.

Be loving! One must love thyself first" Peiter's voice suddenly came across soft spoken. "Tell yourself you are loved by a very loving God. When walking down a dirt path or a cobblestone walkway hold your head up high. Smile at every brother and sister you see. Not only will you generate love from within but you will share this warm feeling with others. If you really want to feel love try smiling at an animal like a stray cat or a roaming squirrel." A few chuckles from the children echoed throughout the room. "Bring the smallest of things into your life to create happiness. Why do some people impose limits on themselves?" Peiter's tone was getting louder. "The changes are real and they are going to start now!" The young minister instructed everyone to stand up. "Without a word, turn to a person next to you and give them a smile. (*a brief moment passed*) Now, turn to someone else near you and smile. Who feels that smile more? Who! You, you are the one creating the happiness. Do you feel richer and fuller? This is about loving yourself. God's love starts with you. Everything starts with you because God has given you everything you need whether you realize this yet or not.

The situation should feel good to give to others even if this is just a smile. Give a smile to yourself and see how it feels! Enlightening I would hope? Start loving yourself more and more. Not just today but always. Break the old patterns. Discover a new you by loving yourself first. Christ is here! No matter who you are, where you came from, you are here! God has not united us together based on our skin color, hair color or the color of our eyes. Love for his words has brought us together. At this time, Missy will read from the Holy Bible, Colossians 3:11."

Missy proceeded to walk towards the front of the room. Thumbing through the pages she came across the marked passages. Her beautiful voice annunciated the short reading.

Lester's mind wandered as he daydreamed. He thought carefully about what the young minister had stated. His head felt as if it had opened up and Peiter had poured new thoughts right into it. The known drunk's feelings were the preacher had directed his sermon specifically to him. There was a lesson in attending the service he thought? Hopefully, the young children caught a glimpse and understanding of this also?

As Missy concluded with the Bible reading, Pieter asked for a joint "Amen!" from the newly formed congregation. "Go with love and always remember 'Christ is Here'." The youngest Miller girl Allie, started to clap as if a performance was over. Lester grabbed her hands as if to stop her as he was quite embarrassed.

"No Sir, she is right." Hattie stated. Along with the young girl, Hattie Mae started to clap loudly. "Peiter, you make me want to cry. My heart is full of joy. That was a beautiful sermon. I not only heard your words but I felt them. Sounds like you been a preacher for many years." Hattie complimented him and gave him a great big hug. There was a 'smile' on her face as she left the church.

Lester hustled the girls out the front door without any further words. Into the carriage they went. Down the dirt path, leading to the country road, they could be seen leaving. Meanwhile, the others gathered outside of the church and shared a few brief words on that sunny, Sunday afternoon.

Chapter 22

PEITER IS IN LOVE

Could the two older teens ever possibly be able to marry? Peiter had fallen deeply in love with his friend Missy. An interracial marriage was just simply unacceptable in this society. The couple would never be able to unite in a legal matrimony.

The bright, warm sun had risen on the early summer Monday morning. Peiter was anxious to head over to the schoolhouse to meet his friend Missy as usual. He slipped on short trousers and sandals were placed on his feet. Dashing across the yard he anticipated greeting his female companion.

Alone in the school, the teacher was busy prepping the room that would welcome the students. As always, Peiter was there to help out and learn as well. The minister was still excited about the previous day's church service that he conducted.

"Missy, we are a special team!" Peiter complimented. "Nowhere else on earth is there a place like this. I mean this room, this farm, your family." He started to spin around like a toddler.

"You think so differently at times Peiter. This place is the only home I really know. When I was a baby we lived in town upstairs in the apartment. The farm is my home as I know it. At times I feel we should share more of your memories from when you lived on that tropical island. Although I know things were hard at times. As a teacher, I am interested in knowing what things were like and how the place was different." Missy compassionately shared.

"Yes Missy, you are always the teacher. Thinking, thinking and more thinking. Guess that is what helps make you so smart?" Peiter held his head down as he recalled some of the dreadful times of his youth back home. "You are right!" Peiter perked up and began to share about his earlier life. "You would not believe the differences, Missy! The land is surrounded by clear water as if you were peering through a glass window. Not like the murky ponds that are seen around here. The trees are tall but do not hold many leaves. The fish. The fish are strange, yet you can eat them all." Peiter busted out in laughter. "Oh how I love to fish. Here, there, just about anywhere. I am off to find my father. Wonder if he wants to go fishing with me this evening? Gonna go catch me some ugly fish to eat for dinner down by the stream."

"You can certainly ask my father as well. He and my grandfathers like to fish also," Missy extended an invite.

Peiter hustled out of the schoolhouse in search of his father. Time to make plans for a fishing adventure. An outing for only for the men. Certainly there would be some willing participant somewhere on the farm.

Doc was tired and still had a few household chores to tend to. Peiter found a few older labors willing to join him on the fishing expedition. Together they gathered poles, bait, and an old rusty bucket. The sounds of the soothing, flowing stream brought a few fish to the men's dangling lines.

The rolling water also hypnotized the young man's thoughts. He turned over the bucket and was seated. With the dusk about to set, he dreamed of his beautiful friend Missy with his eyes lost in the water. Quickly Peiter announced, "Ready to head back? I am getting hungry and these fish need to be filleted. Let's meet back at my house and have dinner, shall we?"

Quite an invitation the elder men thought. "Dinner with the young minister at Doc's house? Sure your Pa won't mind us stopping over there boy?"

"Mind? He's going to enjoy these fish just as we are. My sister Kemica is the one in for a surprise. She doesn't realize we have dinner guests coming." The men were assured they were welcome to come feast on their fresh catch.

Peiter was in a very good mood. An evening of fishing and eating with new friends. A beautiful full moon was expected that night. The teen loved a dark night highlight by a bright lit moon. A sky sprinkled with stars was another favorite of his. Seemed to be a symbol of guidance from God. The moon helped him to understand that God really was out there somewhere.

The next morning, Peiter headed to the school as usual. This time he had a serious agenda. The teacher had not arrived as of yet. He grabbed the drinking bucket that sat near the door. Not his normal chore, he retrieved some fresh water from the pump while waiting for Missy. Next, he swept the wooden platform at the side door with an overused, tattered, straw broom. Then there was the sound of the front door shutting. The teacher had finally arrived on this brisk, Tuesday.

The day had barely begun. Peiter had another request for his friend that he had fallen deeply in love with. Again, he wanted to set up a discrete meeting in the back flower garden after the night set in. The invitation also included she wear something pretty and special. As usual, Missy enjoyed spending time with her male friend and often looked forward to this. She was not sure what the teen boy had planned this particular evening. As he left the schoolhouse, she thanked him for taking care of a few chores. Missy was a little puzzled as Peiter usually stuck around for the school activities.

The day progressed and the darkness was setting in. Missy sat at her ivory-painted vanity and combed her long brown hair. Fresh flowers were fastened to her locks with a few fancy hairpins. Standing up, she notice how pretty she was wearing what was her Sunday best.

Meanwhile, Peiter dressed in a pair of dark trousers. Next, he put on his new white buttoned shirt that went with his tailored suit. That was all he needed to feel dressed up for the night's occasion. He called for his younger sister, Kemica. The two siblings ventured over to the garden. Together they sat with anticipation on the bench in the center of the garden. As instructed, Missy was soon to arrive. In the short distance, Missy's footsteps could be heard approaching closer and closer.

Peiter stood to greet Missy and took her by the hand. There he placed a gentle kiss on top of her wrist. "I know you can't see me very well, hidden by the night. Please take my hand. Do you feel the color of my skin? Of course you do not. All I feel is the softness of yours, Missy." The teen boy then leaned in and gave her a quick kiss on her lips. Missy had never been kissed before. The intimate touch from her friend was somewhat confusing, somewhat strange, yet somewhat comforting. The situation was even stranger as she noticed Kemica seated on the garden's bench. Missy had assumed Peiter had just wanted to meet for some friendly companionship?

A serious conversation was about to begin. Peiter spoke and pronounced his love for his friend, Missy. He explained she would be his loving wife. Poor Missy was surprised, baffled and slightly fearful from what she was hearing.

"My father would never accept this relationship nor let me marry a man of color, Peiter!" Missy cried out.

"I am not asking him, I am not asking in a legal way. I want to be married to you in the eyes of the Lord. We must have this relationship blessed. We can't answer to the government. The government does not understand the meaning of love. This is going to be a private ceremony between the two of us with Kemica as our witness. We will be man and wife in accordance to God's laws. I have brought along my Bible. I will name you my wife and I will be your husband for the rest of our lives." Peiter then instructed his sister to light the big thick candle they brought to the garden.

Standing in the garden were three nervous and scared teens. Peiter instructed Missy to read a few passages from the book. Being unable to read himself he remembered a few phrases that were dear to him. The first reading from the Bible was 1 Peter 4:8; Love covers a multitude of sins. Missy read the words nervously as Kemica held the candle near to shed light on the page. Peiter spoke as a minister would. "Let my love for you Missy shadow over all the sins man has created. God designed men of many different colors and why is this? Who are we to question God? Love is greater than the sins stemmed from love. I have renamed myself P-E-I-T-ER, and I shall speak the special words from him in the Bible." Next he asked her to read one from another favorite section of the book, Colossians 3:2; let heaven fill your thoughts. Do not think only about things down here on earth. Again Peiter started explaining. "Heaven is our final destination. Heaven is full of love, not judgment, not acceptance from others, not the government's laws. The only thing we can take from this earth with us to heaven is love. We shall not be broken down from what others think of our special gift given to the two of us from God."

Missy was impressed with the words shared by Peiter. He truly was Minister Peiter. The teen had learned a lot a long time ago from the traveling missionaries. He appeared before her like a well-educated man. The minister had a great memory and a creative way of expressing his thoughts. Missy, a teacher herself, was proud of her friend's accomplishments. She actually enjoyed listening to him as opposed to the boring Father Murphy who was so hard to understand.

"You are now my wife Missy, with Kemica as God's witness. We can now engage physically and know that we have God's blessing and permission." Peiter announced to his new bride.

Missy stood there trembling feeling uneasy about the ceremony. "Is this real?" she thought. She loved Peiter, yet she loved Kemica also. They were her friends. This is not at all what Missy had dreamed her wedding would be like. Someday, she planned on wearing her mother's wedding dress. She loved that beautiful dress that she had stored in her hope-chest. Over the years, she had tried that dress on many times with expectations of growing into the garment. Thoughts of the dress raged through her mind. Then she remembered her father telling her teachers were not to marry or have children. Her mind was spinning and she seriously felt light headed.

"Can't this ceremony wait?" blasted Missy.

"Wait, this is done and over? Do you not want our love to be a commitment to God and I? I am a minister, I can spiritually marry us."

"I just wanted to wear my mother's wedding dress for such a sacred event."

"Tonight? You want to wear the wedding dress tonight?"

"No! I cannot sneak back into the house to change into a wedding gown. Nor can I sneak the dress out right now." Missy explained.

"Well, I wanted to be married under a full moon." Peiter confided.

The two married teens went back and forth like two little kids arguing selfishly. Neither really wanting to compromise. Peiter had a resolution. The two would consummate the marriage the following night. The moon again would be full and Missy could wear the wedding gown. Kemica stood on the sideline, standing neutral of the married couple's separate requests.

"Meet me here tomorrow night so we can carry on with our spiritual union!" The new husband demanded of his new wife. Peiter leaned forward to kiss his bride good-night. Missy stormed off feeling sickly with butterflies in her stomach.

Arriving at the back door, Missy hoped to sneak in the house. Not that she had any explaining to do. The teen girl was just trying to avoid any curious parents. Greeting her in the dark was Hattie standing proud and tall. "Why you out late all dressed up little one?"

"Just heading back from prayer circle late, I guess?" Missy gave her weak explanation. "We missed you joining us this evening, Hattie Mae."

"Did not hear about no nighttime prayer circle?" Hattie continued to interrogate the older teen.

"Minister Peiter scheduled a nighttime prayer circle twice a week. For folks like you who go to work in the early morning. Come on Hattie, grab your stool and meet me on the front porch." There on the front wrap-around porch, Missy climbed on the porch's swing. Hattie placed her stool near the top step. The two young ladies swapped their daily events as they swatted an army of large mosquitoes.

Hattie Mae retrieved a cotton kitchen-dish cloth from her large apron's front pocket. Lightly she padded the sweat from her face on this awfully muggy evening. "Might be rain tomorrow, the kids will have to play inside for recess?" Hattie Mae suggested.

"Why do you say that?" Kicking and swinging.

"The clouds are hiding the full moon. They are gray. You know, you are the teacher. Gray clouds bring rain. The darker or blacker the clouds, the harder the storm. Hey little one, can I move closer over there by you? I want to be getting some of that breeze you are stirring up from that swing flying." Hattie picked up her stool.

"Come closer, we need to do some more talking about the men," a big sigh followed Missy's statement.

"Oh no, not again. Sure you don't need to talk to your mama 'bout all this?"

"No, this is for the unmarried ladies' ears only." Missy slyly suggested. "And how long are you going to keep calling me, little one? I am a grown woman now!"

"Girl that's how I always known you. You was a little one when I first knew you. Certainly, you are not the big one now, why that would be me. It's dark, late and the bugs are bad. I'm off to bed." Hattie stepped off the porch and then headed to the back of the house.

Missy sat swinging lightly on that humid night. A weird, uneasy feeling was still following her. Was she really married in God's eyes? Could the marriage be real she tried to convince herself? Peiter had taken on the part of a real minister. He was a different type of minister compared to Father Murphy who she had grown up to know. Would the two be considered married in the Roman Catholic Church? Of course not, she agreed. Just as she considered herself to be a real schoolteacher. Schoolteachers can't marry? But who would know other than Kemica? No one else had to know or needed to know. Her own father stated Peiter was not ever going anywhere. Peiter was like family her father acknowledged. Only God would know! God would allow them to always be married in Heaven, as she cleared all her doubts.

The young lady needed to know what to expect from her husband when they consummated the marriage. Who could she talk to about this other than Hattie? Yes, Hattie had to be the-go-to person in the morning. Like the housemaid, Missy slipped in for the night that was highlighted with a bright full moon.

She put on her night clothes and thought about earlier events of the evening. Desperately, she was looking for answers. How was she going to sneak the wedding dress out that was tucked away in her hope-chest? Yes, the dress could be rolled up tightly and hidden in an oversized quilt. The large blanket could then be taken out to the schoolhouse.

Missy cried laying in her bed late that night, frightened and scared. So many questions still needed to be answered. She did not feel secure being Peiter's wife. How could he ever take care of her? They could never have children for fear of not being accepted by their families and society.

The next morning was greeted with sweet, southern sunshine. Missy gracefully dressed for the day and was seated for breakfast. The table in the formal dining room had been nicely set by the butler, John. Arriving next for breakfast were her parents, Charles and Lara. The three would enjoy eating together as a family. Hattie had cooked a full morning meal consisting of golden hotcakes and fried ham. The cakes were smothered in creamy butter and sticky maple syrup.

"Got extra hotcakes if you want to run some out to your friend, little one or I better say M-I-S-S-Y." Hattie extended the leftovers for Peiter.

"Thank you Hattie, I will take those out when we finish here with our breakfast." Missy politely agreed.

"His hotcakes are drizzled with molasses, wrapped up for him on the service window, ready to go." The maid instructed.

"Molasses on hotcakes, Hattie?" Missy questioned the breakfast favorite.

"All this time and I have better known how your grown playmate likes his hotcakes? Goodness, a way to a man's heart starts with his stomach." Laughed the maid.

There seemed to be an opportunity arising. Missy flew up the back staircase. A folded quilt stuffed with the wedding dress was retrieved from her bedroom. Carefully down the steps she came carrying a full load to deliver to the schoolhouse. After dropping the quilt and wedding gown off, she headed back to the house for the plated hotcakes. Again, she walked back to the school to give Peiter some unexpected breakfast. The married couple exchanged a brief, discrete kiss. The quilt was then quickly stuffed in a small closet for possibly later on that night.

Peiter sat at the front table and began to eat. Bite after bite he exchanged a few words in prayer. He reached out for Missy's hand to join his and spoke, "Together we will be one in the eyes of God. We will be man and wife, today and everyday going forward. Please Father, bless our Holy union with a lifetime of love, happiness and health. Thank you for the gifts you have given us. Amen!" Today he was more confident in talking to his wife about their nontraditional marriage.

The school day progressed as usual. A dozen or so students lined-up at the front door. Never seemed to be the same exact group. Every day there were some eager to spend the day with their teacher, Missy. The students were instructed about penmanship, the alphabet, and a brief lesson on the chalkboard involving basic arithmetic. As noon time approached, the sounds of raindrops pinged on the roof. Pellets of rain splashed against the windows.

Missy recalled what Hattie had predicted the night before about the weather. She was correct about the rainy forecast. The teacher announced that the students would be staying in for lunch and recess time because of the inclement weather. Students were instructed to take out the math counters which consisted of dried beans. The younger ones could practice counting. The others could do simple addition problems.

As the end of the school day drew near, the rain came to an end. In moved the white puffy clouds shielding the sun's rays. The time was now, two o'clock, about time to wrap up the learning for the gloomy day.

Straggling behind in the classroom was Peiter waiting to confirm tonight's meeting with Missy. "I expect to meet you here around dark time."

"I am not sure what the plans are at home this evening Peiter." Missy pleaded.

"You are my wife, Missy. Your husband comes first, always first. Remember that when making plans. I know we need to be cautious about our relationship. We are together now and forever." Peiter reminded the bride. "Tonight we will celebrate and be intimate without any consequences from God.

The marriage will be consummated and I just need a little time for making some plans myself."

Peiter offered to walk Missy home across the wet lawn. He grabbed the large, near empty picnic type basket and escorted his friend. Then he headed to the back-barn to his house trying to beat his sister home. Carefully he gathered the new tailored suit, clean socks, and a pair of polished shoes. The clothing was quickly placed in a wadded burlap bag. Back to the schoolhouse he went with the bag over his shoulder. Once at the schoolhouse he put the bag up in the loft to be concealed.

Suppertime was as usual at the Chettsburgs' house. Joseph and Elizabeth had come over to join their son's family for a meal. Hattie had roasted a couple of ducks along with butternut squash. Dinner would not be complete without a tasty treat prepared by the professional baker and chocolatier. On the table waiting was one of Elizabeth's signature chocolate pecan pies.

The grandparents were eager to dash home after eating. Joseph insisted the roads were muddy from the earlier rain. Made for a hard travel for the wagon. Elizabeth agreed on getting an early start back home. She always had chores that needed tending to in their home and at her store. Missy was quick to ask her grandmother if she could share a piece of the leftover pie with her friend, Peiter.

"Of course, dear! Why would you feel as if you ever needed to ask?" The grandmother acted embarrassed.

"Just trying to be polite Ma'am. I know you work hard. Did not want you to think I was just passing off your delicious food to just anyone, you know?"

"Missy, I know you and Peiter are special friends. Of course, I would expect you to share with him. No need to smooth over the topic. I know he is colored, no hiding that. Would not make a difference to me who enjoys my goodies. Whites, blacks, reds, purples." Everyone at the table broke out in laughter at Elizabeth's funny way of expressing no judgment of the young man's color. "Tell me how he likes it Missy, maybe he could use a nice treat every now and then. You know for a fact, your grandfather or I deliver goods to Father Murphy at least twice a week. Maybe the young minister might be as deserving?" The laughter continued.

Hattie called for the butler. There were other leftovers on the table she had plated for Peiter also. "Butler John, you run this plate out to Peiter in the schoolhouse!" The butler just rolled his eyes at the loud woman. He did not like taking demands and orders from her. Was not her place to delegate jobs to him in the first place? Missy intervened. She offered to take the food to Peiter along with a piece of the pie. Seems folks were catching on that Peiter had taken up sleeping quarters at night in the schoolhouse.

Missy was not in a real hurry to head over to the building. She knew Peiter was expecting her after dark. The food was placed on the service window and she assured Hattie the meal would be delivered shortly. Something the butler was pleased to hear.

The items were carefully placed in a luncheon picnic basket. A little awkward to handle with her tiny hands alone.

Quickly, she ran upstairs to her bedroom where she released the tails from her hair. Next, she placed a comb through the long, silky hair. A light coat of lipstick was applied to her lips. She snuck into her mother's room for a little dab of sweet scented perfume. Back to her room she put on a different pair of button leather boots. Down the back stairs she quickly but quietly came down. Hoping not to be noticed by anyone she grabbed the picnic basket and darted towards the schoolhouse.

The building was fairly dark with a slight cast of light from the full moon. Missy assumed that would be enough lightening in order to change her clothes. Over to the closet she went to retrieve the wedding gown bundled in the quilt. Carefully she put on the dress so she did not disturb her neatly combed hair. She twirled around in the dress as she had done several times before. The fit was a little big for the small framed teen girl. Now, she felt distraught not knowing what to expect next. Actually, she felt funny and awkward all dressed up in the dark. Her fears were that no one but Peiter would find her standing there like a princess waiting for the prince. She looked down at the pretty dress but the darkness hindered the true grandness. Standing and pacing was all she knew what to do for the moment. The wooden benches looked inviting to sit on but she feared snagging her attire. The time passed for what seemed like an hour.

Finally the latch on the side door rattled. Peering in was the man she was waiting for. "Peiter!" She quietly whispered.

"Yes, Missy." Answered the voice in the darkness. There in the doorway stood a young handsome, colored man dressed in a magnificent two-piece tailored suit. "My bride has arrived and dressed so nicely from what I can see. Should I light a candle or two?"

"No! We need to be discrete as possible Peiter," shot back Missy.

The new husband approached his somewhat frigid bride. First, he fondled her soft, flowing hair while kissing her forehead for assurance. He stepped back and took off the suit coat. Tightly he embraced Missy and engaged in a deep endless kiss. A real first kiss for her.

In the corner of the room, a shabby mat piled with blankets waited empty. "Tonight I get my gift from God, my virgin wife," Peiter led Missy to the sleeping area. The bride was instructed to disrobe as her husband was standing almost naked. He took the precious piece of apparel from her and gently draped the gown over a table.

The now shy and timid woman spoke up, "Are we really going to do what married couples do? Be physically intimate? I fear I will get pregnant, Peiter! I know about the five-day rule. Hattie told me about what your father knows. Now is not a good time?"

Totally off track, Peiter wondered how Hattie Mae knew of his father's method.

"A woman does not get pregnant when consummating a marriage. Like I said this is God's gift to the husband to take his virgin wife. Remember we now have God's permission and blessings." The words flowed out of Peiter's mouth convincingly. Missy placed trust in his belief.

In the darkness the two gathered on the mat. The bride was positioned on the bottom as her husband rolled on top. Missy was immobile and nervous as her husband explored her warm, soft, body with his hands. His wet lips greeted her small breasts as he gently applied small kisses. Goosebumps coated the bride's back and arms. The eager man took his time anticipating a woman's warmth. Something he had not felt in many years. His hard erect body could not wait much longer. In between her legs he rubbed back and forth with his proud erection trying to stimulate the virgin. Slowly and gradually he thrust into his wife's body. Moans of pleasure cried out loudly from the man and echoed throughout the quiet room. Whines and whimpers came from the woman as the somewhat painful experience was dreadful. Missy was not accepting the act so well. She thought back to Hattie Mae's story about how she enjoyed being intimate with Doc. Peiter called out to his bride, "Are you hurting? The first time may not be so comfortable for a woman. With time this will not be so straining."

All Missy knew is what everyone had told her and that was not much. Her mother Lara never really talked about men. The parent figured, the conversation would be useless since her only daughter would never marry being that she is a teacher. Hattie Mae was bold about everything, even when the subject was intimacy.

With her eyes closed she tried to buffer the marital interaction. "Was this every going to end?"

Missy thought to herself. "Could she ask him to stop, she had enough of this?" She was uncertain how this all was supposed to work. Soon she would find out.

Pieter recited over and over how much he loved Missy. Unfortunately, she was not feeling exactly the same at this particular moment. Finally, a huge sigh of relief came from her sweaty, husband. He grabbed her tightly almost piercing his nails into her delicate skin. Resting on top of the bride, she felt smothered. He was extremely exhausted. Again, the two engaged in a long, deep intimate kiss.

Missy was not sure of her role at the moment. Frantically, she knew she was expected to be home in her own bed. The time was getting late into the night. Yet, she also knew married people slept in the same bed all night together. Seemed to be the norm for married folks?

Peiter's embrace was tight. He was not about to let his bride leave his side yet. The warmth of Missy's body comforted him as her head was placed on his sweaty, drenched, hairy chest. Her long, soft, brown hair glued on him, drawn from his body's perspiration.

"I must go Peiter!" Missy requested of her husband. "You know I can't stay all night. We do not want trouble nor do we want to cause any."

The fragile woman gathered the wedding gown from the table carefully looking in the near darkness. Gently wrapped in the quilt the items were placed back in the closet to recover later. Her fingers combed her hair to smooth out any tangles. Slowly she dressed herself to get ready to leave. Peiter had already fallen asleep on the bedding on the floor. Sounds of his deep breathing filled the room. The warm summer air was the only cover for his body as he slept. The tired and proud man had full-filled his marital duty with his new, young bride.

The two, grown teens, carried out their secret marriage all summer long. The only other person involved in the concealed relationship was Kemica. At times they could laugh at how easy the arrangement worked out. As always the couple spent the week together at the school. Peiter was there to help with the daily duties and to learn as well. On Sundays, Missy was always in attendance for the minister's church service by his side for a Bible reading. A few nights a week the two had their own private "prayer circle." A convenient way for the pair to have privacy in the schoolhouse where the minister mainly lived. Actually, just a covered tale for them to enjoy each other intimately in the late evening hours. The married couple did not share the same roof over their heads. Nor would they legally be allowed to cohabitate. The Chettsburgs' farm provided a homestead large enough for them to be friends, as well as, a family with close enough living quarters.

Chapter 23

THE SURPRISE CHRISTMAS GIFTS

Did you hear about the latest invention? Charles was fascinated with the new sewing machines being mass produced. He was eager to purchase two of the somewhat complicated pieces of equipment. Personally, he knew nothing about sewing or constructing clothes.

One machine would be purchased for his mother and daughter to share. Both women were equally talented seamstresses. On the other hand, his wife had a flare for fashion. Lara was too spoiled to spend her precious time sewing her own clothing. Ready-to-wear garments were her preference. Charles' mother Elizabeth, was already busy enough at her tea room. The new sewing machine would be a time saver for mending and making clothes.

One day brisk day in the fall, Charles arranged to sneak away to a large neighboring town. Heading out, he rounded up Lester to be his traveling companion in the horse drawn carriage. Together they headed to the store where he heard orders could be placed for the sewing machines. He joked to Lester, "I know nothing about sewing, let alone a sewing machine!"

Arriving at the store, Charles relied on the clerk to assist him with the order. The older man mentioned the machines would not be available for several months. A friendly apology was given for the anticipated delay of the product. "Not a problem at all, Sir. I am planning on purchasing two gifts for the ladies. Planned on hiding them until Christmas, anyways." Charles was somewhat relieved, actually. An order and deposit of sale was written out for the purchase. "I'll check back in a month and make another payment, sir?" The two men ventured back to town sharing unrelated stories of their very complicated lives.

The Christmas spirit filled the town. The village of Atlanta and the surrounding areas began to take on the holiday tone. Merchants displayed pine roping with large red bows attached. Lamp posts along the main streets were also festively decorated. Even Charles' horse drawn carriage had a motif wreath tied to the rear. The nights' darkness presented a cool winter chill. Carolers could be seen and heard traveling along the sidewalk as they shared their joyous tunes. In the far distance, the church bells chimed at nine o'clock, signaling the end of another day. Bong, bong, bong!

After months of anticipation the holiday season was celebrated. Tall in the Chettsburgs' formal living room stood an overly decorated pine tree. Strands of popcorn garland were accented with round, shiny bulbs. Tucked away under the tree were gifts to be given and exchanged.

Finally, a chilly Christmas morning had arrived with no need for Saint Nick. For the only child was now grown and no little ones to be found. Charles for one was excited like a kid because of the presents he was about to give.

Discretely, he had the sewing machines located outback and stored in a barn. A couple of laborers were asked to bring one into the house that holiday morning. The machine was placed near the brightly decorated tree. Draped with a blanket so hopefully no one would peak and see what was hiding underneath.

Meanwhile, John the butler, set the formal dinner table with fine china and silver. Carefully, the middle aged man placed the assortment of wares on the linen tablecloth with a stylish table-runner. Hattie Mae was awake early to roast and stuff a wild turkey. Elizabeth was on hand also assisting with the fowl. A special Christmas dressing recipe was recited and specific instructions were given to Hattie Mae. Onions and a granny smith apple were finely diced. Crushed, roasted pecans and cranberries were also added to the bread mixture. Earlier, fresh bread and apple strudel were baked in the out-kitchen by Elizabeth. Glazed yams were also being prepared. Lara acting as the hostess, merely overseeing that the table was set properly.

Everything had be impeccably placed. Including her pretty green, tartan plaid holiday dress.

Elizabeth poked her nose in and out of the kitchen lending a helpful hand.

Platter by platter, Christmas dinner arrived at the table. An invitation to eat followed a long, lengthy prayer of thanks shared by Charles. The Chettsburgs enjoyed the somewhat quiet holiday meal together. "Pass the butter, please!" Was Joseph's request. "Then I'd like some raspberry jam?" Joseph's eyes were feasting just as well. The table looked beautiful and magnificent. "I have been blessed with three lovely ladies." He then blurted out.

"Three? Aren't you a lucky man," Charles added to the pun.

"Seriously Son! I have a loving wife who has cared so unselfishly for me. My daughter-in-law who is very special and dear to my heart. The third, Missy my pride and joy. My granddaughter, who has grown into a compassionate, young woman."

"Come on Father, don't rush things. She is still in her teens." Charles remarked as if not wanting his only daughter to appear grown up already. "We are all lucky if you ask me?"

Everyone commented and agreed with the older man while proceeding to finish their special dinner.

Next on the agenda was the exchange of gifts. First, Charles and Lara gave their daughter a new dictionary. After that came a full-sized globe. Missy was ecstatic about her new Christmas gifts. Not only were they gifts for her but she knew they would likely be new additions to the schoolhouse. She was more grateful that the school had been blessed and gifted new learning tools. That was just her nature, so kind and considerate. The gift exchange continued between the family members.

Finally, the time was for Charles to present the biggest gift yet. He was so overly enthused. He revealed the gift by removing the blanket that was covering this one. The ladies' faces lit up with delight. All three were excited as they viewed the complex mechanism. Elizabeth was more concerned about the expense of the sewing machine. Lara was excited as the gift was truly unique. Missy could not wait to start fidgeting with the mysterious thing. In her mind, she started dreaming about frilly dresses that could be sewn. New dresses made in a fraction of the time were his mother's thoughts. Elizabeth found the sewing machine a little complicated and intimidating. Especially with her eyes not being as good as they use to be. The oldest lady had not sewn much over the recent years either. In the end, the three ladies beamed at the new gift. Charles, knowing his wife would never use the darn thing. He certainly included her as a recipient of the large bulky package though.

Meanwhile, Hattie Mae cleared the formal dining table. Again, the table would be carefully set by Butler John. Later in the evening the Chettsburgs would be hosts to the Machers. The family would be joining them later for tea and holiday desserts. This of course was a time for Elizabeth to shine. She proudly prepared a wide assortment of chocolates, pies, and tortes to be put on display.

Anticipating their arrival, in pranced the Macher family. Butler John stood at the door collecting winter coats, one by one. Everyone's arms were loaded with gifts. Smiles on Leon's and Fia's faces, a sure sign of holiday cheer. Beside them stood Timm, quiet as usual. Along came the twins, Hattie Mae not knowing who was who? "Sure hope your mother and husbands know the difference between you two ladies. My, if I had 'look-a-likes', I'd have to have one girl with short hair and let the other one grow real long hair. How else do you all tell them apart?" the bold maid fussed.

Leon had a comment of his own to add, "Ma'am you get to know their personalities, not their faces." Even Fia smirked for once at her husband's true comment.

There was more to the twins than their facial looks and attitudes. Delores toted in her two young toddlers, Tyler and James. While her plump twin sister Hanna, was expecting her first born within the next few weeks. Another new cousin for Missy was soon to arrive.

"Join us in the dining room everyone!" Lara called out to her parents and siblings.

Missy beamed, "No Mother! Please bring them into the living room first. Come see the decorated tree and my dear father's gift to us women." Missy redirected everyone to showcase the new sewing machine.

Leon was highly amazed with the new piece of machinery. "Charles quit buying my lovely daughter Lara such lavish gifts. My wife is going to expect one also." jokingly.

"Oh father, I do intend on having mother over to learn about the new sewing machine also. She is welcome to use this for her own mending and hemming once we figure out how to function the thing," was Lara's invitation to her mother.

Next, everyone gathered around the dining room. Elizabeth sat tranquil in a chair as she was full of emotions. She was very thankful to have her family together for the winter holiday. Included in her thanks were the Machers, an extension of her immediate family. The holidays had brought together a joyous group. She began to ponder deeper, thinker about her family back in Belgium, her parents, her siblings. They were missed dearly by the aging woman. So much time had passed since she last saw any of them. How many of them were there now? In-laws, nieces, nephews, some she had never met, most she never would. Then she felt empathy for her wonderful husband. Did Joseph ever wish he would return home to be reunited with his other loved ones? The family that was seated at the nicely decorated table was what mattered right now. No time for other wishful thinking.

Hattie Mae poured hot tea for most of the guests, while Elizabeth helped plate desserts. As usual, a quiet argument was brewing from the servants' quarters. Seems Butler John caught Hattie Mae sneaking a delicate chocolate and a few pecan praline candies from one of the nicely arranged serving trays.

"How very rude Hattie Mae to eat from the tray. Shame on you! I will be calling this to the elder Mrs. Chettsburg's attention. She is always awfully nice to you. I know she gave you a slice of her specialty pecan-packed fudge as a holiday treat!" John scolded the feisty maid.

"Why don't you go home?" Hattie Mae demanded. "I do most the work around here anyways. You really gonna tell on me like a little kid?"

"Pardon me Ma'am. You do not tell me to go home. I come to the family farm at Mr. Chettsburg's request. My main profession is the bookkeeper, which is first priority. That is why I rent a room over the law practice office. I am close to work. When things are slow I can assist him with the household duties, especially during the holidays. I am his bookkeeper and butler for a reason, I am t-r-u-s-t-e-d!" The two voices in the servants' area loudened.

Elizabeth excused herself from the company and went to oversee the desserts, as well as, the commotion. Both Hattie Mae and John became silent as she entered the small narrow room. "All I know is I overheard something about being 'trusted'. Now can I trust the both of you to serve our guests quietly? You are well aware the Machers are family and will be treated as such. Keep your little quarrels for later you two!" Elizabeth disciplined them like two little playmates not getting along. Hattie Mae had a personal issue with Butler John's services at the home. She felt the big house was her responsibility. Somehow she thought John was infringing on her territory. The two co-workers had different responsibilities at the home. Hattie Mae constantly felt as if John was intruding, which was not the case. Both had unique jobs to do amongst the tight quarters.

Still there was one more Christmas surprise in store. Another gift was waiting outback. But who was the designated recipient? Yes, there was another new sewing machine that Charles had purchased. The first was for the three ladies to share. Who was going to be gifted the second? The surprise would have to wait until morning. The house was blessed with guests and good food to enjoy for the moment.

The day after Christmas, Charles woke up and headed to the back barn. First stop was at the schoolhouse to find Peiter. He then called for Doc at his home. The two men were needed to help load the other sewing machine onto a wagon.

"Peiter, you be ready in about twenty minutes. We have a Christmas gift to deliver." Charles was tired from the previous late night celebration. Charles then headed back to the house to gather a few things and fetch his jacket. His parents had spent the night and his mother was up early as usual. "Mother you are not headed back to town yet are you? Peiter and I are headed up yonder aways, the other direction." Near the breakfast nook he noticed a large bowl of hard candy. "Those candies a creation of yours, Mother?"

"Yes, there are several treats floating around here Charles. After all this is Christmas. If you are hunger there is pie in the ice box. Maybe a few cookies to nibble on. But so early in the morning, Son?"

"No Mother, 'bout to deliver a late Christmas gift. Wondered if I could take a few treats along for a few needy children."

"Do they need food you are implying?" Elizabeth grew concerned.

"Nah, they have food on their farm. Don't think they get treats too often." Charles sighed.

"How many children are there on this farm?"

"Six."

"Large family like mine used to be growing up, I am guessing? Not an easy task raising a lot of kids" Elizabeth started to gather some small treats. The hard candy was nicely placed in a canning jar and sealed tightly. A leftover ribbon from the night before was tied securely around the jar, a more festive look.

"Thanks Mother, you are as sweet as your chocolate pecan pie." He leaned in and kissed his mother's forehead. "How about a few biscuits or something? No time for breakfast. Peiter is coming with me."

Elizabeth found some leftover dinner rolls, smothered them each with butter and jam. Gently she wrapped them in a kitchen towel tossing in a few molasses cookies. "Hope these will tie you over 'til you get back with the boy?"

Charles gathered everything he needed and again headed outback. Peiter was waiting and pacing. "A little chilly this morning. Mind if I grab a blanket, Sir?"

"Grab a few, what do I care? Keep yourself warm!"

Down the road a piece the wagon went. Within a few minutes Peiter surmised they might be headed to the Miller farm? "Why you asking me to come along, Sir?"

"You know these folks about as well as I do," Charles implied.

"You really taking this expensive sewing machine way out there? That lady gonna know what to do with this thing." Peiter shook his head. "I know Missy sure took a liking to hers."

"When did you find out about her gift? Guess word travels quickly around the farm. Who told you?" Charles interrogated.

"I dunno, must have overheard sometime about it last night?" Peiter played dumb for fearing the father figure. He did not want Charles to know he had seen his daughter late into the Christmas night. Missy had to share the exciting news of the gifted sewing machine with her husband of course!

Minutes later the wagon turned down the narrow road that lead to the Miller's. As usual, the yard was littered with chickens, cats, and kids. As the wagon came closer to the house the children came running to see the visitors. "Go get your Ma, hurry." Charles directed an older child.

"What you come out here for? Sewing more clothes or church?" Questioned the feisty littlest one, Allie pointing. "I know who he is, the man at the little church. He comes to our school also to help the teacher, Missy."

"You never mind. I am waiting for your mother." Charles appeared impatient a quality rarely seen.

"She'll be right out, Sir. Ma's a little busy with Lester." The older child tried to explain.

"Sure explains why all the kids are outside," Charles concluded to himself.

"Why, Sir?" Peiter acted clueless because he was.

"You know what's going on. We both got this thing figured out, now don't we? We'll just sit and wait. Probably won't take Lester too long to finish his business or will it?" Charles shook his head with uncertainty.

"Can't we go join the kids by the fire? It's a little chilly still. Should we wait or head back?" Peiter mumbled.

"No way!" Charles perked up. "We have a surprised for Mrs. Miller on the wagon. You go over there with the kids, don't get too close. Peiter you are acting like a kid yourself. Go talk to them about getting to church more often or something." Charles was intense as he waited. Twenty minutes had to have passed? Finally, Mildred Miller stood in the doorway to greet her visitors. Charles impatiently waved for her to come over to the wagon. Back in the house she went to put on a warm shawl. "Tell Lester to get out here also and quickly!" Charles commanded.

"What brings you out here today and so early in the morning?" Mildred was not clear about why Charles was at the farm.

"Just trying to spread a little Christmas cheer Mrs. Miller. Brought you a present and I hope you will like this?" Charles jumped from the wagon and hollered at Peiter for assistance. The two men uncovered the blanket from the sewing machine. The gift was now presented to Mrs. Miller.

Mrs. Miller stood speechless, Peiter stood speechless, as well as, Charles. A few sighs came from the children. Then the sounds of clapping broke the silence as the littlest one, once again, began clapping her hands together.

"What is it?" The little girl Allie jumped up and down with enthusiasm.

"Why this is a new sewing machine! This is an easier method, or way for sewing and making clothes. Definitely a time saver too for your mother. Your mother does not have to stitch clothes by hand using thread and a needle. The machine does most of the work. All she has to do is guide the fabric while pushing a foot pedal." Charles tried explaining the complicated operation at a child's level and understanding.

Mildred stood in amazement with one hand covering her mouth. The other hand was placed over her heart. She could not sort out the events. First, she was bewildered to actually set eyes on a brand new sewing machine. Secondly, the woman wasn't sure if she properly understood Charles.

"I know you said you brought me a present, Sir. I am delighted that you brought that there machine out here for us all to see." Mildred thanked Charles.

"See? Don't you see? The sewing machine is the present. Your present! Lester was there when I made the purchase. Although he did not know who was the recipient was going to be." Charles thought the situation was getting a little perplexed. Mildred stepped closer to the wagon to get a better view of her Christmas present.

"Why would you give me such a gift? The thing is very expense I assume? Why, I am lucky to have enough spools of threads for all the loose buttons 'round here. I know you are joking though Mr. Chettsburg." Mildred stood baffled. "Don't know how to work such a machine either."

"Mildred, can I speak in private with you?" Charles had some explaining to do.

"Yes Sir, where are my manners. Was not expecting any company so early in the morning. You know there are a lot of chores to do out here on the farm. Guess you do know that for yourself, living on that very large farm of yours. Please step in the house. Might be able to scrounge up some tea. Will the young black man be alright outside with the children for now? No disrespect, never had a color folk in the house." Mildred babbled on nervously.

"Please do not bother but thanks for the hospitality Mrs. Miller. Did not plan on staying long." Charles assured the busy mother of six.

The two headed into the house to discuss Charles' new idea. The sewing machine was very expensive to purchase for someone not very close or dear to him. The attorney and farmer was always thinking of others, the gentle advocate. Again, he thanked the seamstress for previously sewing the tailored suit for Peiter. He felt money alone was not enough payment for the services she provided. Charles knew there was a kind spot in her heart. Something apparently Mr. Perkin's did not have?

In the back of Charles' mind, he had learned a very important lesson about morals and money. There was a proposition in the works for the hard working mother of six children. Along with the gifted machine came another opportunity. The proposal was to set up a new tailoring shop in town. Mildred would be the store's proprietor. She would be able to custom-make clothing, mend, or take on alteration jobs. Of course having a business meant monthly expenses. Part of the profits would be used to pay the low monthly rent. But who was going to be her landlord and where would she find quarters to set up shop? Mr. Chettsburg of course! There was room to set up a small shop adjacent to his law firm's office building that he owned.

Mildred could work at the shop during the week. Obviously Lester was helping out on the farm with the chores and the children. The younger ones could be dropped off at Missy's school in the mornings. The older girl Natasha could learn a new trade with the sewing machine also. Possibly a local woman could be hired to assist with the sewing projects if ever needed. Charles had the answers for everything, almost everything. His sly, personal agenda involved disgracing a man who he felt betrayed him recently. Yes Mr. Perkins, the man who would not sew a tailored suit for a young man because of his skin color. The snooty tailor was about to have some new competition on the west end of town. A seamstress who cared more about the size of her heart and not her pocket book. Things were going to look better financially for the woman. She had no idea taking on that one small project was going to lead to a profitable family business.

"Mr. Chettsburg, I knew nothing about running a business," Mildred tried to convince Charles.

"Mildred, do not sell yourself so short. You have been running a business for years. This here farm is like a business would you not agree? Buying things, making things, organizing, cleaning, schedules, you sound like a business woman to me. You will be placed right next to my office should you need any help or assistance. My partner or I are usually there. Mr. John, my bookkeeper and butler is usually around also. Can't say I ever threaded a needle or sewed on a button. You will be given all the tools you need to have a successful business. Just one last loose thread." Charles smiled. "What shall we call the shop? Think about that. If you cannot come up with a name certainly I can assist you with that. Must get going ma'am. Would you like us to leave the machine here or have it delivered to your new shop?"

"You are very serious about this aren't you sir. Do you think I will be able to handle all this? The farm, kids, and a business." Mildred trembled because of Charles confidence in her. "Never had anyone speak so highly of me before. Always felt like just a wife and a mother."

"Add to that a very fine seamstress. You will have one very good customer when my wife Lara learns of your new business. She has a flair for fashion along with a knack for spending my money!" The eager attorney extended his hand to offer a handshake to seal the deal. "Thanks Mildred."

"No sir, I should be thanking you. And I am!" Mildred softly countered back at Charles.

Charles also leaned over to shake Lester's hand. "Could not have done this without your help my friend."

In parting, the kind-hearted men handed the mother a small wooden crate. In there were the packaged holiday goodies for the children. Charles and Peiter hoisted themselves into the wagon. Both men waved as they departed and hollered to the family, "Merry Christmas!"

Chapter 24

A NEW YEAR, NEW BEGINNINGS

The upcoming year had a lot in store. Charles was preparing to take his wife out of state with him for the spring semester. Again, the smart-witted man was invited to teach a few classes at the out-of-state university.

As always, he knew his family, law firm, and farm were in good hands. Although he couldn't stand the thought of being gone very long. The trip would last for several months. He and Lara would miss their daughter Missy dearly, although she was practically an adult now. Missy had an agenda of her own, teaching school. The pleasant couple dreaded leaving their families behind. Lara would miss the birth of her sister's baby. Charles' law partner was sharp and on his toes. The family farm was loaded with good helpers that would be overseen by Doc and his father Joseph from time to time.

The couple's wagon was carefully packed despite the winter's cool chill. The carriage would gently pull the load, led by a few strong horses. Warm clothing, hats and shoes took up most of the space. Few simple belongings like quilts, pillows and food filled the remainder. This was not the first long trip for the couple. Packing and planning came easier trip after trip. There were plus sides to the long extended stay for Lara. She enjoyed mingling and socializing with the other faculty and the professors' wives.

About five months later, the two would head back home to family and friends. The weather would be warmer than when they left in early winter. The conditions of the roads on the return home should be better for their arrival. Seems someone else was counting the months 'til springtime? Maybe another type of arrival was in the near horizon?

Missy was worried that her parents were leaving the state for several months. Something had been puzzling her since before the holidays. An issue she had rather not discussed with her own mother. Who was the person she needed to talk to? Her husband Peiter of course! The man she knew so well and trusted.

Things were obvious to the frantic woman in her late teens. Even her pretty, peasant type dresses were getting a bit snug. The aprons that tied around her tiny waist weren't so slack. Between work and the holidays she was feeling sluggish. She prayed to God Almighty what she thought was not true. A wife so confident in her husband's counting method.

Together they sat in the schoolhouse building with a small fire burning in the stove. A large, bulky quilt draped around the two of them. The married woman was about to disclose to her husband her biggest fear. Anxiety set in as she tried to sort out the words in her head. This was not a subject she wanted to discuss. She felt her husband failed in a very big way.

"Peiter, I love you dearly like no other. I feel betrayed." The confrontation began. "Could I possibly be pregnant? I trusted your words and we followed the counting method. Look at my belly, it has grown like a pumpkin."

Peiter was not so concerned nor fearful. "I will approach my father in private my dear wife. He will know what to do and what to expect going forward."

"Going forward!" Missy cried out.

"Yes dear, God has blessed us." Peiter confirming the pregnancy. "You will be in good hands with my father. He has acted as a mid-wife for several of the women here on the farm. Were you not aware that he has delivered several babies on the farm besides the animals?" Peiter tried consoling his wife.

"No, you must bring your father here, to the school. We both need to talk to him. He needs to know the whole story that we are married. We are married and need to act like responsible adults now."

"Missy calm down, let's take this slowly. There are possibly too many consequences. Being a man and your husband, I will speak to my father alone." Not too many words needed to be exchanged between the father and son. Doc had his own suspicions of the young teen mother's pregnancy. The true explaining stemmed from Peiter revealing his marriage to Missy, to his father. Doc did not understand the risks the teens had been taken. "God's law doesn't overrule the government's laws." Was the father's quick and fearful comeback. "I do not know who to fear the most? God or this government? My son, what have you gotten us into?"

"God will understand Father, I promise you!" The sympathetic son tried to assure his father.

The months that followed were dreadful for Missy. Most women would be experiencing great happiness to be carrying their husbands' children. Lara was the happiest mother when she was expecting Missy. Concealing this pregnancy was not fun nor an easy task. In the mornings, Missy arrived early to school so no one noticed her now obvious weight gain. The school days became shorter as she spent the days sitting in front of her class shielded behind a table. Visits from her grandparents meant a quick "hello." She tried to hide in her bedroom or just peer out the door at folks. Full petticoat dresses did not camouflage the bulging belly well either. For months she did not attend church service as her small framed body had taken on a new shape.

Months later and late into the night came the new arrival. With the assistance of Doc and Hattie Mae, a healthy baby girl was born to the married couple, Missy and Peiter. Things were going to get more complicated for the young friends who were now deeply in love.

Everyone anticipated Charles' and Lara's late return that spring. The college semester was over and the Chettsburgs once again packed the overloaded wagon with their belongings. The trip home was heavier due to Lara's enthusiasm for shopping. Lara had to spend her time doing something in the big city?

Doc and his family were seriously scared especially since he was given the responsibility of being the head overseer of the farm. They were afraid Charles would be furious when he would find out about the birth of Missy's baby. Peiter feared going to jail for impregnating his white wife. Doc was certain his family would be kicked off the farm with nowhere to go. Possibly be sent back to the island they were so grateful to leave.

Missy's pregnancy was such a controversial, moral issue, only though a few knew of the well-hidden situation. Interracial relationships were so highly frowned upon. A baby produced from this type of affair certainly would be unacceptable!

The decision was to keep the baby at the backhouse. The infant would live there with Doc, Peiter, and Kemica. Missy did not dare take the baby into her father's home out of respect. The main feeling was the baby would be with family; her father, aunt, and paternal-grandfather. The mother, Missy would always be nearby.

Caring for the baby girl was frustrating and challenging at times. Daily, Missy would make several trips to the backhouse to tend and nurse the baby. A routine was in place by everyone who knew the discrete situation.

Missy's biggest concerns were hurting her grandparents. Both sets of them. She knew her Grandmother Chettsburg to be very opinionated, as well as, Grandfather Macher. Certainly they would never welcome this baby as family, was her belief?

Finally, Charles and Lara arrived after a long ride home. Charles could not wait to see his only daughter. First thing he did was rush into the house but Missy was no were to be seen. "She's outback at the little house." Hattie Mae hesitated to disclose. Next, Charles headed towards the school even though the time was way late into the afternoon. No signs of his daughter as he thought for sure she'd be there. He made his rounds to the backhouse as Hattie Mae suggested.

He crossed the green lawn and knocked on the door of Doc's family home. Doc barely opened the door and peeked out. In the background, Charles vaguely saw Missy. Kemica was seated with the tiny baby in her arms. The infant appeared to be about a month old according to Charles' calculations. Everyone was quiet like slate rocks in a pile.

"Oh Kemica, I see you have a new addition? I wasn't aware you were expecting?" Charles cheerfully acknowledged.

"Yes Sir, we do have new baby here." Kemica agreed but could not look into the man's eyes for fear of what was going to happen next. Everyone froze.

Doc revealed to Charles that the baby was a gift and to be able to deliver his very own granddaughter. The new grandfather's eyes watered up. Charles then signaled for Doc to meet him outside. "May I ask who the father of the baby is? Speak up will you! Are you trying to conceal that the father is a white man?"

"Why are you asking me that, Sir?" Doc took a step back.

"It is obvious by the baby's skin color and tone that the baby has a white daddy! Where you not surprised when you delivered the baby she was on the lighter side?" Charles blasted away with questions that Doc was unable to answer truthfully. Charles hindered for a moment at Doc's silence and poked his head back inside the house.

"Well God bless you and your new little one Kemica. I won't impose any longer. Missy, your mother and I would like to see you at the house. Been a long time since we both have seen you my darling daughter." Charles slowly shut the door behind him to not disturb the new baby.

Doc, Kemica, and Missy were startled. "He thinks the baby belongs to Kemica! This lie is getting bigger. What shall we do?" Questioned Doc who was usually well composed and practical.

"We can't tell Mr. Chettsburg the truth now. This is shocking." Kemica blurted out with panic in her voice. "Quickly, someone must find Peiter and tell him what the heck is going on, please and fast!"

"Everyone calm down. We need to pray on this." Doc advocated.

Missy hustled to the house as her father suggested. Greeting her mother, Lara reached out and hugged her daughter. "Oh honey we missed you so much! We stopped in town and seen our parents on the way in. My mother said she has not seen you in over a month. You must have been terribly busy? Look at you! You have packed on a few pounds while we were gone. Either Hattie Mae has been feeding you too well or you have been enjoying plenty of Grandmother's delightful desserts?"

Charles had some questions of his own. "I do not want to intrude but has Kemica recently taken on a boyfriend? Has she been courting? I know the labor community on the farm has not taken to her very well. They seem to treat her like an outsider. Just wondering where she met her mate?"

"No Father, I am do not think she has anyone special?" Missy was promptly responded.

"Honey, did someone take advantage of her of by chance? I hope she is not a victim of some man's greed. What does her father think about the baby?" Charles was concerned about the older teen girl he had salvage from the tropical island.

"Doc loves the baby girl, Father. They all think she is so cute and precious." Missy was nervous with all the questions her father was shooting at her.

"I certainly do not want any funny business going on around this here farm!" Charles firmly stated. "I sure hope that baby was conceived out of love."

"Yes, the baby is loved and well taken care of. Peiter is delighted to have the baby around. He has been staying in the backhouse now to help out. As always, Doc is caring and understanding. The fact, I helped deliver the baby as expected. He has been great about everything." Missy spoke up convincingly.

"Are you aware of anything they might need, a bed, clothes?" As always, Charles was caring and considerate.

"I believe everyone is in good hands, Father. Ummm, there is a doctor, a mother, and Peiter. Mother, you have to come see the baby. She is precious." Missy's voice expressed excitement as she wanted her mother to see the newborn. A baby that was discretely, biologically Lara's granddaughter.

"Missy we were not aware Kemica had a love interest? Do you know of anything else to share with us about the situation? Your father and I are curious and concerned. Do you know anything? The girl is practically like a sister to you. The two of you have grown up together for years. We feel somewhat responsible as we have cared for the family. Hopefully this is something Kemica has come to peace with?" Lara grilled her daughter.

Charles intervened again. "Missy are you sure no man has taken advantage of Kemica? The situation takes a man to produce a child. Never seen her with one, nor has she ever expressed an interest in one, as far as I know."

"Mother and Father, I do not believe she was misled by a man." Missy rushed out of the living room where they all stood. Trying to avoid any further questions that she did not have honest answers for.

Lara told her husband that she felt bad for Kemica. Charles assured her he would speak to Doc about the situation. Meanwhile, Missy hurried off to the backhouse. Feeling flush from running fast she lightly knocked on the door, then entered. "Dear God, my parents think the baby truly is Kemica's."

"Yeah, we thought the same thing by what your father was saying and assuming." Doc agreed with Missy.

"Now what Doc?" Missy picked up the baby to comfort her and to see if she needed nursing.

"Like I said before we need to pray on this and hope all works out well. Peiter can lead us all in prayer?" Doc suggested. "First, we were all afraid to confront your father about the baby. Now he has created a story that is a lie to us. Should we tell him the truth and face grave consequences? Shall we continue with this false story that is a farce? As the head of this family, I say we do what is in the best interest for the baby and the rest of my grown children."

"I just can't face my parents. I can't face my grandparents. Why is it so terrible to be in love and married to a man of another color? Peiter's heart and soul is more important than his skin coloring. He is a man dedicated to God." Missy began to whimper. The baby girl began to cry also. In the hard wooden chair she sat with her infant daughter cradling and comforting the baby. Thinking the baby maybe hungry again, Missy unbuttoned her blouse and began nursing the baby.

Later in the week, Charles had some business to tend to with the new mother, Kemica! As an attorney he knew the baby should have a birth certificate. Early in the morning he headed across the lawn to the backhouse. He confronted the young "mother" as so he thought and was now lead to believe. "How is the new mother doing this morning? Hope you slept well last night. Being a parent is a full-time job and filled with responsibilities. Actually I am here on business." Kemica was uneasy as she felt the worst was coming. "You are aware the baby needs to be registered and a birth certificate filed?"

"No sir. I am not sure of the legal stuff involving, having a baby." The young woman glared with an empty look on her face.

"I need some very important information for the paperwork. First, I need the date the baby was born, approximate time, and the baby's name." Charles demanded quickly as he needed to head to the office. "Come on, let's write this down."

"You will need to write all this down Sir? You write better than I do. The baby was born on April 23rd or maybe the 24th, late into the night. It was a Friday night I remember. There was no school or church the next day. Around midnight or so." Kemica calculated.

"That would make the birthdate April 24th officially." Charles jotted down the information. "What is the baby's name by the way? Guess I never asked you that before."

Again, a blank stare was on the young lady's face. "Come on, you don't' know your own daughter' name? I am kidding with you Kemica. What is her name?" Charles insisted.

"The baby's name is Georgia. Like the state here. This is a great state that you have brought my family to. I am embarrassed Sir, I do not know how to spell the baby's name."

Charles carefully spelled out the name, "G-E-O-R-G-I-A. Here, I will write this down for you to keep and learn how to spell the name for yourself. I know how to spell your name for listing of the mother. I will bring you a copy of the official birth certificate in a week or so."

Kemica was uncertain of the events quickly transpiring before her. Her thoughts were frightening for a timid teen. She was legally going to be listed as the mother of the baby. Secondly, she just legally named Missy's and Pieter's baby after a state. Put on the spot, she could not think of a better name for the baby. For lack of feeling stupid she had to come up with something quick! How could a mother not know the name of her own child?

"Yes Sir, guess I should be thanking you for everything you are doing for 'our' baby. Please see my father for any fees to be paid. You know I do not have any money Sir." Kemica kindly thanked Charles with hesitation.

"You and the baby are like family, Kemica. I would not charge any attorney's fees. Just want to make sure the little one is legal and legit." Charles darted out of the home with the piece of paper in his hand.

Moments later Missy arrived at Kemica's door. This time she had a special guest. Missy had brought along her Grandmother Chettsburg. Kemica grew even more puzzled.

"Grandmother wanted to see the new baby I have been talking about." Missy explained shadily to Kemica.

"Please come in. The precious baby is asleep. You can take a look at her. Missy, are you aware your father was just here? He is kind enough to register the baby for a birth certificate. I do not know much about things like that. He needed all the information." Kemica explained with confusion.

"Information?" Missy abruptly intervened.

"The birth date and the baby's name." Kemica answered feeling intimidated.

"What name did you give him?" Missy demanded.

Elizabeth thought the two ladies were being silly. "Missy of course she gave your father the baby's name? Why are you pressing these questions of Kemica?"

Kemica reached for the piece of paper that Charles had scribbled on and handed it to Missy. "G-E-O-R-G-I-A? You

named the baby Georgia! Sounds like an old lady's name."
Missy was not satisfied with the name Kemica had picked out for
the baby.

"I have picked out a nickname for the baby girl, Gigi.
Sounds kinda cute?" As if asking for permission.

"To me it sounds like you two are squabbling like two
little sisters over a baby's name. Hasn't the mother had this all
figured out already?" Elizabeth tried calming the frustrated
ladies. "The baby is adorable Kemica. I think Georgia fits her
fine, a beautiful name. Gigi is a cute name also. May I hold the
little pecan?"

"Little pecan!" Missy took offense to the pet name.

"Why yes, look at her skin tone. She is not black nor
brown like her mother but a light brown like the beauty of a
pecan's inner meat coloring. How southern can she get? We
have all planted our feet in this here fine state. Along with
planting all those huge pecan trees outback. Her special name
has a story to tell. Do you ladies agree with me?" Both Missy
and Kemica nodded their heads understanding the elder woman's
view point.

Several more weeks of breast feeding the baby took place
in the hard wooden chair. Missy recalled her mother asking if
the baby needed anything.

"Mother can we buy Kemica a rocking chair?"

"A rocking chair?" Lara questioned her daughter's suggestion.

"Yes, so she can rock the baby to sleep?" Missy continued.

"Maybe we can find one at The General Merchant Store. You know your Grandfather Chettsburg would gladly design one. Quicker to buy one." Were Lara's thoughts.

"Kemica and the baby would appreciate the gift, Mother."

"That is a very thoughtful idea. We can look next time we are in town."

The purchase of the new rocking chair was a little too easy. Missy's clever suggestion worked. She now had a new chair to comfort her baby in! With Lara not knowing the furniture purchase was actually for her own biological granddaughter.

Months later the cool fall night was not so quiet. Things were not always going so swiftly for the young mother. Echo's from the baby's cry pierced through the dark southern air. The thin barn boards could not shield the all the fuss. Kemica checked to see if the baby's bottom was dry. Next she tried feeding the baby a tad of warm milk. Baby Gigi did not want the bottle Doc designed. Peiter tried walking and bouncing the baby girl. Still no relief from the baby's tears. Doc took his granddaughter from his son. "Her forehead feels a little warm. Could be from all this fussing? Kemica, please sneak up to the house and wake up Hattie Mae."

Kemica headed to the house in the dark. Slightly she tapped on the window of the back porch with a thin, long stick. "Open the window." She repeated.

"Girl, what are you doing out here so late?" Hattie Mae groaned.

"I urgently need Missy."

"You go wait by the side porch while I creep up the stairs." Hattie instructed the girl.

Minutes later Missy arrived at the door to greet Kemica. "Missy, Gigi will not stop fussing. She has been up for hours and so has everyone else."

"Go get the baby and meet me on the front porch." Missy nervously suggested.

Kemica hustled back to retrieve the baby. She carefully wrapped her in a small quilt. Gigi was then delivered to her mother on the porch. The baby was placed in her mother's arm as Missy sat in the wooden rocking chair out front. The baby obviously needed to be nursed. Her breast was exposed to the little darling. The whimpers slowed down and came to a halt as the baby sucked and drank. Missy rocked and rocked to comfort her baby girl. Soon the mother and daughter were both asleep in the chair. The warmth of their bodies bonded each other. The early, morning bright sunrise woke the sleeping mother. Missy held her baby tight against her chest. Holding her tiny baby girl throughout the night was precious. The baby had to quickly be returned to the home outback. Missy called out quietly for Hattie Mae, "Go get Kemica."

Hattie Mae grabbed a knitted shawl and headed to the backhouse. Soon both women arrived at the steps of the porch. Missy explained to the inexperienced so-called-mother the baby was hungry for breast milk. That is what all the fuss was all about. All the baby needed was her mother. The baby had been sleeping for three hours straight.

The women all seemed to be somewhat upset. Kemica spoke up, "I was frightened and afraid when the baby would not stop crying. She makes me really nervous at times. The baby is delicate, almost fragile."

Missy had a solution as she was bothered by the arrangements also. "We need to get you a nanny, like a caretaker to help out with the baby. This will give you a break and free up some of your time. Truly your brother and I appreciate everything you are undertaking. I will discuss hiring a nanny with Peiter and Doc. At times I can't sleep at night worrying about my precious baby girl. This is so complicated. The baby lives practically out my back door."

Chapter 25
HEADING NORTH

Certainly there could not be a safer compound than the Chettsburgs' farm for the freed slaves? Obviously there was not room for everyone! The young minister Peiter had soon become an advocate like his mentor, Charles Chettsburg. Outside of the church, Peiter was desperately trying to get some of the local freed slaves to relocate to the north.

Overtime Charles had shared stories with Peiter about freed slaves who had headed to the northern states. "There are compassionate and caring people who will help the freed slaves and runaways gain access to Canada. Once arriving on the country's soil, they can truly enjoy their freedom."

Peiter wanted to specifically move some of the freed men to the north for better opportunities. There was a route known as the Underground Railroad for slaves. Concerned people were trying to move black men and women away from slavery in the southern states. To do this, they needed to move from the south and head north. The minister did not know much about the system but he wanted to relocate some freed slaves to safety as well.

From the time he was a young boy he knew slavery was wrong. Even his own mother was a victim. As a minister, Peiter knew slavery was morally wrong. Being a mature adult he knew there would be risks getting involved in helping the black folks relocate. Even locally, he knew there were slaves and freed slaves who still lived in danger.

Peiter continued to have talks with Charles about the idea of moving some people out of the area. The attorney was open to the young minister's ideas. Charles was always helpful too and an advocate for what was right. He had concerns about moving some of the displaced people.

Charles crossed over the street and headed towards the local sheriff's office. Sitting behind the big wooden desk was Sheriff Will Massey proudly displaying his five-point star badge. No introductions needed here. The two men knew each other very well. Although not always on the same page about each other's business.

The local sheriff was a handsome dark haired man with gray highlights. In his late forty's with an athletic built he filled in the uniform rather nicely. The single guy claims he was too busy and too restless to be married and tend to a family. Most local folks believed the man slept at his desk overnight as he rarely took a break from responsibilities and the seriousness of his job.

Charles explained to Sheriff Will his apprehensions about transferring a group of freed slaves. In the conversation he shared Minister Peiter's plans. His church was trying to raise some money and goods to be allocated for travel expenses. The goal would be, when there was enough money for a few people, the process would begin.

Locally, there was a problem with the stagecoaches not wanting to transport color folks. Seemed to be a safety concern having them aboard. Sheriff Will had a solution. The sheriff had been observing Mr. Lester lately. The former town clerk had been changing his ways. The alcoholic's drinks had been washed away by his weekly attendance to the new church. Those 'three young children' started to be a responsibility of his, as well as, taking on the rest of the Miller family. Sheriff Will deputized Mr. Lester with a six-point badge. This was solely done for the purpose and hopes of transporting some of the freed slaves safely.

Within a few months, Minister Peiter had enough money to send five congregants north. All that money certainly did not come from his church that serviced the poor. Charles had given the minister new responsibilities, a job! Peiter was officially to oversee the pecan production and orchard on the Chettsburg family farm. Now he was able to earn a modest living to help out his family and still maintain and operate the church. After all, he discretely had a child to raise along with the help of his sister and father. Charles wanted another ten acres dedicated to the pecan orchard. More trees would be planted, north-east of the existing trees. The idea of planting more trees inspired him for the purpose of the nice wood, something he learned from his father, Joseph. Any old or rotten wood would be used for kindling. He wanted trees available for years in the future. The wood from the very tall trees was perfect for furniture and flooring. The trees in place had been harvesting an abundance of nuts that scattered all over the ground. Peiter's job would be to gather those nuts along with a small managed crew when they flourished, usually in late October. The lavish edible nuts could be sold or traded for other goods. The pecan trees overtime became a signature status for the Chettsburg farm.

For the trip, Lester and Peiter suited several horses for a wagon from the Chettsburg farm. On board were five other men, freed slaves. The men were allowed to take very minimal amounts of belongs with them. Each had a Holy Bible with a cloth cover to conceal a knife and a very small amount of money. Food was packed and a gunnysack was stuffed with assorted clothing for the traveling men.

The cool morning dusk had them all arriving at the stagecoach station. Soon a short, well-dressed man yelled, "Heading north, all aboard!" The five colored men approached to board but the driver was soon to explain, "Can't service the color folks, dealt with too many safely concerns from retaliating white men."

Lester sported his new shiny badge, "Sir, I am a deputy in Atlanta. I am here to see that these appointed men make it safely to their destination. They are headed to Michigan to join the Military Colored Corps. (MCC). The local government is expecting these men of service. You cannot turn down militants can you? I also have a minister here to bless them on their way."

The driver was not very happy with the situation. How could he override the demands and pleas from a deputy and minister? Lester acting confident instructed the driver with a final comment, "The MCC are expecting these fine men to arrive within the next few weeks. Have a pleasant journey."

Lester nudged Peiter to speak up. He added, "May God watch over you and keep everyone safe."

There was one more passenger waiting to fill the coach. Standing nearby was a middle-aged woman dressed in a full pink dress. She would be keeping the men company in her travels to the north. Her destination was to visit her daughter in Ohio. She had just received word that her young daughter was about to give birth. Lester kindly loaded the woman's trunk for her.

After an exchanged of well wishes, Lester and Peiter headed back to the wagon. Both men holding back their nervousness. Deep down they were even a little scared for the men about to travel. Sheriff Will's bluff seemed to be working so far. The tale of the men going to Michigan to join the MCC appeared to work. The sheriff knew that the men being represented by a deputy and a minister were not going to be questioned about their travels. Otherwise, the stagecoach driver might have had to deal with the sheriff himself!

The two men chuckled and admitted to each other they were both nervous. Agreeing though, the sheriff's story of the make believe MCC just might have worked?

"Next time things will be easier." Lester assured Peiter.

"We need more money to send more folks safely to the north." The young minister believed.

The two chummy men chatted on their short ride back to the farm. Peiter was concerned and still felt uneasy. He hoped for the rest of the men's stagecoach changes and travels were to go well? Everything was in God's hands. All he could do was to turn it over to God to be the men's protection and light. "You know Mr. Chettsburg and I tried to take a wagon full of men out of state several months ago. Would you believe we got robbed by a gang of colored men? We were not even an hour down the road. The men outnumbered all of us. They even stole some of the clothing right off our men's backs. Imagine stealing from a minister!

Now we have an armed deputy who has proper authority to handle behavior like those robbers. Those bad men certainly took advantage of us. The situation was scary for folks like us. Mr. Chettsburg did not give up on me or the men. Thank you Mr. Lester for helping this time. Hopefully this plan worked!"

"Didn't Mr. Chettsburg have a gun?" Lester inquired.

"Matter of fact he did! He did not want to harm the robbers. Nor did he want them to know he had one for fear it might have been stolen or fell into their hands. They were only armed with big sticks and large rocks. He agree what they took was not worth human blood shed. He did not care, figuring they could have the stuff. Our men were advised everything taken could be replaced. A human life could not be replaced so it was not worth fighting the hoodlums."

Just before the coach left for departure I addressed the men. I told them to always hold the Holy Bible close to their hearts. Like myself, they may not always be able to read all the words. But we all know what they mean. In their journeys they may find someone to share their special book with. There maybe someone who can read the book to them. Always keep you're your Holy Bible safe and close. The book contains more than words." Peiter chuckled as he knew the cloth covers on the books concealed a thin knife for protection and a little amount of money."

Lester then addressed Peiter. "How did the two of us ever get together to execute this mission? We both have come a long way the past few years together. Furthermore, I rightfully and respectfully think you should start addressing me as 'Deputy Lester!"

Peiter was uncertain of Lester's sincerity, "Good then, I prefer to always be titled Minister Peiter, Deputy Lester. Seems you have jurisdiction from the sheriff like I have authority from God!" Both men shared a quick hoot and a grin then ventured back to town.

Chapter 26

A DARLING FOUR YEAR OLD GIRL

How could a little four year old girl drum up so much curiosity? Some seem to think it was Gigi's softly curled dark brown hair. The shadowing of the hair of Kemica's long mane. Others thought the toddler's skin had a beautiful, golden glow about it. She was different from all the other folks. Colored folks and white ones. Her hair, her skin tone.

In the back of Charles' mind, he had a gut feeling who the father of Gigi might be? His finger was pointing at a Major from the local military. The tall Caucasian, about 30 years old had light blonde hair. He seemed like the aggressive type was Charles thinking. The militant had taken an interest in courting Missy. Charles did not care for the sly man. Matter of fact, he did not want him coming around the farm at all.

Who was Gigi's biological father? Charles thought he now had the mystery solved. The skin on her body made Charles assume the father being Caucasian. He dreaded the assumption that Major Walus could quite possibly be Gigi's father? Now there was concern that maybe Major Walus forced himself on Kemica? The man repeatedly was cocky, arrogant, and demanding. Charles had not noticed any male interaction or interests in Kemica over the years. Certainly someone had an eye on her as kind as she is, were Charles thoughts. These thoughts about the Major began to anger Charles. He promised himself he would take care of that idiot should his analogy proved to be true.

Moments later, Charles considered speaking to Doc about the identity of Gigi's father. Should he confront Doc about all of this? Charles did not want to tap-dance around a family issue, possibly personal? Even though years had passed, he wanted to follow through with the family in case any harm was done. The clever man was so curious to be forward and just wanted to ask Kemica if the father was Major Walus or someone else?

Who else could be the father of that precious little girl? Here and there his mind wandered seeking candidates. The puzzle continued as he could not quite piece anyone to the missing blank. For certain, he did not want Major Walus around in case there was any mishaps towards Kemica. Matter of fact, he did know of any who actually liked the shrewd man anyways. Should he find out anyone caused harm to her they would be punished by law. The Major was not above the law.

Charles recalled having problems with the Major last summer. The member of the Union Army would not leave his only daughter alone. There was constant pestering for her attention and affection towards him. Missy always appeared nice to him but had no personal desires. There was a time when Major Walus had pronounced his love for her and hinted at marriage. He felt Missy would readily fall into his arms because of his rank in the military. The Chettsburgs always welcomed him to stop by for a rest or warm meal out of respect. But they did not really care for what he stood for.

The Major persisted on a relationship with Missy. She herself declined his advances. Right to her father, he went to get permission to marry Charles' daughter. Charles assured the Major that Missy would have a say in who she decides to marry should she someday fall in love. Since she was a teacher, marriage would be a big commitment and a large step into adulthood.

The Major insisted and bugged Charles. The father was not giving in, "You can't make someone love you. I am not a matchmaker. Love is magical, it is a feeling you experience. You will know it when you find it. I can't make this happen for you. Furthermore, I am against the war. The circumstances were preexisting before my family and I came to Georgia and the United States. Don't like war, don't support it. I appreciate your dedication to the Army and war. I have integrity for my family and workers. We have a dissimilar set of values and morals and are headed in a different direction. Major, I do not see you fitting into that pattern. My compassion is for people in a different avenue. That is why I became an attorney, to help folks. I want everyone to do what is right and to know what is legally right."

In the back of his mind, Charles claimed the Major was just a sexually frustrated man. He preyed on Missy like a dog in heat intrigued by her youth and beauty. The man barely knew the kind-hearted woman. Charles knew his daughter deserved someone very special.

Charles' words were not well received by the Major. The Major showed his true negative colors. Off he stormed, appearing upset, mad and threatened.

Like everyone, Charles had a liking for the adorable little girl, Gigi. She was like a pint-size mascot at the farm. How could one not be drawn in by her cute looks and bubbly personality? Kemica on the other hand, was overburdened by the whole complicated situation, acting as the girl's mother. Charles was still baffled as to who Gigi's father was?

Chapter 27

THE WOODEN HOPE CHEST

What treasures were stored in that large wooden trunk? Over the years, miscellaneous things were tucked away by a young, Missy. The hope-chest was crafted by her Grandfather Chettsburg. Originally the trunk belonged to her father, Charles. He used the piece for his travels when he left for college as a teen. The trunk showed some signs of aging. The worldly travels added some tatter to the well-constructed piece. Highlighted on the face of the chest was the word "HOPE". Joseph had neatly etched the term in bold block letters. The craftsman had compassion to add that single, little, word to his design as a constant reminder to his son. A symbol of God's promise and gift for knowing and trusting Him with one's future.

The contents were always kept a secret by Missy since the time she was about eight years old. New things would be added and others discarded over the years. At all times, there was a secured hiding spot for the key to her treasures. Her mother Lara thought Missy's ways were childish the way she still seemed to accumulate her prized belongings. Everything was perfectly stored, wrapped, and stacked in the old trunk. Always fastened to the front of the hope-chest securely was a lock to forever hold all the childish secrets.

Buried in the wooden box was a large assortment of personal belongings. Some items were tokens of gifts and keepsakes. Other things were put away for future usage in case she should ever marry or have children of her own. Bundled up in a piece of twine was a pile of hand-written letters. These writings were from her Grandmother Chettsburg who lived far away when she was a young girl. The letters from Belgium were dear to her heart. They made her grow founder of a woman she did not even know yet at the time. The details outlined promises from a grandmother who would one day meet her only grandchild. A promise that was delivered years later when she finally met her foreign grandparents.

The most valued piece set aside in the large trunk was her own mother's wedding dress. Missy dreamed of a big fairytale wedding. Her tall, handsome prince would take her hand as she stood wearing the pretty gown. This gentleman would spoil her rotten with love, affection, and gifts. Such a fantasy for such a humble kid. Missy had extraordinary thoughts of becoming a special bride for a noble man.

Carefully in place were other things of value. Enclosed was a bulky, old clock her Grandfather Macher had restored. A cute porcelain miniature tea set was carefully wrapped, an earlier gift from her Grandmother Chettsburg. Most of the things in the chest would be on display in her own home someday.

Along with her childish dreams she fantasized of being a mother herself. She would name a daughter "HOPE." A word she recalled seeing almost day engraved on the sentimental wooden-chest. The monogramed chest would then be passed on to Missy's daughter to harbor treasures in.

Looking around her bedroom the older teen reflected about her childhood playtimes. The room neatly displayed her large collection of dolls. Each one assigned a name to match up with their distinct looks and personalities. Acting like a mother, each of the soft sculptured dolls were treated like make-believe children. The toys took the child away with her playful imagination. "Oh what will my girls wear today? Hope, your hair needs to be brushed." Calling out to her pretend playmate.

While scuffling through the chest, Missy realized there was an emptiness to the treasures. None of the contents came from her Grandmother Macher? Maybe she forwarded all her sentimental items to her own daughters? But not one thing for her granddaughter, Missy questioned herself. Grandmother Chettsburg had given her lots of things over the past few years.

Missy knew she had to continue to plant things in the chest for the future. Maybe one day to pass on her own daughter. A child that will never be named Hope. In fact, her own daughter was gifted a name by someone else. The discrete offspring picked up the nickname Gigi, short for Georgia. Would the filled chest be passed on to Gigi someday? Or was there a chance for another daughter to carry that special name, Hope?

Eventually, there were several explorations inside the hope-chest by Gigi. Missy on occasion enjoyed sneaking the child up to her bedroom. Together they would explore the items tucked away. Almost as if Missy did not have a friend to share her collection with. The mother and daughter would rummage through the large piece of furniture seeking lace, ribbons, and stored away toys.

Then the lid would be carefully closed and secured for the next adventure. In her mind, Missy sorted out where the possessions would really end up. Will some end up in her fantasy home? Quite possibly she would pass on some of her gems onto Gigi. Maybe there will be other children to share in the history?

Chapter 28

VISITING GRANDMOTHER'S STORE

Just the smell of chocolate was an invitation into Elizabeth's tea room. The aromas trickled to the sidewalk and then out into the two lane dirt road. Today she was preparing her perfect fudge. Some of the savaged chocolate would be drizzled over whole pecans. Chocolate covered nuts to be sold by the quarter-pound. The sauce pan on the stove was hot heating; syrup, sugar, milk and chocolate of course!

Seated in the dining area were two of Elizabeth's regular guests, Sheriff Will and Deputy Lester. The sheriff was always fascinated with the host's busy work ethics. The older woman had high morals and values. She conformed to having good etiquette, a characteristic she shared with her daughter-in-law, Lara. Elizabeth was modest and tight with money. She did not know any other way since always being a hardworking farm girl.

Elizabeth explained to the men with a smirk, "Proper manners and good etiquette are a must. Keeps you from being snotty or snooty. Just take a look at my precious, well-mannered daughter-in-law!"

The two men had come to know Elizabeth very well and enjoyed her sense of humor. The lady was always neatly dressed and a hair never out of place. They of course knew Lara as well, a local town mascot. Everyone knew Lara Chettsburg, the attorney's wife and Leon's daughter. The law enforcement officials grabbed their hats off the wrought iron hooks. As they exited the tea room, both wished Elizabeth a good day.

Moments later, Missy pranced in the backdoor of her grandmother's establishment. At her side was little Gigi. Since Gigi was three or four years old, Missy loved to take her hush-hush daughter to town. The little one would get dropped off at the tea room. Elizabeth enjoyed the spunky young visitor from time to time. Grandmother Chettsburg would contain and entertain the little girl in the kitchen area. Away and hidden from all the customers of course. To have a young colored girl hanging around the business would not be appropriate or acceptable to some folks. Elizabeth had a little, tiny, wooden stool for Gigi to perch on. Also in the kitchen, was a small box of utensils and toys for Gigi to play with. The girl needed something to keep her busy with while Elizabeth tended to the store's customers. Elizabeth loved to spoil Gigi with special homemade treats during her visits to the tea room.

"Grandmother, I have a few errands to run. I hope you do not mind keeping Gigi for a little while?" Missy inquired to her always accommodating grandmother.

"You go do what you have to, honey. The little girl will be fine with me. I know you'll be turning a few gentlemen's heads while tooling around town. Just do not be gone all day dear."

"Grandmother! I am a teacher." Missy exclaimed.

"Missy, you are too modest. You know there are men after your heart and your daddy's money (chuckling). My granddaughter is sweet, kind-hearted, and pretty. (announcing proudly) What man would pass by you without an obvious glance? Even Peiter seems to sticks to your side. I overheard your mother and father briefly talking a ways back. Your school is a private school, it is not funded locally by the government or the church. Your school does not have to abide by all those conservative rules, laws and policies. Your father is the caretaker of the school. Certainly a nice gentleman will notice all your genuine qualities and make me a great-grandmother some day? I think you could be a great teacher, wife and mother? Do not be too modest, love may be waiting right around the corner for you." Was the grandmother trying to tell Missy something?

Was Missy overdoing Gigi's dress code or is there was such a thing? Did Missy have to dress her young playmate as if she were a toy doll? Missy had been busy at the sewing machine making simple, cotton sundresses for the little girl. Most were made out of colorful remnant fabrics. Her little tag-a-long friend was getting to be the best dressed kid in town. Missy couldn't resist tying loose pieces of ribbon in Gigi's long, curly, dark-brown hair. Heads would turn at the unique pair. Definitely an odd arrangement most folks thought. Missy still stood by her old excuse that she was caring for the girl to give Kemica a break from the child.

Missy had been emotional taken over the years as to how much her grandmother enjoyed being around Gigi. Especially since Elizabeth was known to be shrewd and opinionated on occasion when called for. Not always the most kindhearted woman at times. The comments were never mean-spirited, just frank and truthful, usually. A lot of her compassion was poured into her work at the tea room at times. The owner was always very warm and welcoming to all her guests at her business establishment.

By the time Gigi was five years old, the little girl knew Elizabeth treated her differently than most people. She did not fit in with the white folks. The tenants on the farm did not exactly welcome her into their circle as of yet. The older Mrs. Chettsburg was always real nice to her. Gigi would often question the plump lady with graying hair, "Why are you the nicest to me?"

Elizabeth was not shy to speak up, "The Bible is a special book. The book that Uncle Peiter reads at church. The book tells people to love thy neighbors, meaning everyone. So, the book tells me to love you. (Elizabeth makes a pointing gesture). People should not have a choice to pick certain people to love. Everyone is included." For her age Gigi was still confused about why some folks had skin of color. She was also aware that meant being treated differently most of the time.

Elizabeth tried to share a personal story with the girl. She began to explain to Gigi how she also grew up in farm country. A farm was located in Belgium, far away from the towns and cities. Mistreating people rarely existed. Everyone's skin was white in color, except for an occasional darker-toned Frenchman. Most of the people worked and lived off the farms. People worked hard and lived right. Growing up, Elizabeth never had seen a colored person or knew they even existed, "People are people and they are all the same inside. Equipped with a brain and a heart. People who treat people differently because of their skin color should read the Bible more. You know some people treat me differently because of the way I talk. Folks for years know I am from far away. I do not speak words as clearly as some."

Gigi blurted "I know your words."

"Yes, you are a child learning my little Pecan."

"I am really a pecan?" Gigi was excited.

"Yes, silly. I love you Gigi like the Bible teaches us. Always remember that. You are lucky to have Uncle Peiter, a minister with a church. Listen to him and you will learn many things."

An hour or so later Missy arrived back at the shop to retrieve Gigi. There was one last stop at The General Merchant Store for the pair. Time to buy the tike a new toy and a sweet treat to take home. The store owner, Mr. Richards did not always appreciate the well-to-do customer. Missy had a tendency to disregard an unwritten rule at the place of business. He and his wife did not allow colored folks in the store.

Time after time, Missy bopped into the store with her special, little sidekick as if she was exempt. Wise Mr. Richards was not about to verbally say something. His nonverbal cues gave away his escalated feelings. There was not a smile on his face as he greeted his customers, "Good day Miss Chettsburg." The words stumbled out.

A cheerful response addressed the store owner, "I need two pieces of lightweight cotton fabric, ¾ yards each. Pastels please. Something pink? For little girl's dresses obviously. Chalk if you have some. Finally, twenty assorted flavors of these colorful candy sticks please." Gigi stood close to Missy as she felt a strange glare from the not so friendly gentleman.

Mr. Richards liked the Chettsburg family. More like he liked them spending their money in his store. All of them including Charles' parents. He was quick to remember local merchant Leon Macher who was an in-law to the family. All were loyal customers. Just not the place for a little colored girl to come shopping amongst the white folks! Who was he to chastise Missy? Seems like she is becoming more and more risqué like her mother, Lara.

Who wants to go shopping? Gigi had shared stories with the other children on the farm about her trips to town. None of the colored kids had ever been there. Most never seen a store let alone shop in one.

Gigi playfully bragged about going to Mrs. Chettsburg's tea room and chocolate shop. The small group of about six were fascinated with the little girl as she told of her adventures. The children had a hard time keeping up with all the details about fresh-made muffins and assorted candy.

The five year old tried to describe The General Merchant Store. Her eyes barely met the wooden counters. Looking up there was merchandise everywhere; jumbo pickles, candy jars, boxed soaps, candles, and bolts of pretty fabrics. Every trip included buying candy, of course.

"Why can't all the children come to town?" Was the creative girl's thinking. "Everyone could come shop for candy!" Gigi was excited as a kid might be. She took off running to find her Papa Doc. Maybe he could take all her little buddies to town to see the stores and shop for candy?

Papa Doc, as Gigi called her grandfather, explained he needed to talk to Mr. Chettsburg first. He actually was embarrassed to ask Charles. More humiliated to explain to his granddaughter as to why her innocent request was not a good idea. But why couldn't the children take a trip to town?

Doc approached Charles with Gigi's wild idea about going to town. The outing would involve several of the colored children from the farm. The thought did not go over too well with Charles. The child's idea needed to be thought through some more. Charles explained to Doc he needed to discuss the details with his wife for lack of not wanting to just say "no."

Lara agreed the experience might be good for the children. Get them off the farm and explore the real world. There was life beyond the safe haven of the family farm. Charles was not overly convinced.

"According to Gigi, she wants the kids to see Missy's grandmother's store where they can taste chocolate." Charles appeared frustrated not knowing how his mother would feel.

"I will speak with your mother, Charles. I think this little event should cause no problems what so ever. I will make arrangements with Doc and Missy to go to town in the morning. The children's parents will be told to dress and groom them well. They will need to be on their best behavior. Although, they have never been a problem. Most attend Missy's school and have learned about manners." Lara assured her husband.

Charles was still not convinced about taking a bunch of little colored children to town. He was not sure if his concerns were that they were children, colored, or both. The attorney was all for exposing the kids to new sights. The problem he was focused on was he did not want any snickering from the local white folks. He did not want any confrontation or humiliation for the little ones to witness.

This special morning, school was going to be replaced with a field trip for some students. There would not be enough room for everyone, just the younger classmates. Doc was busy getting the small hay wagon ready for the trip to town. Missy had consulted with the kids' parents. Six children plus Gigi were a manageable bunch for Missy and Doc. Everyone loaded onto the wagon. Off to town they headed. The ride on the wagon was a thrill in itself for the small gang.

Shortly they arrived to visit the town. A new place to experience and explore. First stop was at Mrs. Chettsburg's shop. Doc hitched the wagon securely to a wooden hitching post. Gigi knew the routine. She gathered all the kids in the rear entrance. The children hustled with excitement leaving Missy to catch up with the fast paced tikes. Gigi had them all lined up at the back door. Missy went to the front door to greet her Grandmother Chettsburg.

"Hi Grandmother, we are here!" Yelled Missy into the front entrance.

"I will be right there." Elizabeth yelled back as she finished waiting on a customer. Walking to the rear of the store she noticed a nice line-up of dark haired children. All perfectly quiet. The children were greeted with an open door and instructed to enter the kitchen area. Mrs. Chettsburg explained that the chocolates were made in the kitchen where she also baked.

Excited, Gigi interrupted to point out her special wooden stool. She explained to her young friends she would have to sit there at times while Mrs. Chettsburg, also known as Mrs. C. worked and waited on customers.

In a raspy voice, Elizabeth instructed the kids to sit in a neat row on the floor. "Come on Missy, help me pour lemonade for the children. A glass for Doc, as well." The crew was delighted to have their thirst quenched by such as tasty drink. "Is Doc going to join us in here?" Missy assured her grandmother he would stay outside. Next, Elizabeth handed Gigi a little plate with an assortment of chocolates. The children's faces lit up as they savored the sweet treats. Meanwhile, Missy pitched in and began washing glasses in the big kitchen sink.

Missy then announced for the children to thank her grandmother for the chocolate snacks and the visit to her shop.

She gave her grandmother a departing kiss and guided the children out the backdoor. Once outside she directed them to look across the street. There stood her Grandfather Macher's Time Shoppe. That is where my grandfather and Uncle Timm work. My own mother grew up in that store. The business has been around a long time. "Ok, back to the wagon."

"No!" Gigi pleaded. "We have to go to the other store?"

"For what, Gigi?" Missy questioned the little girl quietly.

"To buy candy for all the kids." Gigi jumped with excitement.

"Do you think Mr. Richards wants all these children in his store?"

"He will if he wants some money. He has a store to get money from everyone."

"Honey, we do not have enough money for everyone to buy candy now do we?" Missy tried to avoid a confrontation with the feisty little one.

"I do, I do have enough money." Gigi moved closer to Missy and proudly displayed a coin in her hand.

"Where did you get that?" Missy snapped.

"Your grandmother."

"My grandmother did not give you a coin?"

Gigi shot back in a snotty toned voice demanding Missy to go back and ask about the coin. A coin Gigi knew the monetary value of. Knowing she had enough money to buy candy sticks for everyone. Gigi instructed the kids to follow her across the street to The General Merchant Store.

"Stop, you cannot cross the street alone!" Missy physically pulled Gigi aside. "You know you can't take all these colored children into Mr. Richards' store? You know that!" She stated firmly.

Gigi struggled to get away. "I know how to do this!" Again the group was instructed to follow her.

Missy was furious with her daughter who had a tendency to be a spoiled brat at times. Gigi passed the front of The General Merchant Store.

"Where are you headed?" Missy shouted sternly from behind the line.

One by one the kids wrapped around the corner of the general store and proceeded to the side of the building. Gigi knocked softly on the side door. Missy was terribly embarrassed at this point.

Gigi's soft voice barely penetrated through the opened side window. "Mr. Richards, we are here for some candy."

Moment later he appeared at the door to question Missy. "Miss Chettsburg, what is this?"

"Apparently the children would like to buy some candy, Sir."

"Do they have money Ma'am.?"

"Yes Sir, Gigi has a coin to spend on candy."

"What would she like?" The owner asked sighing.

"Please ask the paying customer, Sir." Missy suggested. Mr. Richards turned to the little girl and unpleasantly asked for the candy order. Somehow he felt a little funny selling candy to Giga through the side door. But this time she had company, and lots of it.

"We would like red licorice and red lollipops." Gigi spoke up.

"How many of each Miss Gigi?" Mr. Richards waited for a response.

Gigi began to count to Mr. Richards's amazement. "1, 2, 3, 4, 5, 6, 7, Missy, Papa Doc, and Mrs. Chettsburg. Ten red licorice, ten red lollipops." Off he went to gather the order, returning with a sack. In the exchange she handed him the coin. "I get money back." She belted out sharply.

"You certainly are a smart little, girl. Most kids 'round here can barely count to five. This one can even make change." Shaking his head with disbelief.

Missy was even more surprised of Gigi's way around the money. "Where did you learn how to make change out of coins? I know I taught you how to count numbers using the dried beans."

"Your grandmother, Mrs. C. taught me 'bout counting paper and coins." The five year old began to explain. "She has money, we play like pretend school. She had to learn about new money when moving here to Georgia. The store makes the money. She has different money from her other house. You can count coins!" Gigi was obviously getting good at arithmetic. "Mr. Lester doesn't use coins at her store. He gives Mrs. C. eggs and no money for pie and candies." The little girl laughed hysterically about Mr. Lester's bartering process and shouted. "Eggs can buy candy!"

Missy was so proud of Mrs. C.'s little pecan. The girl was smart, bright and kind-hearted. Wonder where she picked up those personality traits?

"Mrs. C. told me about sharing. She says I got a lot of stuff. So, I have to share some my things with the other kids. She made extra candy and lemonade so we could come see her at the store."

Missy was still confused about something. "How did you know about the side door at The General Merchant Store? When you are with me we always go in the front door."

"I watch people from Mrs. C.'s. Out the window I see colored people go to the other door to buy things. If he answers the door? She says they can't go in the store to shop." The little girl had long stories to tell from being at the tea room often.

"So, that is how you learned about using the side door?"

"These kids are colored like me. I only get to go in the store when I am with you, Missy. So, we had to use the side door with all these black kids, right?"

Missy just glared into her daughter's beaming eyes. She was startled as to how her daughter had compared herself to the other children. The little girl knew she somehow fit in with the colored kids. Yet, she was special enough to shop with Missy inside the store. Missy remained puzzled for the moment. Gigi was hardly at all like the others. That upbeat childish personality. She was just too cute. Full of energy with a lot of flounce to her bounce. Gigi had to realize she was different from the others? The color of her skin lumped her into a huge category labeled "Colored." Underneath those layers of darker, baby soft skin, unraveled the girl's true identity. A story played over and over in her head. Wishing for a day her family could live together in a house full of love without prejudices. Her husband beside her in bed for warmth and security way into the nights. The echoes of her daughter calling out to her filled with excitement, "Mommy, Mommy!" Missy leaned over and tightly hugged Gigi. She wiped her tears on the girl's shirt shoulder to shield her emotional feelings.

"Come on Missy, we have go back and give Mrs. C. some candy!" Gigi reminded the group leader and teacher.

Chapter 29

KEMICA'S NEW ADVENTOURS

Seems there is a new place to find local goods. A true trading post was often located on the northeast side of town. The spot was run by a Native American man named Moon Bear. Most days in the early morning you could find him setting up shop on the back of his old, beat-up, flatbed wagon. Everything was hauled in by his big, beautiful palomino horse.

The selection of merchandise would vary from day to day. Moon Bear was a master barter. Daily he would trade his goods for other items. On occasion, he'd take a coin or two.

Kemica enjoyed visiting Moon Bear's makeshift shop. About once a week she would take a thing or two to trade. The most valuable treasure was trading for a nice thick piece of venison for her father. Often she would take a hand-crafted candle or large bag of pecans in hopes of making an exchange.

Overtime, Kemica tried to make friends with man named Moon Bear. Few words were actually exchanged between the two. The young, teen girl was fascinated with his large physical make-up. The tall Native American sported long, shiny, dark brown hair. Although his skin was dark, the tone was like no one else's that she knew of. Rarely did the man make eye contact with her as if his soul was shielding a secret.

The two shared a few common bodily traits that actually had no objective. Kemica just knew they both were different from the local Caucasians and colored folks. She began to find him intriguing and handsome compared to the other men that she lived around.

Doc had concerns about his daughter's trips to the trading post. Most of the time he felt uneasy about her being alone off the farm. Her trips to the trading post were over a mile away. The south was not a safe place for a young, single, colored woman to be traveling by herself alone was his opinion. So, Doc required her trips to have an escort. Her brother or another male from the farm was required to accompany her if he did not tag along.

There was one thing Kemica learned from her acquaintance. Closely she observed how he ran his business. Why couldn't she set up her own business was her new idea? Yes, she could sell and trade her hand-crafted candles, bracelets and rugs. Then she could acquire things for her family's needs.

"How did you get a name like Moon Bear?" Kemica inquired with hesitation.

"Why do you need to know?" Replying as if not liking the interrogation.

"Not common, I suppose?" Kemica shrugged.

"You always have to know so much of me. I do not know your given name? My father saw the small bear roaming around late at night as my mother waited to give birth. Now you know?" The man tried to explain with what little English he knew.

"I am Kemica. I know it is hard to talk with you. You know so few words."

"I do not need a lot of your words. My people have our own language." Moon Bear patted his chest.

"Well, I was hoping you would come closer to town so I could trade with you more often. This is fun for me. Something to do." Kemica smiled and shared with excitement. "Wish I could have a trading post on the farm where I live. Give them folks a place to get more things?"

"I stay far away. I do not trust all men. Too much blood shed over territory." Moon Bear feared tension.

Kemica was enthused to share a story with the man who appeared so gentle. "Once, I traded with Little Star. I gave him a straw hat I made for several large pieces of deer meat. He would wear that hat. Then he traded it to some colored man from down this way. Now the colored man wears it while he works in the hot sunny fields. I can do this too, have a trading post? Sure would beat sitting around the house all day long playing with Gigi."

"You have child? I never see." Moon Bear appeared puzzled.

"Let's just say our family has a little girl who is five and I act like a mother to her." Kemica held up her hand displaying five fingers to signify the girl's age.

"You have no babies?"

Kemica shook her head no. Moon Bear was still puzzled and now frustrated. He thought his words were hindering the conversation. Little did he know the situation with the young girl was truly complicated?

"Someday, I will meet a man and have babies. I do not know where or when? I am so different."

"You are in between?"

Kemica was not sure what Moon Bear meant by the comment. Moon Bear tried to further explain. He extended his arms and held one close to hers. "You are darker than me? Not like night, like the field workers?" Trying to understand her unique skin coloring and tone.

"My family came from another place. We are not as dark as most folks."

Moon Bear pointed at Doc standing off in the distance. "The family head is like you."

"Yes, my father. My mother was like me too."

"Your hair is more like my people. Strange how you are." Moon Bear tried to take notice while being polite about the comparisons. "Not the same? My son is different than me in his heart. You cannot tell by the outside. He does not like to do like his father, hunt and fish. What he does do is sit with mother and weave. Then he tends to the corn at harvest. Not do like father!" Moon Bear pointing both thumbs at himself. "I tell him, no meat, no eat, no clothes for you, son."

In the meantime, Doc patiently waited. By now he was impatient and ready to leave. The father and daughter started a long walk home. Kemica had a few ideas to share with him. She explained to her father the idea of setting up a trading post on the farm for the residents. Her father assured her she would have to consult with Charles and hopefully make some type of arrangements.

Doc had some thinking of his own on the walk home. He was not use to teenagers and their wild ideas. Maybe there were just more opportunities in America he thought? His son was a minister and now his daughter wants to operate a trading post on the farm. The sun warmed his bald head as he kicked and chased a small rolling rock. Kemica found a rock for herself and joined in as if her father had just created a new game. Both were eager to get home. A new enterprise was waiting at the Chettsburgs' farm.

Once reaching the farm, the two took in a long cool drink of water. Then Doc scouted the area for Charles. First stop was at the back porch of the big house.

Doc knocked at the kitchen door in hopes of finding Hattie Mae. There stood the full-figured woman beaming at her discrete lover. Both peering around to see if they were alone. Stepping inside the out-kitchen, Doc zoomed in for a big kiss. Intimately, they engaged for several moments until Hattie Mae abruptly stopped.

"You just had to come by at dinner time when I am very busy?" Hattie Mae scolded Doc.

"Nah, I am looking for Charles but quite glad to see you also."

"Bout dinner time 'round here." She reminded Doc.

"Please pass on a message that I would like to talk to him after dinner if he is available. I will be outback." Doc peered deeply into his lover's eyes wanting to take her immediately into his arms. "Matter of fact, I will be back for you later my dear." Hattie Mae blushed while slapping Doc playfully in the head with a dishcloth.

"Consider it done, Sir. I will let the man know that you need to see him."

Doc headed back to his home and started a small fire in the pit located near the outside. Time for dinner for his family also. Possibly time to grill some chicken? Roast some potatoes on the flames as well.

Hours later, Charles showed up at Doc's home to speak with him. Kemica was the one who actually needed to talk with him. She was somewhat intimidated to talk about her new ideas. Would Charles be keen to her proposal of a small trading post on the farm? Once the conversation was started, she showed sincerity and enthusiasm as she made a few suggestions. First, she explained she was tired of caring for Gigi most of the time. Although the child was fun and rambunctious. School and church provided some socialization. Deep inside she wanted to fill a void.

Kemica began by explaining that the black folks had no place to shop or trade. No one outside of the farm really catered to them. Most colored people would not even venture into town for fear of prejudices? Although most of their food was produced on the farm there was not much access to other necessities, she further explained. Charles listened with an opened mind not quite sure where the conversation was headed yet. Finally, she blurted out the details. She wanted to open a trading post operation similar to her friend, the Native American,

Moon Bear. There would be swapping of items such as candles, decorative bracelets, and fabrics. Kemica was known for weaving nice mats. Something she used to do when Gigi was a baby. All these articles could be traded for other things or coins.

Charles needed no further explanations. The man who advocated for all types of people and situations felt a sense of lack of accomplishment. He had never thought in a way that the young girl did. Immediately he took action.

"Come follow me!" The quick thinking Charles directed the father and daughter to the rear of the overseer's house. In the back of the barn was a small room, a tool shed. "I think this space could be cleaned up."

Kemica's eyes were filled with delight. "Why this could be like a real store on the farm, Sir? I had hoped to just set up a table outside to sell and trade my goods." She jumped up and down and fell into her father's arms for a great big hug.

"This is the perfect location, right next to your house. Close to home and indoors. Convenient for all year round, I suppose? You'll be able to keep a close eye on Gigi while running your new store." Charles reached into his back pocket to recover his leather wallet. Retrieving a five dollar bill, he handed the money to Kemica.

Kemica began to cry. "Sir, this is more money than most folks make in a month."

"Just think of this as an investment for the new business. Hopefully that five dollar bill will multiply into numerous dollars for you and your daughter." Charles began to share the girl's enthusiasm.

Kemica's tears turned into a blank stare. Wishing she could speak out to tell the truth about Gigi. "That's really my niece and your granddaughter, Mr. Chettsburg." She continued to think to herself. "That is not really my child. What a tangled mess my brother has got me into. Will a man ever want me to be his wife knowing I have a child already acclaimed to me? I have been living a big secret, a lie about such a precious gift. I already do not fit in with the black folks here. I am too brown and my hair is long and straight. I am too dark for the Native Americans. No white man would want me? What man would want me with a half-colored kid attached at my side all the time? Even Peiter and Missy have to keep their marriage discrete because of the skin color differences."

"Kemica, Kemica!" Doc spoke up calling to the dreamy girl's attention. "Please thank the gentleman."

"Yes, Father. I drifted off thinking about all the wonderful things I can do here now." Kemica acknowledged.

Charles was quick to break in. "Gee, wonder if I should be the one doing the thanking? I am proud of you young lady for calling this situation to my attention. You will be of service to our family's farm community. God has blessed us over and over again. Let me know if there is anything else you might need. In the morning, I will send a few women over to assist with the clean-up of this area."

Both Doc and Kemica thanked Charles for his generosity and compliance in regards to the new store. The teen was eager to get started with the new business adventure. A sense of purpose set in on her behalf. "Quick Father! Let's go tell Peiter the exciting news."

Chapter 30
FIA BAKES MORE MUFFINS

"Who baked the fresh muffins?" A puzzled Charles questioned looking around the sheriff's office. The attorney had spontaneously stopped by to see Sheriff Will for a moment. Charles had some paperwork in hand. Seems like the man with all the answers had a few questions of his own this time. The property laws were constantly changing as were some of the local deeds.

"Please help yourself to the basket of baked-goods, Charles. Mrs. Macher, your mother-in-law, delivered them earlier this morning." The sheriff began to explain.

"My mother-in-law, Fia Macher?" Charles questioned with amazement. "Not my own mother, Elizabeth right? But my mother-in-law?" Charles zoomed in closer to observe the treats. "Oh yes, those are Fia's muffins for sure. I remember the first time savoring one her delicious pecan muffins. That is a pleasant story to tell."

"Please share then." The sheriff requested.

"I'll make the story short. Mrs. Macher was very hospitable when I opened my first law office in town. Her daughter, now my lovely wife, delivered a goody basket to my front door. That was my first introduction to pecans, had never heard of them, let alone tasted one. Yes, those buttery tasting muffins. I could not wait to tell my own mother who was still in Belgium, about my new found treats here in America. Now years later, my own mother is baking similar goods in her tea room." Charles gave note of.

"Well, well, I did not mean to take away business from your dear mother, who I clearly adore. How could I resist food from your mother-in-law? A man has to eat anyways!" The smirking sheriff teased.

"I just do not get this." Charles began shaking his head. "Fia rarely leaves the house unless one of the children or grandchildren are at her side. She is quite the homebody."

"Nah!" Replied Sheriff Will. "She pays me a visit a couple of times a week. Certainly you know her routine well? About twice a week she delivers food to Father Murphy at the church. Somehow I got in on her weekly schedule of deliveries? Months ago, Fia started dropping off baked goods here also. As a single, busy guy, this has been highly appreciated. I do not know the lady very well. She is so quiet and surreal."

"But this is out of character for her, Will!" Charles demanded.

"One early morning I was relaxing at my desk. Fia came in the office unannounced toting a small basket of baked-goods. She barely spoke to greet me. As you know she still talks to herself in the Italian language." Will chuckled. "I understood her fear of my office. She was afraid the place had a jail cell or two. I assured her it did not. I kiddingly told her I just handcuffed all the bad guys to the hitching post outback. The crooks could just eat hay alongside the horses. She shook her head and smiled at me from that beautiful face of hers. Such a pretty woman, nice tanned-toned skinned and silky smooth hair. Too bad her father pawned her off on her husband, León. They seem like the oddest couple? No disrespect Charles. The distress shows on her face sometimes from losing her original family. I cannot image a father just leaving behind a grown daughter in a strange town, alone yet? The story she tells and the way I understood her, her father was passing through this town. The hardworking man was trying to marry off his daughters. He and his sons were headed north to work and leaving the girls behind. Sure wish someone would have dropped off such a fine woman on my doorstep! She is so pretty for her mature age and stuck with that stern father-in-law of yours."

"Seriously, Leon has a discrete story of his own to share. His background has a sad story also." Charles hinted trying not to take sides.

Sherriff Will abruptly interrupted to continue with his story about Fia. Upcoming parts were going to be news to Charles. "As I tried to understand her broken English, she told of her home far away from this town. Back then, she met a fine boy when she went to grammar school. Sal, Salvatore was the young gentleman's name I believe. The two sweet hearts fell in love and courted. The boy's family was also Italian and spoke the language. Sal's father was a local cobbler and owned a shop. Her humble, dark-haired friend worked alongside of his father to learn the trade of making and repairing shoes, and leather goods. The small store displayed an investment of molds and assorted tools for crafting merchandise, she described.

Her hardworking father was a community minded man. When the local church was built, he helped. The well-put-together man believed business partnering provided for stronger neighborhoods. Along with a few other families he invested in land for farming.

One summer night, her father suddenly began packing the family's belongings. Leaving behind friends, land, and her mother's cherished garden of flowers and plants. Fia never got to say good bye to her special friend who she dreamed and planned on marrying. The father explained he needed to up root his raised family and move on. He felt he done God's work with his by raising his children. Now he felt there was a bigger community to build. But without his own kids? Fia did not understand her father's reasoning or decision. Especially after having her own children she never completely understood how a parent could abandon them and leave some behind?

Fia, had no idea how to get back to that town that she thought was far away. She barely saw the outskirts of the area growing up. Somewhere there was a boy who loved working in a cobbler shop. Not sure how far though? Maybe a two day ride away? Suddenly, Fia was dropped off along her family's travels as if to lighten the load. Falling right into the arms of Leon Macher. A man with the stern face. Certainly not modest and humble like her boyfriend she courted back home. But Leon was a meticulous man though and a good provider for Fia and the children. She dreads him!" The sheriff snickered. "Charles, the lady is bitter and I understand why. She claims your wife Lara is an angel from God. When Lara was born, Leon was so attached to that baby girl. Their daughter's birth seemed to give Fia some space from her demanding husband. The other three children are different she claims. Those are her babied babies. They cling to their mother and not their father. Now she seems to have a little too much space with the children grown and moved out of the home. She pays me a visit about twice a week."

"Seriously!" taunted Charles. "Why is it that you know more about my mother-in-law than I do? I think you are the only one Fia has shared this story with? I know Lara does not know all these particular details. Yes, my beautiful German-Italian bride. A mother's angel. A husband's dream."

"Quit bragging Charles it is not nice." The sheriff was very cheerfully entertaining. "Fia is known to sew on a button or two for me also."

"Sheriff Will, if I did not personally know you, I would swear you are lying and making up stories about my lovely mother-in-law. I seriously do not even think she has one friend outside of the immediate extended family. She socializes and volunteers a little bit at church. This is quite bizarre, Will! The woman rarely speaks to anyone and you seem to know her whole life story. Amazing to me."

"No offense Charles. Your very own mother will testify that I have not been paying her a visit at the tea room as often in the mornings. Not since Fia has been delivering her own bake goods right here to my desk. Fia explained she doesn't mind baking but does not really like to cook. Gee your mother had fed me most mornings, now your mother-in-law is on this? I once teased Fia how I enjoyed fried eggs for breakfast, as well. You would have been surprised with the breakfast she delivered the very next day. She had a piece of your mother's tasty flip-bread. She placed two fried eggs on one-half-side, topped with four thick slices of crisp bacon, then flipped the plain side of the bread over. Guess that's why it's called flipped bread, fold it or flip it over? I felt the egg yolks were a little over done for my liking. But she assured me the yolks needed to be cooked well done in order to deliver them without making a mess. Made perfect sense to me then. I tried explaining to Fia that she needed to show your mother Elizabeth, how to make that flip bread breakfast. The egg meal could be served at the tea room?" Will continued but Charles again interrupted.

"Wait a minute, this woman won't sew a button on her own husband's shirt. She is sewing them on your uniforms, Will? Why I have seen her drop off mending of her husband's at Miller's mending shop although she is a very skilled seamstress. I am not sure if I am confused or impressed Sheriff. She must really have taken a liking to you, Sir!"

Charles thought to himself going forward. "Was Fia delivering something else to the sheriff who was single? No way! She is too shy and timid. Yet, Leon continue the affair with his mistress, Charlotte over the years. Leon admitted he had not had relations with his wife since their son was born. Maybe Fia was just enjoying the sheriff's companionship is all?"

Sheriff Will spoke out, "You know I told Fia she is such a beautiful woman, if only she would smile more often. I think she keeps to herself too much. Such a pretty little thing. Pardon me Sir, but I do know where your wife gets her radiant looks and charm from."

"Charm?" Charles again reflected to himself. "Who is he kidding? Fia is always so somber and timid. Or has she been kidding some of us for a long time now? Were there more secrets Fia was holding to?"

"Charles, you know Fia makes a tasty pecan pie." Will bragged.

"Do not tell me she has baked pecan pies for you too?" Charles scratched his head in disbelief.

"Oh, only a couple times. More like special occasions. Could never get her bake me a fresh apple pie. She stated the pecans were plentiful and at no cost. Her daughter Lara drops them off quite regularly by the bag full." Will further explained. "Damn, I told her I'd even pick some apples for the chance of getting a pie out of them.

"Come on Sheriff, grab your hat. We are headed to my mother's tea room for breakfast, lunch, whatever she has cooked up today. Then we will order an apple pie for you. Mother's apple pie is delicious, mmmmm, with that brown sugar glaze drizzled and baked on the top of that lattice, flakey crust."

The two men left the sheriff's office and headed across the street to pay Charles' mother a visit. Eating was what was on the men's minds now. She would be so pleased to have the two gentlemen stopover.

Fia was attracted to Sheriff Will and was trying to make friends with him. The man was at least ten years younger than herself. Yes the sheriff was fit, handsome and unmarried. Behind his welcoming smile was a humble, modest man. Those were not the only reasons she was drawn to Will though. The sheriff had been in town for about twelve years. Fia's fascination was really in his good quality leather boots. She believed those boots had traveled a ways to this small town. The riding boots the sheriff so carefully polished and buffed. The boots with the heels that were obviously replaced. She noticed the unique style of his boots. Certainly Will's leather hat was custom made, as well. Could they have possibly been crafted by her humble, cobbler friend Sal who was abruptly left behind almost forty years ago? A young man who had to move on. He was living with his short term anger issues. The skilled cobbler felt like he had a run-away-bride. A short period of time later his memory slate was erased about Fia. In the cobbler store, was a new friendly customer who quickly became his bride. The details of the unique stitching on the sheriff's footwear probably was Fia's road map back to finding her long lost friend, Salvatore. The now older woman, still to this day recognized her cobbler friend's signature designs. Quite possibly did Sheriff Will know where her old hometown was located?

Chapter 31

COLORS OF THE RAINBOW

"When are you going to make more time for your husband?" Peiter scolded his wife Missy. "Between teaching school and our daughter Gigi you have been slipping in the area of the marriage vows. I need some intimacy. Can you create some time for me and soon?"

Missy was a little frustrated. Lately, she had been trying to spend more time with their daughter Gigi to free up time for Kemica. The school days seemed more challenging with the dreaded summer heat. Most school days started earlier in the morning to avoid the afternoon's warm sun. Even holding classes under the assorted shade trees did not offer much relief most days.

Who was available to care for the little one for a while? Missy's parents were gone for the day. Doc was busy on the farm. Kemica was running her store outback but Missy did not want to bother the girl. Certainly one of the female laborers could care for the child. Missy knew some of the ladies particularly did have a liking for the smart yet spoiled little girl.

Missy gathered a few things, along with her daughter and headed to town. Her destination was to see her Grandmother Chettsburg. Surely, she would oversee Gigi for a few hours?

"Hattie, I am going to town and may leave Gigi with Grandmother Chettsburg for the rest of the afternoon. As you know my parents are out of town for the day. I will be working on a project with Peiter at the schoolhouse when returning. Is there anything I can get from the store for you?"

"No. Your mother had everything taken care of for the kitchen. Don't need nothing. You gonna be gone a while then?" Hattie Mae inquired.

"Oh 'bout an hour and a half, I'd say. A little while." Missy guessed.

"Ain't it 'bout time Butler John is done for the day?" Hattie demanded.

In the background, John could be heard muttering back to the bossy maid, "What a big mouth you have Hattie Mae! Goes with those big feet of yours. Bet you have to wear men's shoes?"

Hattie defensively shot back, "Best shut up Mr. John or you are gonna be wearing a lady's shoe up your butt!"

Missy intervened as she did not like the negative, ongoing comments between the always feuding pair. "Mr. John, I am heading to town now. Did you care to join Gigi and me for a ride home?"

"Come on Missy, I will hook up a horse or two and attach them to the small wagon. I will drive you into town. I know you can handle the ride back alone. I'll grab the two brown mares, they are very gentle. Your grandfather has spent a lot of time working with them. He loves the horses like household pets."

Hattie Mae's mind was wondering. The second Missy left the house, Hattie began scouting for Doc. The house maid knew no one would be at the home for a while, or however long an hour and half actually was. This was "alone" time to spend with her lover. Frantically, Hattie searched for Doc around the farm. In no time, she located Doc with a group of workers tending to the communal garden.

"Come Doc, come now!" Demanded Hattie in a loud voice. "I need some help with chores at the house and now. Hurry Doc, I think rain is coming"

Doc shook his head at the forward woman. Dropping his garden tool he trailed behind the large framed woman.

"Hurry!" The commands again were getting more anxious from Hattie. "We need to get to my room and fast." The bold woman was excited that the farmhouse would be empty of occupants for a while. This made for the perfect opportunity to make love with Doc. Up the back porch stairs and into her tiny room they went. Next, they quickly disrobed most of their clothing. Standing before her, Hattie glared at her well-endowed man friend. First, Hattie laid on her lumpy high stack of old mattresses. Next, Doc climbed on top of his lover. The two were cramped in the small space but that is all that was needed at the moment for their special activity. Embraced in a kiss the couple proceed to sneak in a love-making session. The small enclosed quarters shielded them from the busy outside world. The walls embraced their moans and giggles. Hattie knew she had a "safe" day to engage sexually with her adult playmate. Certainly she was going to take advantage of that.

Hattie deeply loved sharing intimate moments with Doc. The muscular man felt so good to hold on to. His strong arms comforted her. The feeling of him penetrating her hard was a feeling like no other. The woman enjoyed the sensations her compassionate lover gave her, a racing heart, chills on her forearms. She wondered if this was not love being experienced between the two companions. More importantly, she was unsure if her lover shared the same exact feelings?

The lovers' whimpers and sighs continued. Both drenched in sweat as the small, stuffy room heated up as the summer temperature blazed. Shortly thereafter, sounds of a summer rain could be heard pouncing off the roof of the house. The thuds of the pitter-patter seemed to embrace their secluded moment. Capturing and savoring a rare time together alone. Doc continued to pleasure himself while competing with the extremely warm environment. Holding and clinching on to his lover the heat could not detour him from getting some of the familiar action. Her huge breasts were exposed to his eyes and waiting to be greeted by his warm mouth and tongue.

Hattie was known to be loud and demanding. But during the times of their sexual encounters, she seemed to be actually quieted down and calmer. Doc relished her. This was the only time the outspoken woman remained composed and quieted.

Meanwhile, Missy arrived at the tea room with Gigi at her side. "Grandmother, what smells so delicious." Missy scouted around the kitchen.

"Baking sweet potato pies. You know the kind topped with a strudel of oats, brown sugar, and finely chopped pecans!" Elizabeth proudly announced.

"Grandmother, can Gigi stay for a visit with you for a few hours? I have a few things to do this afternoon."

"Oh course honey. I am not going anywhere." Elizabeth grinned. "I spoke with your parents earlier. Seems your dad is out looking to buy some more livestock. The farm just can't be busy and big enough for him. Buying a couple extra hogs also. Seems his intentions are to roast a few big pigs. He wants to have an upcoming celebration feast for the fall harvest and include the laborers of course. Boy, did I raise a wonderful son or what? Your parents must be going to be gone for a while, the covered coach was led by four stallions. Must have sensed the rain? I noticed tiny sprinkles moments ago while gathering wood for the kitchen stove. Kinda crappy day to be out running errands, Missy? You might want to hustle along?"

"Your grandfather is planning on heading to the farm later this evening. I shall send the little pecan back with him?" Elizabeth's question was more like a statement. As usual, the woman was trying to be practical to save your granddaughter some much needed time. "I will send some of these tasty pies home to you. That is if there is any left."

"Perfect!" Missy smiled with a sigh of relief. "Yes, I will be on my way in hopes of beating the rain." Missy gave departing hugs as she ventured out of the store.

Quickly, Elizabeth directed Gigi back to kitchen area. The wooden stool was placed in the corner for the little one to sit on as usual. Basically trying to conceal her from the store's guests.

"I like how you are always nice to me, Mrs. C.?" Snarled the young, innocent Gigi. "Most people don't like me because I am colored!"

Elizabeth Chettsburg disputed the latter part of the girl's comment. "Now, where is that comment coming from? Who could not like you? Matter of fact, I don't like you either, I love you!" The elder woman reached down and embraced Gigi with a big, warm hug trying to playfully cheer her up.

"You really love me!" An excited Gigi jumped up and down then twirled around.

"I do not think Mr. Richards likes me. People like him give me funny looks all the time. I know it is because of my color." Gigi stretched out her arms to show off her skin tone.

"Maybe folks are jealous of you. Meaning, they do not like that you are truly special, Gigi."

"Why am I special then?" Inquired the little one.

"Seems you have special privileges, you have special people in your life, not like most folks around here. You have a lovely family and live at an exceptionally nice and safe place on our family farm. It is almost as if you have two families."

"Two? How can I have two families?" The girl continued to bombard the elderly lady.

"Now, look at Missy. She has two families because her parents are married. Her father Charles is from the Chettsburg family and her mother from the Macher's. So, when Charles and Lara married, the families came together to make a bigger one." Elizabeth proudly displayed her hands coming together with a loud sudden clap. Gigi clapped back with enthusiasm. "You have Papa Doc's family and my whole entire family. That is what makes you so very special my little pecan!" The two simultaneously clapped hands together. "Do not think so much about what others think. What is important is how you think and how God wants you to think."

"Where is God right now? How does He know what I thinking?" Asked a confused Gigi.

"God is a Spirit not a living human being. You cannot see him but He is always around. That is if you believe in Him. He is here to help us make good choices. People who are not nice to other people are not making good choices in God's eyes. They are only fooling themselves as they tote around the Bible and do not live by the words in the book. God is always watching over us, protecting us. Now how can a little darling such as yourself have any control over what color your eyes, hair, or skin-tone is? You can't, you are God's creation and He made you in a special way. Parents do not have a choice to pick how their babies will look, the hair color, or eye color. It's not like going to the store to buy candy and you only pick your favorite flavors and colors"

"What if you God gave you a colored baby Mrs. C?" Gigi, shot back with a serious yet puzzled look.

"God gave me a colored baby by surprise when you were born on the farm I suppose?" Outside the sky darkened and the sound of thunder roared a distance away.

Elizabeth elaborated and continued to feed the little girl's curiosity. "Where I came from there were no colored folks that lived around there. Remember the story I told you before? Moving to America was my first experience with colored folks.

Never seen one until I arrived here. Did not even know people existed that were black or brown. Not too many people lived by us actually, mostly farmers. Our family never traveled far. Just went to church and to visit a few local relatives.

Moving to America was different for my husband and me. We arrived at the farm and colored folks lived out there on our land, just like neighbors. Didn't bother me at all. People are people. What is in their heart is what matters. Especially when things relate to God. I do not think God intended for white people to live one way and colored another. Yet, as I learned there are different types of people scattered all over the world. I am not sure why there are separate rules and laws for colors, men and even women?"

"Gigi, have you ever seen a rainbow?" Elizabeth continued her stories to the six year old.

"A bow? Like a twisted knot?" Gigi knew what a bow was, but not the details of nature's rainbows.

"No, a rainbow is the most beautiful thing I have ever seen in my lifetime. One might appear after the rain and when the sun peaks out shortly after. The colors are like a ribbon decorating the blue sky. All the pretty colors are stacked on top of each other; violet, blue, green, yellow." Elizabeth motioned with her arms to signify an arch. "I think God created people to be like the rainbow. Placed side-by-side, humans can produce a beautiful rainbow of people."

"Mrs. C., can you show me a rainbow." Gigi expressed with excitement. "Please, I want to see one now!"

"Silly girl, remember I told you they only come out after the rain and high in the sky when the sun is out." Elizabeth reminded her little pal.

"Oh, I really want to see one now!" Exclaimed the interested, stubborn girl.

"The rainbow is dream-like. They are so pretty their existence do not even seem real. Magic created by Mother Nature. Rainbows are really special. Special just like you, my little pecan." Elizabeth pointed down to Gigi perched on her wooden stool listening intensely. "I think you are like a little rainbow from God? I am pretty sure your body is made up of different colors too. Now you are like a rainbow, just created with different shades."

Elizabeth had her own visions of rainbows and reflections. The older woman recalled seeing her first rainbow when she was about eight year's old living in Belgium. There displayed high in the blue, cloudy, sky was the prettiest, vibrant arch reflecting off the North Sea in her homeland.

Playfully as a child, Elizabeth explained to her father she was going to marry a handsome prince in a nearby castle someday. At the time, the girl heard there was a tattered, medieval stone castle about twenty miles away. Tucked away in the dark green pasture was the old fortress. The excite girl would be lucky to someday see the unique mystical structure. On her wedding day, Elizabeth imagined there would be four, colorful arched rainbows dancing in the sky for her special occasion.

As a rural teenaged girl, she had never been to the local thriving city. No chance to search for her special prince. "What are my chances of meeting a prince around here? There are nothing but farmers for miles and miles."

Her father was quick to interrupt the girl's fun with her imagination. As usually, he was short and stern tempered. He tried convincing the child that rainbows were round and not cut off by the land or water to form an arch. A circular beauty embracing a brief moment, reaching far beyond a human's vision. As a child, Elizabeth had no comprehension then of how the rainbows came about. Nor did she make the connection that rainbows were fashioned after a rainfall followed by a shining sun. Certainly, something you could not just demand them to be present in the sky or wished for. Not even for a fairy tale wedding day celebration the young Elizabeth's father concluded.

In the meantime, the child named Elizabeth daydreamed about her prince she would one day marry. She tried to image if what her father was telling her about the magical rainbows was true. Now an elderly woman who still at times seems to enjoy being playful with her little pecan. She still has not found the answer to a question that has lurked her since being that young child. *"Are rainbows really round?"*

Chapter 32

AUTUMN'S CROPS

"What to do with all these pecans?" Was Peiter's concern. The fresh autumn air signified more crops were ready to be harvested. He and his crew laid tarps and tarps of left over burlap bags under the pecan trees to trap the falling nuts. This made for easier gathering of the over plentiful produce. Nearby, the colorful apple trees exhibited red, green and golden yellow fruit like bulbs on a Christmas tree.

On the other end of town, a local woman prepared to bake and cook with the newly harvested collection. Elizabeth also could not wait to prepare her goods with ripe apples and a new batch of pecans. Inventorying her tea room's pantry, she wanted to be well stocked. The prediction was she expected to be busier as the weather cooled down.

To the rear of the tea room, Joseph carefully stacked wood up against the back wall outside. The married couple made a good team no matter the task or situation. Both were hardworking, spiritual individuals. Equally, they needed to slow down in their daily events. Now in their late 60's, the couple did not have the drive and energy they once expressed. The passion still existed but not the vitality. Time had aged the two who had grown to be such great companions.

By late afternoon, Elizabeth began to feel overly exhausted. She kindly asked her compassionate husband to retrieve a shawl for her from the upstairs. The older woman began to feel chilly. "Possibly the change in the weather's temperature?" She assured her husband.

Joseph insisted his wife take a seat in the dining area. "Please relax Elizabeth. I will help you the rest of the day in the kitchen. Think I will look silly wearing your violet apron ma'am?" He gently teased his pale looking wife. Trying to perk his wife up he served her a hot cup of tea. Almost as if he enjoyed being playful wearing the frilly apron. As the afternoon progressed, one by one, Joseph assisted the tea room's few guests. Nearby, his wife supervised every transaction from serving sliced pie to wrapping loaves of bread baked earlier in the morning.

Laying on the overstuffed couch Elizabeth let her hair bun loose. The long locks with gray highlights bounced down on her shoulders. Not long after she had dozed off into a deep sleep. Snoring roared loudly from the exhausted woman, an unfamiliar sound to her husband. "Not like my wife to snore like a man?"

Something did not set right with the man who knew his wife very well after almost fifty years together.

"Honey, should I go get the local medical doctor? Dr. Cameron should be home this time of day. Please let him take a look at you? I am concerned about your symptoms, I'm afraid you are becoming seriously ill, not just tired. Your skin coloring is off, your forehead and cheeks are burning up like a fever. I will return in a few minutes, dear." First, he displayed the 'closed' sign on the front door of the business. Joseph raced across the street to The Time Shoppe. He hollered into Timm for assistance. "Can you send someone to tend to my wife for a few minutes please? I am hoping to find the doctor. Not sure what is wrong with her, if anything? Just know she is running a high fever. I would suggest not going too close to her though?"

Timm was not good about decision making but passed the information on to his father. Leon then instructed his wife to go oversee Elizabeth until Joseph returned. The quiet and meek Fia quickly scrambled across the street with great concern. Without hesitation she was eager to comfort the ill woman who had become part of her extended family for many, many years now.

Quickly, Joseph raced down the road seeking the assistance of Dr. Cameron. The always calm, level-headed man had shifted into a panic mode. His dear wife was ill and he wouldn't want her suffer. The fast paced walk turned into a fast jog. Blocks away he hoped to reach the doctor. Through the big picture of the office window, Joseph spotted the doctor's wife. A sense of relief started to set in for the concerned husband. Firmly he rattled on the doctor's front door. Mrs. Cameron rushed over to see what the commotions was.

"Please, my wife seems to appear very sick. I have never seen her like this before. Is the doctor available to pay her a visit at the family tea room?" The husband inquired with unease.

"The doctor should be back here shortly, Sir. He was headed to Mildred's mending shop to get some farm fresh eggs from her. Maybe you can catch up with him if you hurry. I am surprised you did not pass each other on the street or walkway. Either way, if my husband returns here I will promptly send him over to your place."

Joseph shut the door behind him and headed east down the street to Mildred Miller's shop. The doctor was nowhere to be seen along his short trail. Approaching Miller's Mending's and More, Joseph caught a glimpse of the silver haired doctor wearing a black felt hat. The doctor was heading the same direction ahead of him. Joseph picked up speed as he walked. "Doctor, Doctor." Still too far behind for the doctor to hear his calls. Joseph was getting to old for running he kidded himself. Maybe a little out of shape since slowing down on the work projects?

A couple of short blocks later Joseph caught up with the doctor. "Dr. Cameron can you tend to my wife for a moment. She is across the street at the tea room sleeping."

"Yes, I will be right there. I need to drop off a piece before the Machers' close the shop for the day. This will only take a couple of minutes Mr. Chettsburg." The doctor assured the alarmed husband.

Joseph hustled across the street to the tea room. Relieving Fia from sitting with Elizabeth, he thanked her as she left. Fia confronted the doctor in passing while both crossed the street. "I do not think she is well, Sir." Fia shook her head.

Within minutes the doctor arrived at the store and observed his patient. Elizabeth was still sound asleep on the couch. "A good place for her, Mr. Chettsburg. She may just need some rest. Like any business, there is a lot of stress. Your dear, ambitious, wife needs to relax, take a few days off maybe?" The doctor pulled Joseph aside and quietly spoke. "Could be the influenza also? She has a few symptoms. Let her rest. If this is the flu, rest and sleep should shorten the duration and the severity of the illness. Keep her fever down, we do not want anything contagious to spread. Make sure she is sipping on something all the time to keep her strength up. Something simple like tea, broth, or a light soup. I will stop by first thing in the morning to check on her symptoms. Should things worsen into the night, do not hesitate to come and get me." The doctor leaned in closer to Joseph. "You do not have to knock too loudly. My wife is a light sleeper. I am the one who is a deep sleeper. The lady does not miss a thing even while she is sleeping. Either way, Elizabeth will need to rest and take a few days off. Be away from everyone and everything. See you in the morning around seven o'clock." Doctor Cameron tried to put the worried husband at ease.

Joseph felt somewhat hopeless. Elizabeth was the more caring and compassionate one. Joseph definitely was not a nurse. On the stove was some warm water probably hot enough to make some tea for his ailing wife. The store's front sign still displayed "closed." His heart and his stomach felt empty. What would it be like not having guests at the tea room for a few days? What would he tell the folks?

Soon after, a light knocking could be heard at the front door. Appearing at the door was Leon. He wanted to follow-up about the doctor's visit. Joseph stepped outside to speak with the concerned man. Next, he apologized for putting Fia into harm's way. He hoped Leon's wife was not exposed to the flu if that is the case? Leon assured Joseph he was being too hard on himself.

"Scratch out a small note and posted it to the door. Just tell folks we will be closed a few days due to a family matter, which this is actually. Do not need to feed a frenzy in case she is not sick and just over exhausted. Hopefully the doctor is correct and she just needs a little break. Either way Joseph, maybe she should start slowing down. Maybe I could send my wife over to help out in your shop. Get her out of my hair once in a while." Leon was only kidding with himself. Joseph was not in the mood for joking around.

"Thanks Leon for your concerns. Actually I am grateful. Look at the two of us, how on Earth did our lives ever mingle so tightly? Growing up I never knew being a parent had so many rewards. God gave Elizabeth and me only one gift, our son. But that one and only precious gift has created a whole new life and world for me." Joseph appeared so sentimental and appreciative of his family and the extension of their household. "If you see my son or Lara, please mention that Elizabeth is ill. Tell them I prefer no one to stop by except for the doctor. I fear someone else could possibly get infected."

Leon patted his friend on the shoulder as he departed. "I will send you a plated dinner later." Leon called out. "Make sure to take care of yourself as well." Leon advised his close acquaintance.

The worried husband poured two cups of freshly brewed tea. For certain he knew Elizabeth would not be awake anytime soon. Carefully he placed a pretty tea cup within her reach on the side table. Beside the hot drink he left her a biscuit. Slouched in a winged-backed chair, Joseph sipped on a cup of tea. Effortlessly, he watched his sleeping sick wife. Then scrounging around the room, he lit a few candles as night was due to set in soon. Time was dragging for the man who was always ambitious and had to keep busy.

Quickly he scooted upstairs to retrieve an old book or outdated newspapers. Anything to keep him busy through the night. More candles were grabbed just in case they might be needed. A couple of pillows and quilts were tossed down the stairwell. Looks like Joseph and Elizabeth Chettsburg were spending the night in the tea room. Food and treats were not lacking. At his side sat a half-eaten meal of ham hocks and mushy buttered beans. The favorite part of the plated dinner was Fia's sweet, golden cornbread. The bread slathered with butter would have been enough to satisfy Joseph's appetite. Waiting throughout the night were several other baked good tucked away in the kitchen. No one to scold him for eating too many goodies since his wife was fast asleep.

Around eleven o'clock, the kindhearted husband covered his sleeping wife with one of her handmade quilts. Gently he placed a pillow under her head in hopes she could breathe better being propped up. Joseph was tempted to wake her. Concerned she may need a drink or need a bite to eat.

Time for dessert! Quietly he patrolled the kitchen. In the icebox, an apple pie was staged. The pie had not been cut into yet. Diving into the treat would be a big give away as to who cut into the pastry and how much was eaten, were his thoughts. Snooping around he found a large bowl covered with a linen kitchen towel. Peeking under the towel Joseph began to smile. Smiling back at him was a bowl of Elizabeth's tasty praline pecans. No need to be modest. This was going to be a long night. He headed back to the chair with the whole damn bowl!

"Cock-a-doodle-doo." Echoed with the morning sunrise. Moments later Dr. Cameron arrived as promised. A very tired Joseph was relieved to see him. The doctor gently awakened Elizabeth to ask about her condition. The startled woman looked around at the surroundings.

"Joseph, did I fall asleep on the couch last night?" The wife questioned with a slight cough. "Dr. Cameron, are you here for bread this early in the morning?"

The doctor began to explain to the woman, "Mrs. Chettsburg, you were running a high fever yesterday evening. You were sound asleep when I paid you a visit. Was not sure if you were just overworked and tired. Now I am certain you have influenza. A few days off from work is prescribed for you my dear lady. I suggest that you have very little contact with other people for the next week or so. Do not want the illness to spread to others is my suggestion. Your husband is aware to keep you feed and healthy. He will have to make a choice. He will have to either tend to you or the business but not both. Hopefully he is not infected also. By now he probably would have shown some symptoms."

Joseph stood there feeling silly. He sadly displayed the pretty calico, lilac apron that he forgot to take off the previous evening. Most embarrassing was that he recalled Leon had seen him wearing the garment the night before also. "I am sure Leon got a big laugh out of me wearing my wife's apron?" The husband not so proudly announced. "Will my wife be alright to sleep upstairs in the apartment if the store remains open?"

The doctor was quick to not agree. "Too many germs floating around. Either the store needs to be closed a few days or she will need to be removed from the premises."

"So, my options are to close the store while she recovers, is what you are saying?"

"Just a few days, Sir." Assured Dr. Cameron. "Three to five days should be sufficient, as long as she is recovering fairly well."

That seemed like a long time to be closed for the couple. The store was typically open six days a week and closed on Sundays for worship and family. The couple agreed a short break was in order for the both of them.

By mid-day, Charles and Lara had arrived in town not knowing Elizabeth was very ill with the flu. Her son was stunned when he saw the hand scratched notice attached to the front door, "closed until next Monday, family matter." Charles hustled around to the back door of the tea room. Quietly, he let himself into the kitchen area. Calling upstairs to his parents. "Mother, mother, father?"

Joseph appeared at the top of the stairwell. "Please meet me outside in the back, I will be right out, Son."

"Outside?" Charles muttered to himself. "Since when do we meet outside?"

Back to the front of the building Charles went first. He offered a suggestion that his wife cross the street to her parents' home. Charles was puzzled with the day's events starting with the tea room being closed. Again he went to the back of the store to meet up with his father.

Joseph explained to his son that Elizabeth was ill and all the circumstances surrounding her condition. Charles desperately wanted to see his mother. Joseph had his say in the matter. "One sick Chettsburg is enough for the time being. Please, we must follow Dr. Cameron's instructions. Your mother is ill and this allows for no visitors, not even from her own son."

Charles abruptly left and headed to the Machers'. By this time, Leon and Fia had already explained to Lara about her mother-in-law's condition. Leon spoke up and addressed his son-in-law. The business man had a plan and a good one he thought. He explained to Charles that he felt Elizabeth should return to the family farm to be better attended to during her illness. In the meantime, Fia and Lara could run the tea room for a few days. Charles almost found the suggestion to be hysterical. "My dear wife does not bake nor cook. Although I know your wife, Fia can bake some mighty tasty treats, Leon."

Leon was quick to intervene. "The two will make a good team. This will only be for a few days. Let me remind you, my daughter is a good business woman. She helped build my business since being a very young teen. Those two could never replace what your mother does alone. Together I think they can master things until your mother gets back on her feet in a very short time. Not good business to be closed. Just a deterrent for the customers."

The mother and daughter team discussed the possibilities of operating the tea room for about a week. Yes, the two would make a good team, one baking while the other managed the business end. Only for a few days? Of course, Charles would be on hand for any assistance or needed help for the ladies. So, the family agreed to keep the store closed for two days to let the air freshen indoors. Joseph packed a few things for his wife's stay at the farm. More relaxing, more room, more helpers were his thoughts. A very somber feeling for the older gentleman though. He felt a little broken down not having his wife feeling well. Off to the Chettsburgs' family farm the older couple went.

The next four days were followed by trial and mishaps at the tea room. Fia was busy baking items from her own recipes.

The known spoiled Mrs. Lara Chettsburg was helpful serving and waiting on guests. "Been a long time since I put in a long day of work at a store, Mother." Lara shared.

Her mother Fia was actually enjoying herself. Busy in the kitchen she made a double batch of her buttery pecan muffins. Next in line, were a few pecan pies to be baked. Fia was actually relaxed in Elizabeth's kitchen, no husband, no kids, and no grandchildren to tend to. The kitchen was spacious and well organized. The shy baker was not accustomed to dealing with so many people throughout the day. On the other hand, her daughter Lara had a flare for customer service. Good service meant good revenue was her philosophy. The new, two woman team seemed to manage the business without too many awkward incidences. The guests were overly accommodating and accepting about the tea room's provisional changes. Many loyal customers welcomed a few new changes to the menu. Most flattering was being attended to by Mrs. Lara Chettsburg, a local favorite. Lara personally would rather have been shopping herself than working! Certainly she owed her mother-in-law Elizabeth the respect to tend to her business while she was ill. Tucked away in the kitchen was her own mother. Fia. Proudly the older woman worked baking her basic creations. Furthermore, the temporary job released her from duties and time spent at home with husband, Leon.

Back at the farm, Elizabeth was feeling better and gaining strength. No need to rush and get better too soon was the doctor's advice. Confined to an upstairs bedroom, she enjoyed the view of the farm's daily activities. Each day played out like a short story. Doc headed to the main barn to milk a few heifers. A group of men would head south into the fields to gather the daily crops. Hours later, Missy would be seen gathering her students for the day. From there on, her stories changed throughout the week.

Who could resist eyeballing little Pecan? Elizabeth was content just watching the pint-sized girl play. She joked to herself and commented, "Good thing her skin tone was not chocolate brown. I would have had to call her Cocoa? Three of my favorite things; pecans, chocolate, and Gigi." Yes, the elderly lady admitted a liking for the brown skinned girl with eyes to match. The cutest little darling with a smile you just want to kiss. Who could resist that cute, bubbly personality?

Elizabeth lounged around all week in the same nightgown. Hollering down the staircase she tried for Hattie's attention. She relayed to Hattie for someone to purchase a few yards of lightweight flannel fabric. Feeling somewhat better, Elizabeth recalled the sewing machine set up in the living room. Reminiscing, she remembered that special Christmas gift her son presented the ladies years ago. Sewing a new nightgown during her stay at farm would be relaxing. The project could occupy some of the days' long boring hours was her thought.

Hattie questioned Elizabeth's plan thinking the doctor order her to bed rest. "I will speak with your husband or Missy, ma'am. Matter fact, I'll be looking for one of them. Missy has been sleeping in the newly constructed school house located to the east of the main house. Joseph has been sleeping between the parlor's couch and the far shanty. Your coughing all night kept him wide awake."

"Wait a minute, are you trying to tell me my husband has been sleeping in a shanty because of me?" Firmly, Elizabeth was in disbelief.

"I don't think that would be a bad thing ma'am. Been out there? He had been out there early on this year, fixing on the place. Got real wood floors, screen in the window, and a latch on the door. He did real nice. I think he plans on moving you in with him!" Hattie's sense of humor was delightful at times.

"Probably not much smaller than our first home. A tiny little cottage, sitting beside the road. Nothing but pastures wrapped around there. My husband had bigger plans for our family although it did not grow by much." Elizabeth's face lighted up thinking back to her youthful days as a bride.

"You best get back to bed or I am telling the doctor on you." Hattie shook her index finger as if scolding a child. "Go!"

She demanded. The doctor was due back for a visit to the farm in a few days to check on his patient's recovery.

"How are things at the tea room?" Were the men's thoughts. Earlier, Charles and Joseph had headed to town. Their main focus and concern was possibly hiring a helper for the establishment. Either way, Elizabeth needed to slow down and spend less time working. Although she enjoyed running her business and waiting on the guests. The men wanted to free up some of her time to relax and relish more with the family. Fia and Lara were doing remarkably well at the tea room. Their much appreciated assistance was only temporary though. Now was the time to start looking for a helper or partner for Elizabeth's business.

Imagine sleeping without your wife for a whole week? Elizabeth's illness made way for the married couple to inconveniently spend several nights apart. This was something most traditional marriages did not experience every night. The conversation going on in the new schoolhouse was quite different one evening. Peiter began to share some thoughts with his wife, Missy. As a child, an imaginary story about the farm was created. "You know, I would dream the farm was like an island. An island like the place I use to live on. I would pretend the farm was surrounded by beautiful blue waters. The land would be protected and kept everyone secure and safe. I knew at some point early on Missy that you were going to be my wife. I had to marry you and only you my dear. There was no one else here on the farm for me but you. What if nobody else ever came to our private island? The only new person is our daughter Gigi, God's creation. Here, we are surrounded by family and the workers."

Peiter sprung up and darted for the door, "I need to talk to your father, Missy."

The young man's first stop was at the main barn. No sign of Charles there. A few laborers suggested Peiter look in the other outbuilding. They knew Charles and Joseph had a few of the horses out earlier.

"Mr. Chettsburg!" Peiter called out. "If you are not too busy I have a few questions?" The man had a smart but unusual request according to Charles. Peiter was interested in knowing the exact perimeter of the farm's property.

Charles grabbed a shot gun and a dog, "Never know when you might come across a nice fat bird. We can walk part of the way with Buck Edwards, one of the farm's overseers. Doesn't hurt to have an extra man along. To this day still, I still do not trust a lot of folks. Certainly not safe to be traveling alone, especially with colored folks like yourself, Peiter. People still carry prejudices and hatred for no apparent reasons. Let's just be cautious all the time."

As the three men walked, Peiter started to share his concerns with Charles. "Who will take care of the farm when you are too old?"

"You, silly!" Charles jokingly kidded.

"Will Missy know how much land belongs to the farm? Really, how big is it?"

"Peiter, there are legal papers and deeds that show or illustrate the land ownership. Don't worry, as an attorney that is my job and responsibility. Missy has secured copies of all the paperwork for the farm."

"She has the papers for the farm already?" Peiter acted bewildered.

"Why not? This farm will be all hers someday." Charles proudly announced.

Buried deep in the bottom of a young lady's hope-chest was a bountiful treasure. Tuck away with her other prized possessions the land deeds were safe and out of sight. A hidden secret, undisclosed from her husband, concealed but not forgotten.

Chapter 33

THE FINAL CHAPTER

"If only she would have slowed down?" Joseph questioned his wife's busy business practices. "She had to keep busy all the time, baking, cooking, or sewing something. Always helping someone. Now I wish she would have spent a lot more time on herself.

Dressed in his loose overalls, Joseph headed to town. Slowly, he traveled to town on his favorite horse and companion. With his head held low he tried to disguise his sorrow. The General Merchant Store was his destination but he was in no hurry to get there. The casket that he was designing for his wife was in need of some hardware.

While pacing the store's floor, Joseph had an inquiry for Mr. Richards the man he's always known as a jack-ass. "I'll need to place an order for a headstone I suppose. How much for a small one, Mr. Richards?"

"'Bout five dollars. Are you sure I can't interest you in the larger size, Mr. Chettsburg? Your lovely wife certainly is deserving of something special."

"Oh, she would not want me fussing and purchasing one at all. I could make something real nice out of wood is my guess?" Joseph walked with his hand in his pockets.

"My wife and I wish to pay for the stone. We've discussed this and will not take "no" for an answer. Elizabeth was a very special lady, so caring and giving. It is our turn now. Go ahead pick something from this catalog. Please, we need to be modest but we can budget for about $25. You know the fancy ones go for as much as $100?" The Richards' were losing a friend also. Mr. Richards liked to sneak down to the tea room for a delicious morning snack on occasion. No blame on the wife for not fixing him breakfast. The two had a busy business to run.

Joseph was overwhelmed by the Richards' generous offer. "May I come back in a day or two? Few things I want to think about before making a selection and placing the order." The saddened husband shook his head. He felt like this conversation was meant for Elizabeth herself. What would she pick out for her own headstone? Looks like he needed some family input?

The trip back to the farm was just as slow moving on this autumn day. Knowing his wife would not be there to greet him ever again, when he would arrive. Over and over he questioned himself and prayed. "God, why have you taken my wife so soon, our life together was not supposed to be over yet?" The faithful husband was not ready for his wife's sudden departure. His heart already began to feel empty and lonely without her.

There was no regaining strength for Elizabeth's weak body. For weeks she was feeling fine after recovering from influenza. Then a bad case of pneumonia set in. The short battle took her quickly and quietly.

The farmhouse was full of chitter-chatter. Everyone was making plans with every little detail. Charles graciously took over preparation plans from his father. Lara had made contact with Father Murphy to make arrangements at the church. The priest had a vested interest with the deceased, dear mother-in-law. Seemed to be another component to the scheduled mass. Why would the family have to consent to a formal consultation with Father Murphy after the burial?

In the meantime, the skilled carpenter discretely crafted a casket for his wife. Planks of plentiful pecan wood was specially selected for the project. He remembered to taper the corners to help keep the body in place. Placed on top of the coffin would be one of those signature wooden crosses. Like the ones he taught the laborers to make and apply on top of their designed wooden boxes.

Days later, a wake was scheduled at the farmhouse for Elizabeth. A couple of farm laborers were called upon to prepare and dig a grave. The burial would take place in the north-east corner of the farm. A specific plot of land that would now be known as the family cemetery going forward.

Other arrangements were also being made. Missy was overly emotional due to her grandmother's passing. Sobbing to her father, she pleaded with him. She wanted him to allow Doc and his grown children to pay their respects in the house where Elizabeth's body was on display.

Her husband Peiter had earlier made arrangements with Charles for the farm laborers to pay their last respects. Charles had agreed that the laborers could gather after the official wake viewing. The small crowd was allowed that night to meet in front of the house near the living room window close to where Elizabeth's body was laid out. Many of the laborers recalled a lady who at times could be strict with rules and stuck by them. Yet, a woman compassionate enough to deliver flavorful baked goods on rare occasions. As the darkness set in, the colored folks from the farm assembled in the front yard. Prayers were led by Minister Peiter. A chorus of songs were sung in her praise. All the words were not understood as they sang hymns only known from their first language. The beautiful chanting did not need an organ or musical instrument to accompany them. The heart-warming gathering was a clear reminder of Elizabeth's concern for love among all mankind.

The somber time was a wakeup call for Missy. Deep inside she wanted and needed the comfort of her husband and dear friend, Peiter. Back in the house she openly cringed onto her husband's shirt and wept. Tightly she grabbed onto him with her tight fists seeking support from her sadness.

Hattie Mae stood in the background as usual. A stream of tears rolled down her face also. Reflecting the hidden dark secrets kept from the decreased woman. Now feeling guilty like a bold faced liar. How could everyone be so deceptive all these years? Her thoughts were that Elizabeth will never know some of life's truths. How could a woman live life without having knowledge of being a great-grandmother to the precious Gigi? Hattie's face began to feel flush and butterflies set in her stomach as she felt guilty. She now feared God for carrying on with the long, fabricated stories about Missy's and Peiter's marriage and the birth of their baby. She prayed God was loving and forgiving of her ongoing sins and shame. Hopefully, God would weigh out the sins that were committed in hopes of protection and not causing harm.

Later on in the night, Doc and his children gathered together at his home. Peiter directly spoke to his sister, Kemica. "If God never gives you children of your own, at least He has given you the opportunity to raise and rear my daughter, Gigi. Kemica, you are a special sister. So far I have only been gifted one child."

"I miss our mother." The young man hugged his sister and began to cry. "I miss how I use to sit on her lap as she swayed back and forth. Usually she would make up a silly song to sing in hopes of me falling asleep. Father must miss her terribly also? I am not sure if you are lucky for barely knowing her. You cannot miss what you do not know. You did not really know or remember her right? You were too young then when she was snatched away from us. Father was left to raise us both alone. A big undertaking for a young man."

Finally, the burial of a wonderful woman named Elizabeth Chettsburg was now laid to rest. A woman whose uncertain travels lead her to a home far away from home. A new life where she and her husband followed in her son's ambitious path. A journey of new places and faces. Her final destination, *"Chettsburgs' Farm, where pecans are plentiful."*

The next morning, there still was some uncertain business to take up with Father Murphy. The family was scheduled to meet him at ten o'clock at St. Michael's Roman Catholic Church. What to wear troubled the women, funeral attire or their Sunday best?

As an attorney, Charles had an additional plan. From now on, Leon and Fia Macher were to be included in most of the Chettsburgs' business affairs. Should something drastic happen to Charles or Joseph, all the assets would fall into the laps of Lara or Missy. Mr. Macher would then be able to assist with finances and legal guidance for his daughter or granddaughter. Charles trusted the father of his wife. He knew Lara and Missy

would always be well taken care of when in the hands of Leon.
Charles sincerely had faith in Leon. Except when things
involved Leon's discrete lover, Miss Charlotte.

Everyone crowded around the cramp office of Father
Murphy. Lara and Missy were seated at his desk. The others
stood uncomfortably around the room. In the priest's hands were
several sheets of paper. He started off by stating that Elizabeth
was a cherished friend of his. She was special member of the
church's congregation. This was a woman who did not like the
neighboring wars. One day she wished to take a long train ride
once the battle fields cleared. Next, he began to describe what
Elizabeth had explained to him many years ago. "Although I am
not an attorney, there were a few things that Mrs. Chettsburg
wanted me to handle for her. At times she appeared to have more
faith in God than the government. She prepared a document
referred to as her "Wish List." Her personal request was for me
to share this information with her family after her heavenly
departure."

The first short note was read by the priest, "Dear Joseph,
I know there will come the day when I will not wake up to wish
you a good morning. May a warm cup of coffee be in your hand
everyday like usual. Missing will be our good conversation and
our daily prayers. I have thanked God every day for embracing
me with a wonderful husband."

The woman's next wishes were very serious as the priest read on with the notes. Missy was quiet confused. "Dad, why would Grandmother Chettsburg want the family to leave Gigi the pecan trees, meaning the east end orchard? Why so much, and why Gigi?"

"Your grandmother often stated that our family owed a lot to Doc and his family. We would not have been able to run the farm efficiently without them all. Since Gigi is their youngest family member, I will make sure the property gets titled accordingly." Charles noted to the entire crowd.

"Father, does this not bother you?" Missy was confused about her grandmother's well wishes.

"Gee, we elders have had ongoing conversations over this. We have been overly blessed in many ways. Down the road someday we knew the land might have to be divided up. I have no son to inherit the farm." Charles recalled talking to his older parents. Missy sobbed as her father gave explanation. "Daughter why are you being so greedy about parting with some of the farm's property one day?"

"No father, I am crying because I am happy. I did not realize Grandmother would want to gift so much to Doc's family. She never talked about this matter with me. I am overwhelmed as to how thoughtful she really was. This is a stunning gesture."

"Yes, the woman was wise and genuine. She worked hard all her life. Always saving money when she really did not need to. The tea room earned income for the family also. So this is fair that she desires to distribute some of the family's wealth."

Father Murphy had one more piece to share. Afterwards, the elderly man handed Missy a personalized handwritten letter to be read to Gigi.

> *Gigi, you are special like the rainbows that decorate the sky.*
>
> *You are made of many different colors also.*
>
> *When put all together, they are beautiful.*
>
> *Rainbows are rare and few,*
>
> *Just like you, my little Pecan.*
>
> *With love from my heart, Mrs. C.*

Several years ago with a pen in her hand, Elizabeth drafted that short note to her bubbly companion. The girl, also known as, Little Pecan was more than her buddy. The woman sat in the tea room and recollected to herself one early, chilly spring morning.

Thinking back, Elizabeth remembered returning to the farm around daybreak. *"I had gone to the family farm house to retrieve an old kettle I thought I had left behind. I was going to need the pan for soup that day. I had decided to make the soup the night before but the time was late. My thoughts were to get up early and quietly sneak over to the farm's out-kitchen. Joseph would have been angry with me if he had known I had ventured out in the near darkness. I did not want to disturb anyone at the household so early on, it was barely dawn. Arriving, I parked the carriage at the end of the driveway. I walked up the dirt path. Then I entered the out-kitchen though the side door.*

I was not finding what I was looking for in the out-kitchen. So, I headed into the house in hopes of finding the kettle in the serving area. I crept around like a little mouse trying not to wake my dear granddaughter or any of the farm's servants. My son and his wife were out of town at the university for several months already.

Too my sudden surprise, I heard what appeared to be gurgling noises coming from the formal sitting room. I could not image that anyone was awake and up in the household so early in the morning. I tip-toed and peeked around the corner into the sitting room and looked out the window. To my sudden surprise, my granddaughter Missy was seated in the wooden rocking chair on the front porch. In her arms, she cradled the baby known as Georgia. Missy's long brown hair flowed over the baby's tiny head. She continued to rock in the chair soothing the infant. I was startled by what I was seeing. My chest pound harder and harder. Missy was breast feeding the baby! I panicked. My eyes were not playing tricks on me. What I viewed was real. A cool chill rushed through my entire body. My emotions ran wild. I quickly and quietly raced to the side door hoping the baby's coos would hide my patters. I shuffled back to the carriage parked near the road.

I was furious! Who created this lie everyone was living? Some very deceitful people. How blind have I been?" Things started to add up and make sense to the older woman who was always practical. *"Yes, Missy had gained some weight. The impression was she was acting distant for several months over the winter. The two of us have always been close. Shucks, I traveled across the frightening ocean to reach and be with my lovely granddaughter. How could she have betrayed the whole family by having a baby out-of-wedlock? That was like asking for a free ride to hell.*

Never, ever did I imagine the tiny colored baby was my great-granddaughter? The precious infant was partially made of my own flesh and blood. I was furious and angry about the lies. Back to my house I went. My face felt flush like a fever. Pounding so hard, I thought my chest was going to explode. When I arrived home, I snuck into the tea room and fell to my knees. I knelt in a praying like position until my husband woke me up to rise for the day. All I could do was bury the untruth deep in my heart and leave this one in God's hands.

Years ago, I never foreseen our family growing any bigger. There would be no more children, no grandchildren quite possibly. I understand what a wonderful wife Lara has been to my son Charles. The woman really was not highly interested in being a mother first. She loved to socialize at events, attend church, and travel. I think more children would have tried Lara down. May have taken away from her delightful, fun spirit. I figured my cherished granddaughter Missy would never marry. The smart lady was dedicated to education and her career as a teacher.

That little baby that I named and called Pecan was a joy in my life at times. She is always playful, silly, and a bit on the sassy side. Since I made the discovery that Gigi was physically part of my family, I could not deny her as my own.

My son Charles, constantly but modestly brags about his pecan trees. The orchards are his main cash crop. He is proud of his gold mine. The Chettsburg Farm in itself was a good investment, as well as, the storefronts in town. Lara has had all the money she could imagine to play with. Missy will never need a thing, everything has been provided for her. Maybe a lot to manage someday?" Elizabeth sighed from her thoughts.

"For these reasons, I want to make sure there are conditions for my little Pecan. My husband and son will be instructed to do so at my request. Certainly they will honor my wishes. The majority of the east end property will be gifted to the pintsized girl. Yes, the young orchards behind the farmhouse." The great-grandmother had security concerns for

her great-granddaughter and wanted the little one to be well provided for.

"I know Doc and his children will always be there for Gigi. I am highly troubled at the thought of a young colored girl growing up here in the southern states. What is the future going to hold for her? Maybe she will be a bride, be a mother, have an occupation, or be a teacher like her mother? I dread the thought of Pecan living in one of those old shanties in the rear of the farm. I could not imagine her becoming a farm worker.

With the Devil resting on my shoulder, I prayed to God intensely. My eyes closed so tightly as I knelt next to our bed many dark nights. My quiet pleas to Him at times were that Mr. Leon Macher never find out the facts like I have. I feared he may have a hidden temper as his face often that appears so harsh most of the times. Not never really knowing what that smug mug had in store. My thoughts were terrifying to think what would happen if he discover to be the great-grandfather to a colored grandchild. Lord prove I am wrong as I pray hoping to be wrong about the local watch maker's beliefs.

For these reasons, I must write a note to my family about my wishes. Time after time, I have lied to my loving husband about something I kept to myself for years. There never seemed to be the right moment to discuss my discovery with him. My little Pecan who I love and adore. My little secret." Elizabeth gathered her notes and her "Wish List" as she sat quietly in the tea room. The only person she would trust with the documentations was Father Murphy. Shortly after, she made arrangements to meet with the man of faith. Then and there she put trust in Father Murphy to pass on her personal requests when the time was appropriate.

After Father Murphy disclosed all of Elizabeth's wishes to the Chettsburg family the somber group returned to the farm. Joseph was saddened by the loss of his dear wife. Granddaughter Missy was experiencing an upset stomachache and felt light-headed. Charles and Lara were compassionate and consoling as usual. Their love was their biggest strength, always.

At the end of the village was a casual acquaintance eager to help out the newly widowed, Joseph. Miss Charlotte, the flower lady, was ready to start a new life of her own. Although the timing was too soon, she was aware Joseph would eventually be a good catch. Single, handsome, and very well to do, yet a modest man. Her sly approach was to plant some flowers in honor of dear Elizabeth when the grave's dirt settled. Extending a kind gesture in hopes of landing in his arms before long. Her best friend Henrietta, thought Charlotte was being silly and getting too old for a new romance. Charlotte referenced her current affair with Leon, "I have been able to afford to grow beautiful flowers while others struggle to produce food. I think I am the only woman in this town who seems to have time to tend to a surplus of bulbs, flowering shrubs, roses and peonies? Why I have even made *a wilted blossom bloom* before! Are you challenging me my friend?" The two older ladies laugh quietly as Miss Charlotte continued to share her upcoming plans. The gray highlights in Joseph's hair added to his mature fine look, the women both agreed.

In all the confusion of Elizabeth's sudden death, there were other problems to solve on the farm. Doc had to approach Charles about a personal problem, although the timing was not good. At his side stood the broad woman named Hattie Mae. "I need to marry Hattie Mae, Sir. She has been experiencing symptoms of being pregnant. Afraid I am going to be a father again at this mature age. Your family has been so accommodating to all of us. We are all grateful for all that you have offered. May I ask that Hattie Mae and I relocate to one of the newer shanties, one with a porch, Sir? Maybe easier to set up a household there. Get established as a new family. My other two children are grown and both have their own living quarters. Hattie has been very light-headed and constantly complaining of a weak stomach. Her body is adjusting to the pregnancy is why she is not feeling well."

In the background, Missy began weeping intensely as she feared to face her own truths. Tears streamed down her warm, pale, face. She cradled her queasy stomach with both hands and cried at the top of her voice, "Oh, no?"

THE CONCLUSION

Late in the fall, the college courses were coming to an end for Laney Walker. Purposely, she was one of the last students to turn in her final exam. Wearing a tan cowl necked sweater with metallic threading, she approached the professor's desk, "Mr. Seely, I am surprised at how much I learned in this class. I will admit, I did not know my family's extensive personal history. My family tree now appears full and tall like a southern pecan tree ready for harvest." Smiling at her instructor.

"I also learned a lot about you, as well as, all the other students in this class. That rare extra-credit assignment added some value to the course's discussions. Going forward in life, do not assume things nor make false judgments until you have done your research. Sometimes that comes in the form of soul searching. So, you do not have to look far for the answers." Mr. Seely addressed the occasionally sassy student.

"This course has changed my life and spirit forever! I am not physically who I thought I was?" Laney stretched out her arms and shook them like willows in the wind and giggled,

"If I did not know better Mr. Seely, after completing my family research project, I feel like my skin is *changing colors*?"

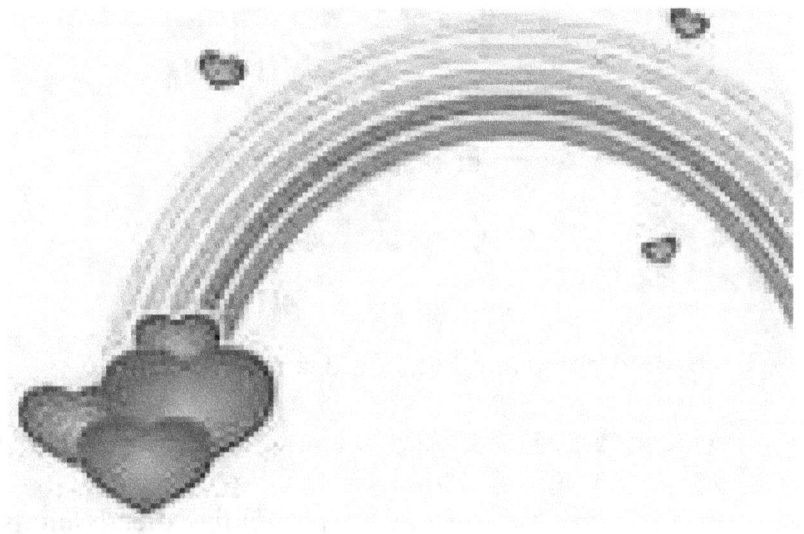

Elizabeth's Special Christmas Dressing

Ingredients

Two loafs of bread (stale/air dry)

One granny smith apple

Three Onions

Sage

One pint warm water

Two cups roasted pecan

Two cups of cranberries

Take dried bread and break into small, cube, size pieces. Place in large bowl. Add one pint of warm to bread, mix well but gentle. In a separate bowl combine diced onions and apple, crushed pecans, and homemade jarred cranberries, sprinkle with dried or fresh sage, slowly add bread mixture. Stuff the prepared fowl.

ELIZABETH'S SIGNATURE CHOCOLATE PECAN PIE

Ingredients

3 eggs beaten

1 cup maple syrup (corn syrup if available)

1 cup sugar

1 large pat of butter

2 cups fresh pecans

1 cup cocoa powder

Prepare your pie crust. Stir in all the ingredients listed above, add the pecans last. Carefully pour into the pie crust shell. Bake in a very warm oven for over an hour.

PRALINE PECAN CANDY

Ingredients

One cup of farm fresh heavy cream

2 cups brown sugar

1 splash of vanilla

2 ½ cups toasted pecans

On the stove heat in a sauce pan; brown sugar, cream and stir with a wooden spoon. Remove pan and place safely on a table or counter. Add vanilla and pecans. Drop small amounts of the mixture on a metal cooking tray. Cool at room temperature. If desired, drizzle warm chocolate on top of the praline candies, allow to cool.

A Story about the Story . . . .

At times, people watching can be interesting. Whether there is a crowd at a public event or a private gathering. The situations at times can seem curious. Take note how people sometimes start to segregate themselves into smaller different groups. The process is simple every now and then. The groups may be set apart solely by gender, age, culture, or race.

Let me reflect back to my first day of kindergarten. My mother Bettie, kindly reminded me that there might be '*colored*' students in the class. She assured me they were just like everyone else and to treat them as such.

That afternoon my two neighbor girlfriends and I walked Main Street until arriving to North Grade School located in Romeo, Michigan. Greeting the three of us was our teacher Mrs. Frappier. The tall thin lady was friendly, fun and talented. As a five year old, I was amazed as she sang and played at the piano. Mostly, I enjoyed the creative crafts that she incorporated into the daily lessons at times.

Located near the front of the large classroom were six short table, each with little four chairs. The two tables placed by the windows were full. One middle table remained empty. The other middle table was occupied by three colored boys, Calvin, Rudy (Anthony), and Tony. My two friends proceeded to sit at the empty table on the end. Sitting alone at the last table was Kimberly a quiet sweet little girl, who was colored. I suggested to my two pals that we sit with the other girl to fill her table. There were three seats left and three of us. The four of us girls shared that table for the remainder of the year.

Next, Mrs. Frappier passed out a new box of crayons to each of the students. Those big eight packs in the gold and green boxes. Our table was last to receive the crayons and seems the teacher was short a package? Scouring around the teacher handed my friend Carrie a purple off-brand box of crayons. Time after time, Carrie pouted about having a different color box. The rest of us girls at the table tried to convince her the color of the box did not matter. (*You know how some little kids just have to have the 'same thing'*?). All the crayons were the same inside the boxes I tried to convince her.

As a five year old, I wondered if Kimberly felt like the boxes of crayons, a different color on the outside. She appeared to be like the rest of the girls and she was. Back to those colored boys who were seated at the table next to us. Well, I had made two new friends for life it seemed. Calvin and Rudy loved to push the four of us girls on the merry-go-round at recess. How fun was that! Yes, Calvin and Rudy were acquaintances of mine well past high school graduation. Unfortunately, both of them passed on as young adults due to health issues.

Does it really matter what color the crayon box really is? What should matter is how one has the opportunity to color life with their assortment that is contained inside, not just the outside. How well have you colored your life.......?

Meet the Author

Welcome to the author's page. Janice Fouchey is an inspiring writer who enjoys a variety of genres. Her titles include romantic adventures and historical fiction. Another interest of hers is writing and reading poetry. Currently she also the author of <u>A Wilted Blossom Blooms</u>.

As graduate of Central Michigan University, she had a diverse educational background. Earning a Bachelor's of Science degree with a Major in Community Development and a concentration in Public Administration. A Home Economics Major in the area of Family Management and Consumer Studies, and a Marketing Minor were also completed.

Ms. Fouchey grew up and currently resides in the historic town of Romeo, Michigan. She has enjoyed a variety of careers paths in management, sales, marketing, and education. As a writer, she continues to execute her talents. Other personal interests of hers include a passion for art, sewing, and crafts that also express her creative side. Outside from these activities she enjoys the companionship of her dear family and good friends. A special thanks to Jean and John for all the assistance.

janicefoucheyenterprises@yahoo.com

Janice Fouchey Enterprises on FB

www.ingramcontent.com/pod-product-compliance
Lightning Source LLC
Chambersburg PA
CBHW070206260626
47160CB00002B/469

* 9 7 8 0 9 9 1 1 1 8 7 2 4 *